THE GATES

John Connolly

THE GATES

A strange novel for strange young people

HODDER &
STOUGHTON

First published in Great Britain in 2009 Hodder & Stoughton
An Hachette UK company

1

Copyright © John Connolly 2009

The right of John Connolly to be identified as the Author of the
Work has been asserted by him in accordance with the Copyright,
Designs and Patents Act 1988.

Photograph of Albert Einstein on page 50, © Bettmann Corbis

A CIP catalogue record for this title is available from the British Library

ISBN 978 1444 7 09414

Typeset in Garamond MT by
Palimpsest Book Production Limited, Grangemouth, Stirlingshire

Printed and bound by
Clays Ltd, St Ives plc

Hodder & Stoughton policy is to use papers that are natural, renewable and
recyclable products and made from wood grown in sustainable forests. The
logging and manufacturing processes are expected to conform to the
environmental regulations of the country of origin.

Hodder & Stoughton Ltd
338 Euston Road
London NW1 3BH

www.hodder.co.uk

For Cameron and Alistair

'Scientists are not after the truth; it is the truth that is after scientists.'

Dr Karl Schlecta (1904–1985)

One

In Which the Universe Forms,
Which Seems Like a Very Good Place to Start

In the beginning, about 13.7 billion years ago, to be reasonably precise, there was a very, very small dot.[1] The dot, which was hot and incredibly heavy, contained everything that was, and everything that ever would be, all crammed into the tiniest area possible. The dot, which was under enormous pressure due to all that it contained, exploded, and it duly scattered everything that was, or would be, across what was now about to become the Universe. Scientists call this the 'Big Bang', although it wasn't really a big bang at all because it happened everywhere, and all at once.

Oh, and just one more thing about that 'age of the universe' stuff. There are people who will try to tell you that the Earth is only about 10,000 years old; that humans and dinosaurs were around at more or less the same time, a bit like in the movies *Jurassic Park* and *One Million Years B.C.*; and that evolution, the change in the inherited traits of organisms passed from

[1] Scientists call the dot the 'singularity'. People who are religious might call it the mote in God's eye. Some scientists will say you can't believe in the singularity and the idea of a god, or gods. Some religious people will try to tell you the same thing. Still, you can believe in the singularity *and* a god, if you like. It's entirely up to you. One requires evidence, the other faith. They're not the same thing, but as long as you don't get the two mixed up, then everything should be fine.

one generation to the next, does not, and never did, happen. Given the evidence, it's hard not to feel that they're probably wrong. Many of them also believe that the Universe was created in seven days by an old chap with a beard, perhaps with breaks for tea and sandwiches. This may be true but, if it was created in this way, they were very long days: about two billion years long, give or take a few million years, which is a lot of sandwiches.

Anyway, to return to the dot, let's be clear on one thing, because it's very important. The building blocks of all that you can see around you, and a great deal more that you can't see at all, were blasted from that little dot at a speed so fast that, within a minute, the Universe was a million billion miles in size and still expanding, as the dot was responsible for bringing into being planets and asteroids; whales and budgerigars; you, and Julius Caesar, and Elvis Presley.[2]

Oh, and Evil.

Because somewhere in there was all the bad stuff as well, the stuff that makes otherwise sensible people hurt one another. There's a little of it in all of us, and the best that we can do is to try not to let it govern our actions too often.

But just as the planets began to take on a certain shape, and the asteroids, and the whales and the budgerigars and you, so too, in the darkest of dark places, Evil took on a

---

[2] In fact, about one per cent of the static that sometimes appears on your television set is a relic of the Big Bang and, if your eyes were sensitive to microwave light instead of just visible light, then the sky at night would appear white instead of black, as it continues to glow from the heat of the Big Bang. And because atoms are so small, and are constantly recycled, every breath you take contains atoms that were once breathed by Julius Caesar and Elvis Presley. So a little bit of you once ruled Rome, and sang 'Blue Suede Shoes'.

form. It did it while the Earth was cooling, while tectonic plates shifted, until, at last, life appeared, and Evil found a target for its rage.

Yet it could not reach us, for the Universe was not ordered in its favour, or so it seemed. But the thing in the darkness was very patient. It stoked the fires of its fury, and it waited for a chance to strike . . .

Two

In Which We Encounter a Small Boy, His Dog, and Some People Who Are Up to No Good

On the night in question, Mr Abernathy answered the door to find a small figure dressed in a white sheet standing on his porch. The sheet had two holes cut into it at eye level so that the small figure could walk around without bumping into things, a precaution that seemed wise given that the small figure was also wearing rather thick glasses. The glasses were balanced on its nose, outside the sheet, giving it the appearance of a shortsighted, and not terribly frightening, ghost. A mismatched pair of trainers, the left blue, the right red, poked out from the bottom of the sheet.

In its left hand, the figure held an empty bucket. From its right stretched a dog lead, ending at a red collar that encircled the neck of a little dachshund. The dachshund stared up at Mr Abernathy with what Mr Abernathy felt was a troubling degree of self-awareness. If he hadn't known better, Mr Abernathy might have taken the view that this was a dog that knew it was a dog, and wasn't very happy about it, all things considered. Equally, the dog appeared to know that Mr Abernathy was not a dog (for, in general, dogs view humans just as large dogs that have learned the neat trick of walking on two legs, which only impresses dogs for a short period of

4

time. This suggested to Mr Abernathy that here was a very smart dog indeed – freakishly so. There was something disapproving in the way the dog was staring at Mr Abernathy. Mr Abernathy sensed that the dog was not terribly keen on him, and he found himself feeling both annoyed and slightly depressed that he had somehow disappointed the animal.

Mr Abernathy looked from the dog to the small figure, then back again, as though unsure as to which one of them was going to speak.

'Trick or treat,' said the small figure eventually, from beneath the sheet.

Mr Abernathy's face betrayed utter bafflement.

'What?' said Mr Abernathy.

'Trick or treat,' the small figure repeated.

Mr Abernathy's mouth opened once, then closed again. He looked like a fish having an afterthought. He appeared to grow even more confused. He glanced at his watch and checked the date, wondering if he had somehow lost a few days between hearing the doorbell ring and opening the door.

'It's only October the twenty-eighth,' he said.

'I know,' said the small figure. 'I thought I'd get a head start on everyone else.'

'What?' said Mr Abernathy.

'What?' said the small figure.

'Why are you saying "what"?', said Mr Abernathy. 'I just said "what".'

'I know. Why?'

'Why what?'

'My question exactly,' said the small figure.

'Who *are* you?' asked Mr Abernathy. His head was starting to hurt.

5

'I'm a ghost,' said the small figure, then added, a little uncertainly: 'Boo?'

'No, not "What are you?" *Who* are you?'

'Oh.' The small figure removed the glasses and lifted up its sheet, revealing a pale boy of perhaps eleven, with wispy blond hair and very blue eyes. 'I'm Samuel Johnson. I live in number five hundred and one. And this is Boswell,' he added, indicating the dachshund by raising his lead.

Mr Abernathy, who was new to the town, nodded as though this piece of information had suddenly confirmed all of his suspicions. Upon hearing its name spoken, the dog shuffled its bottom on Mr Abernathy's porch and gave a bow. Mr Abernathy regarded it suspiciously.

'Your shoes don't match,' said Mr Abernathy to Samuel.

'I know. I couldn't decide which pair to wear, so I wore one of each.'

Mr Abernathy raised an eyebrow. He didn't trust people, especially children, who displayed signs of individuality.

'So,' said Samuel. 'Trick or treat?'

'Neither,' said Mr Abernathy.

'Why not?'

'Because it's not Halloween yet, that's why not.'

'But I was showing initiative.' Samuel's teacher, Mr Hume, often spoke about the importance of showing initiative, although any time Samuel showed initiative Mr Hume seemed to disapprove of it, which Samuel found very puzzling.

'No, you weren't,' said Mr Abernathy. 'You're just too early. It's not the same thing.'

'Oh, please. A chocolate bar?'

'No.'

'Not even an apple?'

'No.'

'I can come back tomorrow, if that helps.'

'No! Go away.'

With that, Mr Abernathy slammed the front door, leaving Samuel and Boswell to stare at the flaking paintwork. Samuel let the sheet drop down once more, restoring himself to ghost-liness, and replaced his glasses. He looked down at Boswell. Boswell looked up at him. Samuel shook the empty bucket sadly.

'I thought people might like an early fright,' he said to Boswell.

Boswell sighed in response, as if to say, 'I told you so.'

Samuel gave one final, hopeful glance at Mr Abernathy's front door, willing him to change his mind and appear with something for the bucket, even if it was just a single, solitary nut, but the door remained firmly closed. The Abernathys hadn't lived in the street for very long, and their house was the biggest and oldest in town. Samuel had rather hoped that the Abernathys would decorate it for Halloween, or perhaps turn it into a haunted house, but after his recent encounter with Mr Abernathy he didn't think this was very likely. Mr Abernathy's wife, meanwhile, sometimes looked like she had just been fed a very bitter slice of lemon, and was looking for somewhere to spit it out discreetly. No, thought Samuel, the Abernathy house would not be playing a very big part in this year's Halloween festivities.

As things turned out, he was very, very wrong.

Mr Abernathy stood, silent and unmoving, at the door. He peered through the peephole until he was certain that the boy and his dog were leaving, then locked the door and turned away. Hanging from the end of the banister behind him was a black, hooded robe, not unlike something a bad monk might wear to scare people into behaving themselves. Mr Abernathy put the robe back on as he walked down the stairs to his basement. Had Samuel seen Mr Abernathy in his robe, he might have reconsidered his position on Mr Abernathy's willingness to enter into the spirit of Halloween.

Mr Abernathy was not a happy man. He had married the woman who became Mrs Abernathy because he wanted someone to look after him, someone who would advise him on the right clothes to wear, and the proper food to eat, thus allowing Mr Abernathy more time to spend thinking about things. Mr Abernathy wrote books advising people how to make their lives happier. He was quite successful at this, mainly because he spent every day dreaming about what might have made him happier, including not being married to Mrs Abernathy. He also made sure that nobody who read his work ever met his wife. If they did, they would immediately guess how unhappy Mr Abernathy really was, and stop buying his books.

Now, his robe heavy on his shoulders, he made his way down the stairs into the darkened room below. Waiting for him were three other people, all dressed in similar robes. Painted on the floor was a five-pointed star, at the centre of which stood an iron burner filled with glowing charcoal. Incense grains had been sprinkled across the coals, so that the basement was filled with a thick, perfumed smoke.

'Who was it, dear?' asked one of the hooded figures. She said the word 'dear' the way an executioner's axe might say the word 'thud' if it could speak as it was lopping off someone's head.

'That weird kid from number five hundred and one,' said Mr Abernathy to his wife, for it was she who had spoken. 'And his dog.'

'What did he want?'

'He was trick or treating.'

'But it's not even Halloween yet.'

'I know. I told him that. I think there's something wrong with him. And his dog,' Mr Abernathy added.

'Well, he's gone now. Foolish child.'

'Can we get on with it?' said a male voice from beneath another hood. 'I want to go home and watch the football.' The man in question was quite fat, and his robe was stretched taut across his belly. His name was Reginald Renfield, and he wasn't quite sure what he was doing standing around in a smoke-filled basement dressed in a robe that was at least two sizes too small for him. His wife had made him come along, and nobody argued with Doris Renfield. She was even bigger and fatter than her husband, but not half as nice, and since Mr Renfield wasn't very nice at all, that made Mrs Renfield very unpleasant indeed.

'Oh, Reginald, do keep quiet,' said Mrs Renfield. 'All you do is complain. We're having fun.'

'Are we?' said Reginald.

He didn't see anything particularly amusing about standing in a cold basement wearing a scratchy robe, trying to summon up demons from the beyond. Mr Renfield didn't believe in demons, although he sometimes wondered if his friend Mr Abernathy might have married one by accident. Mrs Abernathy frightened him, the way strong women will often frighten weak men. Still, Doris had insisted that they come along and join their new friends, who had recently moved to the town of Biddlecombe, for an evening of 'fun'. Mrs Abernathy and Mrs Renfield had met in a bookshop, where they were both buying books about ghosts and angels. From then on their friendship had grown, eventually drawing in their husbands as well. Mr Renfield didn't exactly like the Abernathys but a funny thing about adults is that they will spend time with people they don't like very much if they think it might benefit them. In this case, Mr Renfield was hoping that Mr Abernathy might buy an expensive new television from Mr Renfield's electrical shop.

'Well, some of us are having fun,' said Mrs Renfield. 'You wouldn't know fun if it ran up and tickled you under the arm.' She laughed loudly. It sounded to her husband like someone pushing a witch in a barrel over a waterfall. He pictured his wife in a barrel falling into very deep water, and this cheered him up a bit.

'Enough!' said Mrs Abernathy.

Everyone went quiet. Mrs Abernathy, stern and beautiful, peered from beneath her hood.

'Join hands,' she said, and they did so, forming a circle around the star. 'Now, let us begin.'

And, as one, they started to chant.

Most people are not bad. Oh, they do bad things sometimes, and everyone has a little badness in them, but very few people are unspeakably evil, and most of the bad things they do seem perfectly reasonable to them at the time. Perhaps they're bored, or selfish, or greedy, but, for the most part, they don't actually want to hurt anyone when they do bad things. They just want to make their own lives a little easier.

The four people in the basement fell into the category of

'bored'. They had boring jobs. They drove boring cars. They ate boring food. Their friends were boring. For them, everything was just, well, *dull*.

So when Mrs Abernathy produced an old book that she had bought in a second-hand bookshop, and suggested, first to her husband, and then to their slightly-less-boring-than-the-rest friends the Renfields, that the book's contents might make for an interesting evening, everyone had pronounced it a splendid idea.

The book didn't have a name. Its cover was made of worn black leather, emblazoned with a star not unlike the one painted on the basement floor, and its pages had turned yellow with age. It was written in a language none of them had ever seen, and which they were unable to understand.

And yet, and yet . . .

Somehow Mrs Abernathy had looked at the book and known exactly what they were meant to do. It was almost as if the book had been speaking to her in her head, translating its odd scratches and symbols into words that she could comprehend. The book had told her to bring her friends and her husband to the basement on this particular night, to paint the star and light the charcoal, and to chant the series of strange sounds that were now coming from each of their mouths. It was all very odd.

The Abernathys and the Renfields weren't looking for trouble. Neither were they trying to do anything bad. They weren't evil, or vicious, or cruel. They were just bored people with too much time on their hands, and such people will, in the end, get up to mischief

But just as someone who wears a sign saying 'Kick Me!' will, in the normal course of events, eventually be kicked,

so too there was enough mischief being done in that basement to attract something unusually bad, something with
more than mischief on its mind. It had been waiting for a
long time. Now that wait was about to come to an end.

Three

*In Which We Learn About Particle Accelerators,
and the Playing of 'Battleships'*

Deep beneath a mountain in the heart of Europe, nothing was happening.

Well, that wasn't entirely true. Lots of things were happening, some of them quite spectacular, but because they were happening at an infinitesimally small level, it was quite hard for most people to get excited about them.

The Large Hadron Collider was, as its name suggested, very big. It was, in fact, some 17 miles long, and stretched inside a ring-shaped tunnel burrowed through rock near Geneva in Switzerland. The LHC was a particle accelerator, the largest ever constructed: a device for smashing protons together in a vacuum, consisting of 1,600 electromagnets chilled to -271 degrees Celcius (or, to you and me, 'Crumbs, that's *really* cold. Anybody got a sweater I can borrow?'), producing a powerful electromagnetic field. Basically, two beams of hydrogen ions, atoms that have been stripped of their electrons, would whiz around the ring in opposite directions at about 186,000 miles per second, or close to the speed of light, and then collide. When they met, each beam would have the energy of a big car travelling at 1000 miles per hour.

You don't want to be in a car travelling at 1000 miles per hour that crashes into another car travelling at the same speed. That would not be good.

When the beams collided, enormous amounts of energy would be released from all of the protons they contained, and that was where things got really interesting. The reason scientists had built the LHC was in order to study the aftermath of that collision, which would produce very small particles: smaller than atoms, and atoms are already so small that it would take ten million of them laid end to end to cover the full stop at the end of this sentence. Ultimately, they hoped to discover the Higgs boson, sometimes called the 'God Particle', the most basic component of everything in the material world.

Take our two cars travelling at 1000 miles per hour before pounding into each other. After the crash, there isn't likely to be much of the cars left. In fact, there will probably only be very small pieces of car (and possibly very small pieces of anyone who was unfortunate enough to be inside the cars at the time) scattered all over the place. What the scientists at CERN, the European Organization for Nuclear Research, hoped was that the colliding beams would leave behind little patches of energy resembling those that existed seconds after the Big Bang, when the dot of which we spoke at the start exploded, and among them might be the Higgs boson. The Higgs boson would stick out because it would actually be much bigger than the two colliding protons that created it, but it wouldn't hang about for very long as it would vanish almost instantly. It would be as though our two colliding cars had come together and formed a truck, which then immediately collapsed.

In other words, the scientists hoped to understand just how the Universe came into being, which is a big question that is a lot easier to ask than to answer. You see, scientists – even the clever ones – only understand about four per cent of the matter and energy in the universe, which accounts for all the stuff we can see around us: mountains, lakes, bears, artichokes, that kind of thing.[3] That leaves them scratching their heads over the remaining 96 per cent, which is a lot of scratching. To save time, and prevent unnecessary head injuries, the scientists decided that about 23 per cent of what remained should be called 'dark matter'. Although they couldn't see it, they knew that it existed because it bent starlight.

But if dark matter was interesting to them, whatever accounted for the remaining 73 per cent of everything in the universe was more interesting still. It was known as 'dark energy', and it was invisible; entirely hidden. Nobody knew where it came from, but they had a pretty good idea of what it was doing. It was driving galaxies farther and farther apart, causing the universe to expand. This would lead to two things: the first was that human beings, if they didn't start inventing fast ways to move somewhere else, would eventually find themselves alone, as all the neighbouring galaxies would have disappeared beyond the edge of the visible

---

[3] And even all that stuff added together still amounts to much less than one per cent of not very much at all, since more than 99 per cent of the volume of ordinary matter is empty space. If we could get rid of all the empty space in the atoms of our bodies, the whole of humanity could be squeezed into a matchbox, with room left over for most of the animal kingdom too. Mind you, there would be nobody left to look after the matchbox.

universe. After that, the universe would start to cool, and everything in it would freeze to death. Thankfully, that's likely to happen hundreds of billions of years in the future, so there's no need to buy a thick coat just yet, but it's worth remembering the next time you feel the need to complain about the cold.

The LHC would probably be able to help scientists better understand all of this, as well as providing evidence of other really fascinating stuff like extra dimensions, which as everyone knows are filled with monsters and aliens and big spaceships with laser cannons and . . .

Well, you get the picture.

At this point, it's a good idea to mention the whole Might-Cause-The-Destruction-Of-The-Earth-and-The-End-Of-Life-As-We-Know-It issue. It's a minor thing, but you can't be too careful.

Basically, while the LHC was being built, and lots of men in white coats were chatting about dark matter and high-speed collisions, someone suggested the collider might create a black hole that would swallow the earth. Or instead it could cause particles of matter so strange they're called 'strangelets' to appear and turn the earth into a lump of dead grey stuff. It's safe to say that this chap wasn't invited to the scientists' Christmas party.

Now you or I, if told we were about to do something that might, just might, bring about the end of the world, would probably pause for a moment and wonder if it was a good idea after all. Scientists, though, are not like you or me. Instead the scientists pointed out that there was only a tiny chance the collider might bring about the end of all life on Earth. Hardly worth bothering about, really, they said.

Not to worry. Take a look at this big spinning thing. Isn't it pretty?[4]

All of which brings us back to the important things happening in the Large Hadron Collider. The experiments were being monitored by a machine called VELO. VELO detected all of the little particles given off when the beams crashed. It could tell their position to within one two-hundredth of a millimetre, or one-tenth of the thickness of a human hair. It was all terribly exciting, although not exciting enough for two of the men who were responsible for watching the screens monitoring what was happening, so they were doing what men often do in such situations.

They were playing Battleships.

'B Four', said Victor, who was German and blessed with lots of hair that he wore in a ponytail, with some left over for his chin and upper lip.

'Miss,' said Ed, who was British and blessed with hardly any hair at all, and certainly none that could be spared for

---

[4] Anyway, the scientists figured, if the end of the world did happen, there wouldn't be anybody left to blame them. There would probably be just enough time for someone to say, 'Hey, you said it wouldn't cause the end of—' before there was a bit of a bang, and then silence. Scientists, while very intelligent, don't always think things through. Take, for example, the first caveman who found a nice rock, tied it to a stick with a piece of vine, and thought, 'Hmm, I've just invented a Thing For Banging Other Things Into Things With. I feel certain that nobody will use this to hit someone over the head with instead.' Which someone promptly did. In fact, they probably hit *him* with it so that they could steal it. This is how we end up with nuclear weapons, and scientists claiming that they'd only set out to invent something that steamed radishes.

his face. Nevertheless, Ed quite liked Victor, even if he felt Victor had been given some of the hair that should, by rights, have come his way.

Victor's face creased in concentration. Somewhere in the not very vast vastness of Ed's board lay a submarine, a destroyer, and an aircraft carrier, yet, for the life of him, Victor couldn't seem to hit them. He wondered if Ed was lying about all those misses, then decided that Ed wasn't the kind of person who lied. Ed wasn't very imaginative and, in Victor's experience, it was imaginative people who tended to lie. Lying required making stuff up, and only imaginative people were good at that. Victor had a little more imagination than Ed, and therefore lied more. Not much, but certainly a bit.

Ed heard Victor sniff loudly.

'Ugh!' said Victor. 'Was that you?'

Now Ed smelt it too. There was a distinct whiff of rotten eggs in the room.

'No, it wasn't me,' said Ed, somewhat offended.

For the second time in as many minutes, Victor wondered if Ed might be lying.

'Anyway,' said Ed, 'it's my turn. E Three.'

'Miss.'

Beep.

'What was that?'

Victor didn't look up. 'I said it was a miss. That's what it was: a miss.'

'No,' said Ed. 'I meant, what was *that?*'

His right index finger was pointing at the computer screen, which was occupied by a visual representation of all of the exciting things happening in the particle accelerator, and which had just beeped. The image on the screen looked like a tornado, albeit one that was the same width throughout instead of resembling a funnel.

'I don't see anything wrong,' said Victor.

'A bit just whizzed off,' said Ed. 'And it went *beep.*'

'A *bit?*' said Victor. 'It's not a bicycle. Bits don't just whizz off.'

'Right then,' said Ed, looking miffed. 'A particle of some kind appears to have disengaged itself from the whole and exited the accelerator. Is that better?'

'You mean that a bit just whizzed off?' said Victor, thinking: who said we Germans don't have a sense of humour?

Ed just looked at him. Victor stared back, then sighed.

'It's not possible,' he said. 'It's a contained environment. Particles don't simply leave it to go off, well, somewhere else. It must have been a glitch.'[5]

'It wasn't a glitch,' said Ed. He abandoned the game and began furiously tapping buttons on a keyboard. On a second screen he pulled up another version of the visual representation, checked the time, then began running it backward. Twenty seconds into the rewind a small glowing particle came into view from the left of the screen and appeared to rejoin the whole. Ed paused the image, then allowed it to run forward again at half-speed. Together, he and Victor watched as the bit whizzed off.

---

[5] Whenever someone uses the word 'glitch', which means a fault of some kind in a system, you should immediately be suspicious, because it means that they don't know what it is. A technician who uses the term 'glitch' is like a doctor who tells you you're suffering from a 'thingy', except the doctor won't tell you to go home and try turning yourself on and off again.

'That's not good,' said Victor.

'No,' said Ed. 'It shouldn't even be possible.'

'What do you think it is?'

Ed examined the data. 'I don't know.'

Both men were now working on keyboards. Simultaneously, they pulled up the same string of data on the screen as they tried to pinpoint a reason for the anomaly.

'I'm not seeing anything,' said Ed. 'It must be buried deep.'

'Wait,' said Victor. 'I'm seeing— No! What's this? What's happening?'

As he and Ed watched, the data seemed to rewrite itself. Strings of code changed; zeros became ones, and ones became zeros. Frantically, both men tried to arrest the progress of the changes, but to no avail.

'It must be a bug,' said Victor. 'It's covering its own tracks.'

'Someone must have hacked into the system,' said Ed.

'I helped to build this system,' said Victor, 'and even I couldn't hack into it, not like this.'

And then, less than a minute after it began, the changes to the code were completed. Ed tried rerunning the image of the particle separating itself from the accelerator, but this time only the great tunnel of energy appeared on the screen, filled with protons behaving exactly as they should.

'We'll have to report it,' said Ed.

'I know,' said Victor. 'But there's no evidence. There's just our word.'

'Won't that be enough?'

Victor nodded. 'Probably, but –' He stared at the screen. 'What did it mean? And, more to the point, where did it go?'

'And what is that *smell* . . . ?'

* * *

Scientists were not the only ones who had been monitoring the collider.

Down in the dark places where the worst things hid, an ancient Evil had been watching the construction of the collider with great interest. The entity that existed in the darkness had many names: Satan, Beelzebub, the Devil. To the creatures that dwelt with it, he was known as the Great Malevolence.[6]

The Great Malevolence had been squatting in the blackness for a very long time. He was there billions of years before people, or dinosaurs, or small, single-celled organisms that decided one day to become larger, multi-celled organisms so they could, at some point in the future, invent literature, painting, and annoying ringtones for mobile phones. He had watched from the depths of space and time – for rock and fire and earth, vacuums and stars and planets were no obstacle to him – as life appeared on earth, as trees sprouted and the

---

[6] 'Malevolence' for those of you who were off 'sick' from school that day means 'hatred', but hatred of a very vicious, evil kind. Incidentally, when you put inverted commas round a word in this way, as I just did round the work 'sick', it means that you don't believe that the word in question is true. In this case, I know that you weren't really sick that day; you just felt like having a morning off to watch children's television in your pyjamas. Hence 'sick', instead of, well, sick. If you really want to annoy someone, you can make little inverted commas by holding up two fingers of each hand and twitching them gently, as though you're tickling an invisible elf under the armpits. For example, when your mother calls you for dinner, and dinner turns out to be boiled fish and broccoli, you can say to her 'Well, I'll just eat my "dinner", then', and do the little inverted commas sign. She'll love it. Seriously. I can hear her laughing already.

oceans teemed, and hated all that he saw. He wanted to bring it to an end, but could not. He was trapped in a place of flame and stone, surrounded by those like him, some of whom he had created from his own flesh, and others who had been banished there because they were foul and evil, although none quite as foul or as evil as the Great Malevolence himself. Few of the legions of demons who dwelt with him in that distant, fiery realm had even laid eyes upon the Great Malevolence, for he existed in the deepest, darkest corner of Hell, brooding and plotting, waiting for his chance to escape.

Now, after so long, he had just made his first move.

Four

In Which We Learn About the Inadvisability of Attempting to Summon Up Demons, and of Generally Messing About With the Afterlife

Samuel and Boswell sat on the wall outside the Abernathy house and watched the world go by. As it was a quiet evening, and most people were indoors having their tea, there wasn't a whole lot of the world to watch, and what there was wasn't doing very much. Samuel shook his bucket and heard the sound of emptiness which, as anyone knows, is not the same thing as no sound, since it includes all the noise that someone was expecting to hear, but doesn't.[7]

---

[7] This is similar to the old problem about whether or not a tree falling in a forest makes any noise if there is nobody there to hear it. This, of course, assumes that the only creatures worth being concerned about when it comes to falling trees are human beings, and ignores the plight of small birds, assorted rodents, and rabbits who happen to be in the wrong place at the wrong time and find a tree landing on their heads.

In the eighteenth century, a man named Bishop Berkeley claimed that objects only exist because people are there to see them. This led a lot of scientists to laugh at Bishop Berkeley and his ideas, because they found them silly. But according to quantum theory, which is a very advanced branch of physics involving atoms, parallel universes,

Samuel didn't want to go home. His mother had been preparing to go out for the evening when Samuel left the house. It was the first time that she had dressed up to go out since Samuel's dad had left, and something about the sight of it had made Samuel sad. He didn't know who she was going to meet, but she was putting on lipstick and making herself look nice, and she didn't go to that kind of trouble when she was heading out to play bingo with her friends. She hadn't questioned why her son was dressed as a ghost and carrying a Halloween bucket when it was not yet Halloween, for she was well used to her son doing things that might be regarded as somewhat unusual.

The previous week Samuel's teacher, Mr Hume, had rung her at home to have what he described as a 'serious conversation' about Samuel. Samuel, it emerged, had arrived for show-and-tell that day carrying only a straight pin. When Mr Hume had called him to the front of the class, Samuel had proudly held up the pin.

'What's that?' Mr Hume had asked.

'It's a pin,' said Samuel.

'I can see that, Samuel, but it's hardly the most exciting of show and tells, now is it? I mean, it's not exactly a rocket ship, like the one that Bobby made, or Helen's volcano.'

Samuel hadn't thought much of Bobby Goddard's rocket

---

and other such matters, Bishop Berkeley may have had a point. Quantum theory suggests that the tree exists in all possible states at the same time: burnt, sawdust, fallen, or in the shape of a small wooden duck that quacks as it's pulled along. You don't know what state it's in until you observe it. In other words, you can't separate the observer from the thing being observed.

ship, which looked to him like a series of toilet-rolls covered in foil, or for that matter Helen's volcano, even if it did produce white smoke when water was poured into its crater. Helen's father was a chemist, and Samuel was pretty sure he'd had a hand in creating that volcano. Helen, Samuel knew, couldn't even put together a bowl made of lollipop sticks without detailed instructions, and a large supply of solvent remover to get the glue, and assorted lollipop sticks, off her fingers afterwards.

Samuel had stepped forward and held the pin under Mr Hume's nose.

'It's not just a pin,' he said solemnly. Mr Hume looked unconvinced, and also a little nervous at having a pin rather closer to his face than he might have liked. There was no telling what some of these kids might do, given half a chance.

'Er, what is it, then?' said Mr Hume.

'Well, if you look closely . . .'

Despite his better judgement, Mr Hume found himself leaning forward to examine the pin.

'Really closely . . .'

Mr Hume squinted. Someone had once given him a grain of rice with his name written upon it, which Mr Hume had considered interesting but pointless, and he wondered if Samuel had somehow managed a similar trick.

'You might just be able to see an infinite number of angels dancing on the head of this pin,' finished Samuel.[8]

---

[8] It was St Thomas Aquinas, a most learned man who died in 1274, who was supposed to have suggested that an infinite number of angels could dance on the head of a pin. In fact he didn't, although he spent a lot of time thinking about whether or not angels had bodies (he

Mr Hume looked at Samuel. Samuel looked back at him. 'Are you trying to be funny?' asked Mr Hume.

This was a question Samuel heard quite often, usually when he wasn't trying to be funny at all.

'No,' said Samuel. 'I read it somewhere. Theoretically, you can fit an infinite number of angels on the head of a pin.'

'That doesn't mean that they're actually there,' said Mr Hume.

'No, but they might be,' said Samuel reasonably.

'Equally, they might not.'

'You can't prove that they're not there, though,' said Samuel.

'But you can't prove that they *are*.'

Samuel thought about this for a couple of seconds, then said: 'You can't prove a negative proposition.'

'What?' asked Mr Hume.

'You can't prove that something doesn't exist. You can only prove that something *does* exist.'

'Did you read that somewhere too?' Mr Hume was having trouble keeping the sarcasm from his voice.

'I think so,' said Samuel, who, like most honest, straight-forward people, had trouble recognising sarcasm. 'But it's true, isn't it?'

'I suppose so,' said Mr Hume. He realised that he sounded

---

seemed to think not), and how many of them there might be up in heaven (rather a lot, he concluded). The problem with St Thomas Aquinas was that he liked arguing with himself, and it's very hard to nail down exactly what he thought about anything at all. Still, the question of how many angels can dance on the head of a pin is probably of interest mainly to philosophers and, one presumes, dancing angels, since the last thing an angel doing the foxtrot wants to worry about is how crowded the pin is getting, and the possibility of falling off the edge and doing himself an injury.

distinctly sulky, so he coughed, then said with more force: 'Yes, I suppose you're right.'[9]

Samuel continued: 'Which means that I have as much chance of proving that there are angels on the head of this pin as you have of proving that there aren't.'

Mr Hume rubbed his forehead in frustration. 'Are you sure you're only eleven?' he asked.

'Positive,' said Samuel.

Mr Hume shook his head wearily.

'Thank you for that, Samuel. You can take your pin – and your angels – back to your desk now.'

'Are you certain you don't want to keep it?' asked Samuel.

'Yes, I'm certain.'

'I have lots more.'

'*Sit down*, Samuel,' said Mr Hume, who had a way of making a hiss sound like a shout, a sign of barely controlled rage that even Samuel was able to recognise. He went back to his chair

[9] Actually, this is not entirely true. It may well be the case that one cannot prove the existence of a nine-eyed, multi-tentacled pink monster named Herbert, but that does not mean that, somewhere in the universe, there is not a nine-eyed, multi-tentacled pink monster named Herbert wondering why nobody writes to him. Just because he hadn't been seen doesn't mean he isn't out there. This is known as an *inductive argument*. But the argument is probable, not definite. If there's actually a pretty good chance he exists, there's at least as good a chance that he doesn't exist. So you can prove a negative, at least as much as you can prove anything at all.

In addition, again according to quantum theory, there is a probability that all possible events, no matter how strange, may occur, so there is a probability, however small, that Herbert may exist after all.

Still, it's a good argument with which to confuse schoolteachers and parents, and on that basis alone Samuel is to be applauded.

and carefully impaled his desk with the pin, so that the angels, if they were actually there, wouldn't fall off.

'Anyone else got anything they'd like to share with us?' asked Mr Hume. 'An imaginary bunny, perhaps? An invisible duck named Percy?'

Everyone laughed. Bobby Goddard kicked the back of Samuel's seat.

Samuel sighed.

So that was why Mr Hume had called Samuel's mother, and afterwards she had given Samuel a talking to about taking school seriously, and not teasing Mr Hume, who appeared to be, she said, 'a little sensitive'.

Samuel glanced at his watch. His mother would be gone by now, which meant that Stephanie the babysitter would be waiting for him when he returned. Stephanie had been OK when she had first started looking after Samuel a couple of years before, but recently she had become horrible in the way that only certain teenage girls can. She had a boyfriend named Garth who would sometimes come over to 'keep her company', which meant that Samuel would be rushed off to bed well before his bedtime. Even when Garth wasn't around, Stephanie would spend hours talking on the phone while watching reality TV shows in which people competed to become models, singers, dancers, actors, builders, or anything other than what they really were, and she preferred to do so without the benefit of Samuel's company.

It was now dark. Samuel should have been home fifteen minutes ago, but the house wasn't the same any more. He missed his dad, but he was also angry at him and his mum.

'We should be getting back,' he told Boswell. Boswell

wagged his tail. It was getting chilly, and Boswell didn't like the cold.

At which point there was a bright blue flash from somewhere behind them, accompanied by a smell like a fire in a rotten-egg factory. Boswell nearly fell off the wall in shock, saved only by Samuel's arms.

'Right,' said Samuel, sensing an opportunity to delay returning home, 'let's go and see what *that* was . . .'

In the basement of 666 Crowley Avenue, a number of cloaked figures were covering their faces with their sleeves and spluttering.

'Oh, that's disgusting,' said Mrs Renfield. 'How horrid!'

The smell really was terrible, particularly in such an enclosed space, even though Mr Abernathy had earlier opened the basement window a crack to let in some air. Now he rushed to open it wider and, slowly, the stench began to weaken, or perhaps it was just that there was now something else to distract the attention of the four people in the basement from it.

Hanging in the air at the very centre of the room was a small, rotating circle of pale blue light. It twinkled, then grew in strength and size. Slowly, it became a perfect disc, about two feet in diameter, from which wisps of smoke were emerging.

It was Mrs Abernathy who took the first step forward.

'Careful, dear,' said her husband.

'Oh, do be quiet,' said Mrs Abernathy.

She kept advancing until she was mere inches from the circle. 'I think I can see something,' she said. 'Wait a minute.' She drew closer. 'There's . . . *land* there. It's like a window.

I can see mud, and stones, and the bars of some huge gates.

'And now there's something moving—'

Outside, Samuel crouched by the small window looking down on the basement. Boswell, who was a very intelligent dog, was hiding by the hedge. In fact Boswell was *under* the hedge, and had he been a larger dog, one capable of restraining an eleven-year-old boy, for example, Samuel would have been right there beside him; that, or both of them would have been well on their way home, where there were no nasty smells, no flashing blue lights, and no hints that something bad had just happened, and was likely to get considerably worse, Boswell also being a melancholic, even pessimistic dog by nature.

The window was only a foot long, and opened barely two inches on its metal hinge, but the gap was wide enough for Samuel to be able to view and hear all that was going on inside. He was a little surprised to see the Abernathys and two other people wearing what looked like black bathrobes in a cold basement, but he had long ago learned not to be too shocked by anything adults did. He heard Mrs Abernathy describe what she was seeing, but all that was visible to Samuel was the glowing circle itself. It seemed to be filled with a white fog, as if someone had blown a very big, very dense smoke ring in the Abernathys' basement.

Samuel was anxious to discover what else Mrs Abernathy might have been able to glimpse. Unfortunately those details were destined to remain unknown, apart from the fact that whatever it was had grey, scaly skin and three large, clawed fingers for that was what reached out from the glowing circle, grabbed Mrs Abernathy's head and dragged her through. She didn't even have time to scream.

Mrs Renfield screamed instead. Mr Abernathy ran towards the glowing circle, then seemed to think better of whatever he was planning to do and settled for plaintively calling out his wife's name.

'Evelyn?' he said. 'Are you all right, dear?'

There was no response from the hole, but he could hear an unpleasant sound from within, like someone squishing ripe fruit. His wife had been correct, though: something was visible through the hole. It did indeed look like a pair of enormous gates, ones which had developed a hole that was now bubbling with molten metal. Through it, Mr Abernathy could see a dreadful landscape, all ruined trees and black mud. Shapes moved across it, shadowy figures that had no place except in horror stories and nightmares. Of his wife there was no sign.

'Let's get out of here,' said Mr Renfield. He began bustling his wife towards the stairs, then stopped as a movement in the corner of the basement caught his eye.

'Eric,' he said.

Mr Abernathy was too concerned with the whereabouts of his wife to pay attention.

'Evelyn?' he called again. 'Are you in there, dear?'

'Eric,' said Mr Renfield again, this time with more force. 'I think you may want to see this.'

Mr Abernathy turned and saw what Mr Renfield and his wife were looking at. As soon as he did so he decided that, all things considered, he might rather not have seen it, but by then, of course, it was too late.

There was a shape in the corner of the cellar, rimmed with

blue light. It resembled a large, Mrs Abernathy-shaped balloon, although one that was being filled with water and then jiggled by some unseen force so that it bulged in all the wrong places. In addition its skin, visible only at its face and hands where they emerged from the now tattered and bloodied cloak, were grey and scaly, and the fingernails of each hand were yellow and hooked.

As they watched, the transformation was completed. A tentacle, its surface covered in sharp suckers that moved like mouths, coiled around the figure's legs for a moment, and then was absorbed into the main body. The skin became white, the nails went from yellow to painted red, and something that was almost Mrs Abernathy stood before them. Even Samuel, from where he watched, could see that she wasn't the same. Mrs Abernathy had been quite pretty for someone his mum's age, but now she was more attractive than ever. She seemed to radiate beauty, as though someone had turned on a light inside her body and it was now glowing through her skin. Her eyes were very bright, and some of that blue energy flickered in their depths, like lightning glimpsed in the blackest night.

She was also, Samuel realised, quite terrifying. *Power*, he thought. She's full of *power*.

'Evelyn?' said Mr Abernathy uncertainly.

The thing that looked like Mrs Abernathy smiled.

'Evelyn is gone,' she said. Her voice was deeper than Samuel remembered, and made him shiver.

'Well, where is she?' demanded Mr Abernathy.

The woman raised her right hand and pointed her finger at the glowing hole.

'In there, on the other side of the portal.'

'And what is "in there"?' said Mr Abernathy. To his credit, he was being rather brave when faced with something that was clearly beyond his experience and, indeed, beyond this world.

'In there is . . . Hell,' said the woman.

'Hell?' said Mrs Renfield, entering the conversation. 'Are you sure? It doesn't sound very likely.' She peered into the hole. 'It looks a bit like that place on the moors where your mother lives, Reginald.'

Mr Renfield took a careful look. 'You know, you're right, it does a bit.'

'Bring Evelyn back,' said Mr Abernathy, ignoring the Renfields.

'Your wife is gone. I will take her place.'

Mr Abernathy regarded the thing in the corner.

'What do you *want*?' asked Mr Abernathy, who was cleverer than Mr and Mrs Renfield, and all the little Renfields, had they been there, put together.

'To open the gates.'

'The gates?' said Mr Abernathy in puzzlement, then the expression on his face changed. 'The gates . . . of *Hell*?'

'Yes. We have four days to prepare the way.'

'Right,' said Mr Renfield, 'we're off. Come along, Doris.' He took his wife's arm and together they began ascending the steps from the basement. 'Thanks for an, um, *interesting* night, Eric. We must do it again some time.'

Mr and Mrs Renfield got as far as the third step when what looked like twin strands of spider web flew from the glowing blue hole, wrapped themselves round the waists of the unfortunate pair, then plucked them from the steps and dragged them through the portal. With a puff of foul-smelling smoke they were gone. The portal grew larger for an instant before the blue rim seemed to disappear entirely.

'Where is it?' shouted Mr Abernathy. 'Where has it gone?'

'It's still there,' said the woman. 'But it's better that it should remain hidden for now.'

Mr Abernathy reached towards where the circle had been, and his hand vanished in mid-air. Quickly he pulled it back again, then held it up before his face. It was coated in a clear, sticky fluid.

'I want my wife back,' he said. 'I want the Renfields back.' He reconsidered. 'Actually, you can keep the Renfields. I just want Evelyn back. Please.' Mr Abernathy might not have been fond of his wife, but having her around was easier than being forced to look after himself.

The woman merely shook her head. There were twin flashes of blue behind her, and two large hairy things moved in the shadows of the basement. From where he crouched, Samuel glimpsed black eyes glittering – too many eyes for two people – and some bony, jointed limbs. While Samuel watched, the shapes gradually assumed the form of Mr and Mrs Renfield, although they seemed to have a bit of trouble finding somewhere to store all their legs.

'I won't help you,' said Mr Abernathy. 'You can't make me.'

The woman sighed. 'We don't want your help,' she said. 'We just want your body.'

With that a long pink tongue slithered from the portal, and Mr Abernathy was yanked from his feet and disappeared into thin air. Moments later a fat blob, green and large-eyed, assumed his shape and took its place beside what looked, to the casual observer, like Mrs Abernathy and the Renfields.

By then Samuel had seen enough, and he and Boswell were running as fast as they could for the safety of home. Had he waited, Samuel might have seen the creature that was now Mrs Abernathy staring in the direction of the small window, and at the faint shape of a boy that hung in the still night air where Samuel been hiding.

Five

In Which We Meet Nurd, Who is Not Quite As Terrifying As He Would Like to Be, but a Great Deal Unluckier

Nurd, the Scourge of Five Deities, sat on his gilded throne, his servant Wormwood at his feet and his kingdom spread before him, and sighed.

'Bored, Your Scourgeness?' enquired Wormwood.

'Actually,' said Nurd. 'I am extremely excited. I cannot remember the last time I felt so enthused about anything.'

'Really?' asked Wormwood hopefully, and received a painful tap on the head from Nurd's Sceptre of Terrible and Awesome Might for his trouble.

'No, you idiot,' said Nurd. 'Of course I'm bored. What else is there to be?'

It was an entirely understandable question, for Nurd was not in a happy place. In fact, the place in which Nurd happened to be was so far from Happy that even if one walked for a very long time – centuries, millennia – one still would not be able to see even Slightly Less Unhappy from wherever one ended up.

Nurd's kingdom, the Wasteland, consisted of mile upon mile of flat, grey stone, unbroken by anything at all, apart from the odd rock that was less grey, and some pools of viscous, bubbling black liquid. At the horizon, the rock met a slate-grey sky across which lightning occasionally flashed without ever bringing the sound of thunder, or the feel of rain.

It wasn't even a kingdom as such. Nurd, the Scourge of Five Deities, had simply been banished to it for being, as his name had it, a Scourge, although the nature of Nurd's offences was open to some doubt.[10]

The title 'Scourge of Five Deities', which Nurd had come up with all by himself, was technically true. Nurd had been something of a bother to five different demonic entities, but they were relatively minor ones: Schwell, the Demon of Uncomfortable Shoes; Ick, the Demon of Unpleasant Things Discovered in Plugholes During Cleaning; Graham, the Demon of Stale Biscuits and Crackers; Mavis, the Demon of Inappropriate Names for Men; and last, and quite possibly least, Erics', the Demon of Bad Punctuation.

Nurd had been less of a scourge to these worthies and more of a minor irritation, like a fly buzzing against a window in summer or, well, like a stale biscuit that one had rather been looking forward to having with a nice cup of tea, but thanks to the demon Graham, turns out to taste soggy and a bit dusty. Eventually, because he wouldn't go away, and kept trying to muscle in on their operations, the five deities appealed

---

[10] A deity, pronounced 'day-it-tee', is a kind of god. There are good deities, and bad deities. Nurd was a bad deity, but in general none of them is to be trusted. The playwright William Shakespeare wrote, in *King Lear*, that 'As flies to wanton boys are we to the gods; they kill us for their sport.' Nasty lot, deities. Don't say that you haven't learned something new by reading this page.

to an aide to the Great Malevolence himself, which was how Nurd came to be occupying a not-very-interesting piece of nowhere-in-particular with not-very-much-to-do, but had decided to make the best of it by calling it his kingdom. To keep him company, his faithful servant Wormwood had been expelled along with him, an expulsion that Wormwood considered more than a bit unfair because he hadn't done anything wrong at all, except to be careless in his choice of employer.

The Great Malevolence was not entirely without mercy (or, indeed, a sense of humour), for he had seen fit to give Nurd a slightly used throne upon which to sit, and a cushion for Wormwood, as well as a box in which Nurd could keep various bits and pieces that had proved of no use whatsoever during his banishment. Thus it was that Nurd and Wormwood had been sitting in the middle of nowhere, if not for eternity, then since a few minutes past. They had never had very much to talk about. Now they had even less.

Wormwood rubbed his head, where a new bump had been added to the already impressive collection that adorned his misshapen skull, and not for the first time thought that Nurd, the Scourge of Five Deities, really was a bit of a sod.

Nurd, heedless of Wormwood's resentment, sighed once more, and promptly disappeared.

There wasn't a name for the bundle of blue energy that had managed to escape from the Large Hadron Collider. It was part of that 96 per cent of matter and energy unknown to science, and it wasn't an intended result of the collider experiment at all. Rather, in attempting to recreate the circumstances of the Big Bang, the multiple explosions in the collider had, very briefly, opened a portal, and on the other side of the portal the Great Malevolence had been waiting for precisely that moment. The little bundle of energy was the equivalent of a piece of wood that has been wedged beneath a door to keep it open. Now the challenge was to start putting pressure on the door in order to open it wider, because the Great Malevolence was an immense being. What Mrs Abernathy had glimpsed, before she met her unfortunate end, were the gates of Hell, which had been put in place to keep the Great Malevolence within the boundaries of that awful place. The shard of blue energy had created a small hole in those gates, large enough for some of the Great Malevolence's agents to pass through. They were scouts, and guardians of the portal. They also represented the first step in the Great Malevolence's plan to leave his own place of banishment, which wasn't much better than that of Nurd, the Scourge of Five Deities, but did at least have a view, and a few more chairs.

Unfortunately, as soon as anyone or anything starts sending random bursts of energy whizzing through portals between dimensions without being sure of the consequences, there's a good chance that some of that energy may end up in places that it shouldn't, like the sparks from a welder's torch as he works on a piece of metal. In an act of grave misfortune, one of those sparks of energy had ended up creating a small fissure between our world and the space occupied by Nurd's throne or, more particularly, Nurd himself.

The Great Malevolence had managed to wedge open a door, just as he had hoped.

He had also, unintentionally, managed to open a window. Nurd, the Scourge of Five Deities, was free.

* * *

Nurd was feeling dizzy, and somewhat sick, as though he had just climbed off a roundabout.[11] He wasn't sure what had happened, except that it had been very painful, but he knew that he was no longer occupying a throne in a dull, grey world accompanied only by a small demon who looked like a weasel with mange, which meant that this could only be a good thing. He felt air on his skin. (Nurd was vaguely human in appearance, although his ears were too long and pointed, and his head, shaped like a quarter-moon, was too large for his body, and bore a distinctly greenish tinge.) Although he was in darkness, his eyes were already beginning to make out the shapes of unfamiliar things.

'I'm . . . somewhere else,' said Nurd. Although he had never been anywhere other than the Wasteland and, briefly, until he'd irritated the Great Malevolence, certain far-flung regions of Hell itself, he understood instinctively where he was. He was in the Place of People, of Humans. He was a demon of great power let loose among those who, next to him, were powerless and insignificant. He began to channel all his rage and hurt and loneliness, creating from them an energy that he could use to rule this new world. His skin cracked and glowed red, like streams of lava glimpsed beneath the shifting rock of a volcanic eruption. The glow moved to his eyes, giving them a ferocity they had not had for a very long time. Steam erupted from his ears, and he opened wide his jaws as he prepared to announce his presence on Earth to all those

---

[11] There was a demon for that feeling too: Ulp, the Demon of Things That Go Round for Slightly Too Long, with additional responsibility for the Smell of Candyfloss When You're Not Feeling Yourself, and the Lingering Odour of Small Children Being Unwell.

who would soon know his wrath.

'I am Nurd!' he cried. 'You will bow down before me!'

Light appeared. It was disturbingly regular, forming a huge rectangle, the outline of a door larger than Nurd had ever seen, even in the depths of Hell itself. Then the door opened, flooding Nurd's new world with illumination. A giant being towered above him, a colossus in a pink skirt and white blouse. It had something in its hands, a squat, eyeless creature with a long nose and square jaws.

'Oh, bug—' began Nurd, all he got to say before Mrs Johnson's vacuum cleaner dropped on him, and everything went dark again.

Back in the Wasteland, Wormwood was still trying to work out what, precisely, had happened to his unloved master. He poked the space on the throne that Nurd usually occupied, wondering if Nurd had been hiding the art of invisibility for all this time, and had only now decided to use it in order to break the monotony, but there was nothing there.

Nurd, it appeared, was gone.

And if Nurd was gone, then he, Wormwood, was now ruler of all he surveyed.

Wormwood picked up the Sceptre of Terrible and Awesome Might from the foot of the throne. With his other hand, he grasped the Crown of Misdeeds which had fallen from Nurd's head as he slipped out of existence. He stared at them both, then faced the Wasteland and raised the sceptre and the crown above his head.

'I am Wormwood!' he cried. 'I am –'

There was a sound behind him, as though a Nurd-shaped object were being forced through a very small hole, and wasn't feeling terribly pleased about the process.

– 'very happy to see you again, Master,' concluded Wormwood, as he turned and saw Nurd, seated, once again, on his throne, and looking like a very big Thing of Some Kind had fallen on him. He seemed bewildered and somewhat broken in places.

'Wormwood,' said Nurd. 'I feel ill.'

And he sneezed a single, dusty sneeze.

Six

In Which We Encounter Stephanie, Who is Not a
Demon But is Still Not Terribly Nice

The front door opened while Samuel was still fumbling for his key. He had only recently been entrusted with his own house key, and he was so terrified of losing it that he kept it round his neck on a piece of string. Unfortunately it was proving rather difficult to find it while dressed as a ghost and holding on to a small, worried dog, so he was still searching beneath various layers of sheet, sweater, and shirt when Stephanie the babysitter appeared in his line of sight.

'Where have you been?' she said. 'You should have been back half an hour ago.' The expression on her face changed. 'And why are you dressed like a ghost?'

Samuel shuffled past her, but didn't answer immediately. First of all, he set Boswell free of his lead and divested himself of his sheet.

'I thought I'd get an early start for Halloween,' he said, gasping, 'but that doesn't matter now. I've seen some-thing—'

'Forget it,' said Stephanie.

'But—'

'Not interested.'

'It's important.'

'Go to bed.'

'What?' Samuel was momentarily distracted from what he had witnessed in the Abernathys' basement by the injustice of this order. 'It's half-term. I don't have to go to school tomorrow. Mum said—'

'"Mum said, Mum said,"' mimicked Stephanie. 'Well, your mum isn't here now. I'm in charge, and I say that you have to go to bed.'

'But the Abernathys. Their basement. Monsters. Gates. You don't understand.'

Stephanie leaned in very close to Samuel's face and Samuel recognised that there were things even more terrifying than what he had seen at the Abernathys' house, if only because they were very close and their anger was directed entirely at him. Stephanie's face was going red, her nostrils were flaring, and her eyes had grown narrow, like the slits in a castle wall before someone begins firing flaming arrows out of them. She spoke very precisely, through gritted teeth.

'Go. To. *Bed.*'

The final word was delivered at such ear-splittingly high volume that Samuel felt certain his glasses were about to crack. Even Boswell, who was used to Stephanie by now, looked disturbed.

With no other option, Samuel stomped up the stairs to bed, closely followed by Boswell. He was about to slam his door behind him when he heard Stephanie shout: 'And don't you dare slam that door!'

Although sorely tempted to disobey, Samuel decided to err on the side of discretion. There was not a great deal that

Stephanie could do to him, although he sometimes wondered what she might have done if she thought that she could get away with it, like burying him in the back garden after drowning him in the bathtub.[12] Still, Stephanie was a tattle-tale and when Samuel had crossed her in the past he had found himself dealing with his mother the following morning. Unlike Stephanie, there were a great many things she could do to make his life uncomfortable, such as denying him television, or his allowance, or, as on one particularly grim occasion after he had dropped a plastic snake down Stephanie's back, both of the above. How was he to know that Stephanie was afraid of snakes, he had argued, even though he had been fully aware of how much she disliked them, and that had been half the fun. He still treasured the memory of her leaping from the couch in shock, and the strange noise that had come from deep within her, a sound that was barely human, as if someone were playing a violin inside her very, very badly. In fact, he could trace the serious deterioration of his relationship with Stephanie to that particular occasion. Not only had his mother punished him but the odious Garth had threatened to stick his head down the toilet and flush him to China if he ever pulled a stunt like that again. Samuel, having no

[12] It is a curious fact that small boys are more terrified of their babysitters than small girls are. In part, this is because small girls and babysitters, who are usually slightly larger girls, belong to the same species, and therefore understand each other. Small boys, on the other hand, do not understand girls, and therefore being looked after by one is a little like a hamster being looked after by a shark. If you are a small boy it may be some consolation to you to know that even large boys do not understand girls, and girls, by and large, do not understand boys. This makes adult life very interesting.

great desire to be flushed to China, had not pulled a stunt like that again.[13]

Samuel changed into his pyjamas, brushed his teeth, and climbed between his sheets. Boswell curled up in his basket at the foot of the bed. Usually Samuel would read before turning off the light and going to sleep, but not tonight. He was determined to stay up until his mother returned home, and then he would confront her with what he had learned.

Samuel managed to stay awake for two and a half hours before sleep eventually took him. He thought of all that he had seen and heard in the Abernathys' basement. He wondered if he should go to the police, but he was not an unintelligent boy and he knew that the police would take a dim view of an eleven-year-old with a dachshund who claimed that his neighbours had been transformed into demons intent upon opening the gates of Hell. So it was that Samuel did not hear his mother come in, nor did he hear Stephanie leave, after first informing Samuel's mother that Samuel had broken curfew.

Nor did he see, after all the lights were turned off and his mother was, like him, asleep in bed, the figure of a woman standing at the garden gate, staring intently at his bedroom window, her eyes burning with a cold blue fire.

[13] It is not possible to flush someone to China. Or Australia. Well, not unless they're already there. It is not a good idea, though, to point this out to someone who is threatening to flush you to China or Australia, as there is a good chance that they will try it anyway just to prove you wrong.

Seven

*In Which the Scientists Wonder What the Bit Was,
And Where It Might Have Gone*

While Samuel slept, a group of scientists huddled over a series
of screens and printouts. Behind them, an uncompleted game
of Battleships lay forgotten.

'But there's no record of anything unusual occurring,' said
one. His name was Professor Hilbert, and he had become a
scientist for two reasons. The first was that he had always
been fascinated by science, particularly physics, which is
science for people who like numbers more than – well, more
than people, probably. The other reason why Professor Hilbert
had become a scientist was that he had always *looked* like a
scientist. Even as a small boy he had worn glasses, been unable
to comb his hair properly, and had a fondness for storing
pens in his shirt pockets. He was also very interested in taking
things apart to find out how they worked, although he had
never discovered how to put any of them back together again
in quite the same way. Instead he was always trying to find
some means to improve them, even if they had worked
perfectly well to begin with. Thus it was that, when he
'improved' his parents' toaster, the toaster had incinerated the
bread, and then burst into flames so hot they had melted the
kitchen counter. The kitchen had always smelled funny after

that, and he was required to eat his bread untoasted unless supervised. After he spent an hour with their radio, it had begun picking up signals from passing military aircraft, leading to a visit from a couple of stern men in uniforms who were under the impression that the Hilberts were Russian spies. Finally young Hilbert was sent to a special school for very bright people, where, to his heart's content, he was allowed to take things apart and put them together again in odd combinations. He had started only one or two fires at the special school, but they were small, and easily extinguished.

Now Professor Hilbert was trying to make sense of what Ed and Victor were telling him. The collider had been shut down as a precaution, which annoyed Professor Hilbert greatly. Turning the collider on and off wasn't like flipping a light switch. It was a complicated and expensive business. Furthermore, it generated bad publicity for everyone involved in the experiment, especially as there were still people who were convinced that the collider would be responsible for the end of the world.

'You say that a particle of some kind separated itself from the beams in the collider?'

'That's right,' said Ed.

'Then somehow passed through the walls of the collider itself, and the solid rock around it, before disappearing.'

'Right again,' said Ed.

'Then the system began rewriting itself to eliminate any evidence of this occurrence?'

'Yes.'

'Fascinating,' said Professor Hilbert.

What was strange about this conversation was that at no point did Professor Hilbert doubt the truth of what Ed and

Victor were telling him. Nothing about the Large Hadron Collider and what it was revealing about the nature of the universe was surprising to Professor Hilbert. Delightful, yes. Troubling, sometimes. But never surprising. He was not a man who was easily surprised, and he suspected that the universe was a much stranger place than anyone imagined, which made him anxious to prove just how extraordinary it really was.

'What do you think it might be?' asked Ed.

'Evidence,' said Professor Hilbert.

'Of what?'

'I don't know,' said Professor Hilbert, and rambled off sucking his pencil.

Hours later Professor Hilbert was still at his desk, surrounded by pieces of paper on which he had constructed diagrams, created complex equations, and drawn little stick men fighting one another with swords. He had also gone over the system records for the past few hours and had discovered something curious. The system had overwritten itself, as Ed and Victor had suggested, but it had not done so perfectly. Like someone rubbing out a couple of lines written in pencil, the shadow of what had been there before still remained. Slowly, Professor Hilbert had begun reconstructing it. While he was not able to recreate it completely, he found that, at the precise moment that Ed and Victor had witnessed what was now being termed 'the Event', a batch of strange code had found its way into the system. It was this code that Professor Hilbert was now attempting to reconstruct.

The problem was that the code was not in any known computer language. In fact, it didn't appear to be in any recognisable language at all.

Professor Hilbert's particular area of interest was dimensions. Specifically, he was fascinated by the possibility that there might be a great many universes out there, of which ours was only one. He was part of a group of scientists who believed that our universe might exist in an ocean of other universes, some being born, some already in existence, and others about to come to an end. Instead of a universe, he believed in the possibility of a multiverse. His life's work had been devoted to this belief, which he hoped the collider might help him to prove. If a mini black hole, one that did not swallow up the Earth, say one thousand times the mass of an electron and existing for only 10^{-23} seconds, were created in the collider, Professor Hilbert believed that it would provide evidence for the existence of parallel universes.

Now, as he sat at his desk, he looked at the strange code, written in symbols that seemed at once modern yet very, very old and wondered: Is this the proof that I have been seeking? Is this a message from another universe, another dimension?

And if it is, then what does it mean?

Some of you may know who Albert Einstein was. For those who don't, here is a picture of him:

Einstein was a very famous scientist, the kind of scientist who even people who know nothing about science can probably name. He is most famous for his General Theory of Relativity, which concluded that mass is a form of energy, and goes e=mc^2 (or energy = mass by the speed of light squared) but he also had a sense of humour. He once said that we were all ignorant, but each of us was ignorant in a different way, which is very wise when you think about it.[14]

It was Einstein who predicted the existence of black holes (there is one at the heart of our Milky Way, but it's obscured by dust clouds; otherwise it would be visible every night as a fireball in the constellation of Sagittarius), but Einstein's black holes came with their own inbuilt problem. They had, at their centre, a singularity (there's that word again, remember footnote 1?), a point at which time came to an end and all known rules of physics broke down. You can't make a rule that breaks all the rules. Science just doesn't work that way.

Einstein wasn't happy about this at all. He liked things to work according to the rules. In fact, the whole point of his life's work was to prove that there were rules governing the known universe, and he couldn't very well leave things like singularities hanging about making the place look untidy.

[14] As you can see from his picture, Einstein didn't take himself too seriously, at least not all of the time. In general, it's a good idea to avoid people who take themselves too seriously. As individuals, we have only so much seriousness to go round, and people who take themselves very seriously don't have enough seriousness left over to take other people seriously. Instead they tend to look down on them, and are secretly pleased when they get stuff wrong, because they just prove to the too-serious types that they were right not to take them seriously to begin with.

So, like any good scientist, Einstein went back over his work and tried to find a way to prove the singularities didn't exist or, if they did, that they played by the rules. So, after a bit of fiddling with his sums he came to the conclusion that the singularities might in fact be bridges between two different universes. This solved the problem of the singularities as far as Einstein was concerned, but nobody really believed that this bridge, known as an Einstein–Rosen bridge, could actually be used to travel between the universes, mainly because, if it existed at all, it would be very unstable, like building a bridge made from chewing gum and bits of chocolate over a very long drop, then suggesting that someone in a big truck might like to give it a try. The bridge would also be very small – 10^{-34} metres, or so small that it would hardly be there at all – and it would exist only for an instant, so driving a truck across it (a space truck, obviously) would be difficult and, frankly, fatal.

Mathematicians have also suggested the possibility of what are known as 'multiply-connected spaces', or wormholes – literally, tunnels between universes – that exist at the centre of black holes.[15] In 1963 a New Zealand mathematician named Roy Kerr suggested that a spinning black hole would collapse into a stable ring of neutrons because the centrifugal force pushing out would cancel the inward force of gravity.

---

[15] In *Alice Through the Looking Glass*, the book by Lewis Carroll, the looking glass is, in effect, a wormhole. Carroll, whose real name was Charles Dodgson, was a mathematician, and was aware of the theory of wormholes. He liked injecting puzzles into his maths classes. One of his most famous goes as follows: A cup contains 50 spoonfuls of brandy, and another contains 50 spoonfuls of water. A spoonful of brandy is taken from the first cup and added to the second cup.

The black hole wouldn't fall in on itself, and you wouldn't be crushed to death, but it would be a one-way trip, as the gravity would be sufficient to prevent you from returning the way you had come.

Nevertheless, the whole debate was another stage in the great discussion about wormholes, and black holes, and parallel universes, places where the rules of physics might not be quite the same as ours but might work perfectly well in that universe.

Now Professor Hilbert was wondering if something in a universe other than our own might have found a way of breaking through, using a hole or a bridge as yet unthought of in our science, and tried to make contact. If that was the case, then, if the bridge still existed, there would be an opening in its world, and another opening in ours.

The questions that followed from this were: where was that opening, and what exactly was going to emerge from it?

Back in the basement of 666 Crowley Avenue, four figures stood staring at where there had been, until recently, a spinning circle of blue. Mrs Abernathy had returned from her visit to Samuel Johnson's house to find her three companions in a state of some distress.

'The portal has closed,' said Mr Renfield, who no longer looked or sounded quite like the Mr Renfield of old. His

---

Then a spoonful of that mixture is taken from the second cup and mixed into the first. Is there more or less brandy in the second cup than there is water in the first cup? If you'd like to know the answer – and, I warn you, it will make your head ache more than drinking all of the brandy would – it's at the end of this chapter . . .*

voice emerged from his throat in a series of hoarse clicks, and his skin had already taken on the wrinkled, unhealthy appearance of a rotting apple. The change in his appearance had begun almost as soon as the blue light had disappeared, and a similar decay could be seen in Mrs Renfield and Mr Abernathy. Only Mrs Abernathy remained unaffected.

'They have shut down the collider,' said Mrs Abernathy, a strange expression on her face as she spoke, which she hid from the Renfields, 'as the Great One predicted that they would. But now we know that travel between this world and ours is possible. Even as we speak, our master is assembling his army, and when he is ready the portal will open once again, and he will cross over and claim this place as his own.'

'But we grow weak,' said Mrs Renfield. Her breath smelled bad, as if something inside her was festering.

'*You* grow weak,' said Mrs Abernathy. 'You are here only to serve my needs. Your energy will fuel me, and when the portal opens once more you will be renewed.'

This was not entirely true. Mrs Abernathy was a more extraordinary demon than her three companions, older and wiser and more powerful than ever they could have imagined. The portal had not closed, not entirely. Mrs Abernathy's will and strength were keeping it open just a crack. Nevertheless, she was content to suck energy from the others as required, and to use the portal only when necessary. She would be the one to explore this new world in advance of her master's coming, and it was important that she blended in without attracting attention. After so long in the darkness, she wanted to experience something of the Earth before it was turned to ash and fire.

---

* Okay, back to Lewis Carroll's brandy and water problem. Mathematically speaking, the answer is that there will be just as much brandy in the water as there is water in the brandy, so both mixtures will be the same. But – and this is where your head may start to ache – when equal quantities of water and alcohol are mixed the sum of them is more compact than their parts because the brandy penetrates the spaces between the water molecules, and the water penetrates the spaces between the brandy molecules, a bit like the way two matching pieces of a jigsaw fit together so that they occupy less space than if you just laid the same pieces side by side. In other words, the mixture becomes more concentrated, so if you add 50 spoonfuls of water and 50 spoonfuls of brandy, you actually end up with less than 100 spoonfuls of the mixture in total. Adding a spoonful of brandy to 50 spoonfuls of water will give you less than 51 spoonfuls of the mixture, because, like we said earlier, it's more concentrated. If you take a spoonful from *that* mixture, it will leave less than 50 spoonfuls in the cup. Then, if you add that spoonful from the concentrated mixture to the cup of brandy, it means that there's more brandy in the brandy cup than there is more water in the water cup. I warned you . . .

Eight

In Which Samuel Learns That Someone Trying to Open the Gates of Hell is Not of Particular Concern to His Mum

Samuel awoke shortly after eight to the sound of plates banging in the kitchen. He dressed quickly, then went downstairs. Boswell was waiting expectantly for scraps from the breakfast table. He glanced at Samuel, wagged his tail in greeting, then went back to gazing intently at Mrs Johnson and the remains of the bacon on her plate.

'Mum—' Samuel began, but he was immediately cut off.

'Stephanie says that you came in late last night,' said his mother.

'I know, and I'm sorry, but—'

'No buts. You know I don't like you being out late by yourself.'

'But—'

'What did I just say? No "buts." Now sit down and eat your cereal.'

Samuel wondered if he would ever be allowed to complete a sentence again. First Stephanie, and now his mother. If this continued, he'd be forced to communicate entirely through sign language, or notes scribbled on pieces of paper, like someone in solitary confinement.

'Mum,' said Samuel, in his most serious and grown-up of tones. 'I have something important to tell you.'

'Uh-huh.' His mother stood and carried her plate to the sink, disappointing Boswell considerably.

'Mother, please.'

Samuel almost never called his mum 'Mother'. It always sounded wrong, but it had the effect, on this occasion, of attracting her attention. She turned round and folded her arms.

'Well?'

Samuel gestured at the kitchen chair opposite him, the way he saw grown-ups on television do when they invited people into their office to tell them they were about to be fired.

'Please, take a seat.'

Mrs Johnson gave a long-suffering sigh, but did as she was asked.

'It's about the Abernathys,' said Samuel.

'The Abernathys? The people at number six hundred and sixty-six?'

'Yes, and their friends.'

'What friends?'

'Well, I don't know their friends' names, but they were a man and a woman, and they were both fat.'

'And?'

'They are no more,' said Samuel, solemnly. He had read that phrase somewhere, and had always fancied using it.

'What does that mean?'

'They've been taken.'

'Taken where?'

'To Hell.'

'Oh, Samuel!' His mother rose and returned to the sink.

'You had me worried there for a minute. I thought you were being serious. Where do you get these ideas from? I really will have to keep a closer eye on what you're watching on television.'

'But it's true, Mum,' said Samuel. 'They were all in the Abernathys' basement dressed in robes, and then there was a blue light and a hole in the air, and a big claw reached out and pulled Mrs Abernathy inside, and then she appeared again except it wasn't her but something that looked like her. Then spiderwebs took their fat friends and, finally, Mr Abernathy was yanked in by a big tongue, and when it was all over there were four of them again, but it wasn't them, not really.'

'And,' he finished, playing his trump card, 'they're trying to open the gates of Hell. I heard Mrs Abernathy say so, or the thing that looks like Mrs Abernathy.'

He took a deep breath and waited for a response.

'And that's why you were half an hour late coming back last night?' asked his mother.

'Yes.'

'You know that you're not supposed to be out past eight, especially now that the evenings are getting dark.'

'Mum, they're trying to open the *gates* of *Hell*. You know: Hell. Demons, and stuff. Monsters.' He paused for effect, then added: 'The Devil!'

'And you didn't eat your dinner,' said his mum.

'What?' Samuel was floored. He knew that his mother tended to ignore a lot of what he said, but he had never lied to her. Well, hardly ever. There were some things she didn't need to know, such as where her private stash of chocolate kept disappearing to, or how the rug in the living room had been moved slightly to cover some nasty burn marks after an experiment involving match heads.

'Don't say "what", say "pardon",' his mother corrected. 'I said you didn't eat your dinner.'

'That's because Stephanie sent me to bed early, but that's not the point.'

'Excuse me, Samuel Johnson, but that's precisely the point. You came in so late that you couldn't eat your dinner. There was spinach. I know you don't like it, but it's very healthy. And you annoyed Stephanie, and it's hard to get good baby-sitters these days.'

Samuel was by now completely bewildered. His mother could be very strange. According to her, this was how the world worked:

THINGS THAT ARE BAD

1. Coming in late.
2. Not eating spinach.
3. Annoying Stephanie.
4. Trying to confuse Mr Hume with talk of angels and pins.
5. Not wearing the hat his grandmother had knitted for him, even if it was purple and made him look like he had a swollen head.
6–99. Lots of other stuff.
100. Trying to open the gates of Hell.

'Mum, haven't you heard anything I've said?' asked Samuel.

'I've heard everything that you've said, Samuel, and it's more than enough. Now eat your breakfast. I have a lot to do today. If you want to, you can help me with the shopping later. Otherwise you can just stay here, but no television and no video games. I want you to read a book, or do something useful with your time. It's all those cartoons and monster-killing games that have given you these ideas. Honestly, dear, you live in a world of your own sometimes.'

And then she did something completely unexpected. Having spent the last five minutes complaining about him, and not believing anything that he'd told her, she came over and hugged him, and kissed his hair.

'You do make me laugh, though,' she said. She looked into his eyes, and her face grew sad. 'Samuel, all this stuff – these stories, the angels on the pin – it's not to do with your dad, is it? I know you miss him, and things have been a bit difficult since he left. You know I love you, don't you? You don't need to go looking for attention from me. I'm here, and you're the most important person in my world. You will remember that, won't you?'

Samuel nodded. His eyes felt hot. They always did when his mum talked about his dad. He'd been gone for two months and three days now. Samuel wished that he'd come back, but at the same time he was angry with him. He wasn't sure what had happened between his mum and dad, but his dad was now living up north, and Samuel had only seen him twice since the break-up. From a whispered but angry phone conversation that he'd overheard between his mum and dad, someone called Elaine was involved. Samuel's mum had called Elaine a very bad name during the conversation, and then had hung up the phone and started crying. Samuel was sometimes angry at his mum too, because he wondered if she might have done something to drive his dad away. And, on occasion, when he was feeling particularly sad, Samuel would try to remember if he himself had done anything to make his dad leave, if he'd been bad, or mean to him, or had let his dad down in some way. For the most part, though, he sensed that his dad was the one who was most to blame, and he hated the fact that his dad made his mum cry.

'Now eat your bacon,' said Samuel's mum. 'I've left it under the grill for you.'

She kissed him on the head again, then went upstairs.

Samuel ate his bacon. Sometimes he just didn't understand adults. He wondered if he ever would, or if there would come a time, after he become a grown-up himself, when it would all suddenly make sense to him.

He finished his food, fed the scraps to Boswell, then washed his plate and sat down at the table again. He looked at Boswell. Boswell looked at him. There was still the not-so-small matter of the opening of the gates of Hell to be dealt with, and his mum had been no help at all with that.

'Now what are we supposed to do?' asked Samuel.

If Boswell could have shrugged, he would have.

The doorbell rang at number 666. It was Mrs Abernathy who answered. Standing before her was the postman, holding a large parcel. He wasn't the usual postman, who was on holiday in Spain, and he had never seen Mrs Abernathy before, but he thought she was extremely good-looking.

'Parcel for Mr Abernathy,' he said.

'That would be my –' Mrs Abernathy, unused to talking to someone who wasn't another demon, had to think for a moment – 'husband,' she finished. 'He's not here at the moment.'

'No problem. You can sign for it.'

He handed Mrs Abernathy a pen, and a form on a clipboard. Mrs Abernathy looked confused.

'Just sign, er, there,' said the postman, pointing to a line at the bottom of the form.

'I don't seem to have my glasses,' said Mrs Abernathy. 'Would you mind stepping inside for a moment while I look for them?'

'It's just a signature,' said the postman. 'On a line. That line.' Once again, he pointed helpfully at the line in question.

'I don't like signing anything that I haven't read,' said Mrs Abernathy.

It takes all sorts, thought the postman. 'Right you are, then, ma'am. I'll wait here while you look for your glasses.'

'Oh, please, come inside. I insist. It's so cold out, and it may take me a moment or two to find them.' She moved further into the house, still holding the clipboard. That clipboard was very important to the postman. It contained details of all of the parcels and registered letters that he had delivered that day, and he wasn't supposed to let it out of his sight. Reluctantly he followed Mrs Abernathy into the house. He noticed that the blinds and curtains were drawn in the rooms adjoining the hall, and there was a funny smell, like rotten eggs and recently struck matches.

'Bit dark in here,' he said.

'Really?' said Mrs Abernathy. 'I rather like it this way.'

And the postman noticed, for the first time, that there seemed to be a blue glow to Mrs Abernathy's eyes.

The door closed behind him.

But Mrs Abernathy was in front of him, so who could have closed it?

He was turning to find out when a tentacle curled itself round his neck and lifted him off the floor. The postman tried to say something, but the tentacle was very tight. He had a brief glimpse of a huge mouth, and some big teeth, and then everything went dark for ever.

Humans were puny, thought Mrs Abernathy. She had been sent to find out their strengths and weaknesses, but already she could tell that the latter far outweighed the former.

On the other hand, they didn't taste bad at all.

Mrs Abernathy licked her lips and went into the dining room, where the curtains were also drawn. Three figures sat upon chairs, doing nothing in particular apart from smelling funny. Mr Abernathy and the Renfields were starting to turn an ugly shade of purple, like meat that was going bad, and their fingernails had begun to drop off. That was the trouble with destroying the life force of another being, and taking on its shape. It was like opening a banana, throwing away the fruit, and then sewing up the skin in the hope that it would continue to look like a banana. It would for a while, but then it would start turning black.

'I'm concerned about the boy,' said Mrs Abernathy.

Her husband looked at her. His eyes were milky.

'Why?' he asked, his voice little more than a croak as his vocal cords began to decay 'He's just a child.'

'He will talk.'

'Nobody will believe him.'

'Somebody might.'

'And if they do? We are more powerful than they can ever be.'

Mrs Abernathy snorted in disgust. 'Have you looked in a mirror lately?' she said. 'The only powerful thing about you is your smell.'

She shook her head and walked away. That was the problem with lower demons: they had no cunning, and no imagination.

Mrs Abernathy was of the highest order of demons, only a level below the Great Malevolence himself. She had knowledge of humans, for the Great Malevolence had spoken of them to her, and with him she had watched them from afar, as if through a dark window. What he saw fed his hatred and jealousy. He rejoiced when men and women did bad things, and howled with rage when they did good. He wanted to reduce their world to rubble and scarred earth, and destroy every living thing in it that walked, crawled, swam, or flew. It was Mrs Abernathy who would pave the way for him. The Great Malevolence, and the human's machine with its beams and particles, would do the rest.

But there remained the problem of the boy. Children were dangerous, Mrs Abernathy knew, more so than adults. They believed in things like right and wrong, good and evil. They were persistent. They interfered.

First she would find out what Samuel Johnson knew. If he had been a naughty little boy, one who had been sticking his nose in where he had no business sticking it, he would have to be dealt with.

Nine

In Which We Learn a Little About the Gates of Hell,
None of Which is Entirely Helpful

After his mother left to do her shopping, Samuel spent
some time at the kitchen table, his chin cupped in his hands,
considering his options. He knew that Mrs Abernathy, or
the entity that now occupied her body, was up to no good,
but he was facing a problem encountered by young people
the world over: how to convince adults that you were telling
the truth about something in which they just did not want
to believe.

His mother had told him not to play computer games, but
that didn't mean he couldn't use his computer at all. With
Boswell at his heels Samuel went up to his bedroom, sat at
his desk, and began to search the Internet. He decided to
start with what he knew for certain, so he typed 'gates of
Hell' into the search engine.

The first reference that came up was to a huge bronze
sculpture entitled *La Porte de l'Enfer*, which in English means
The Gate of Hell, by an artist named Auguste Rodin. Apparently
Rodin was asked to create the sculpture in 1880, and prom-
ised to deliver it by 1885. Instead Rodin had still been working
on it when he died in 1917. Samuel did a small calculation
and discovered that Rodin had been 32 years late in deliv-

ering the sculpture. He wondered if Rodin might have been related to Mr Armitage, their local painter, who had been supposed to paint their living room and dining room over a single weekend and had in fact taken six months to do it, and even then had left one wall and part of the ceiling unfinished. Samuel's father and Mr Armitage had had a big argument about it when they met in the street. 'It's not the ceiling of the Sistine Chapel,' Mr Armitage had said. 'I'll get round to it when I can. You'll want me flat on my back painting angels next.'[16]

[16] The artist Michelangelo painted the ceiling of the Sistine Chapel in Rome between 1508 and 1512. He had to use scaffolding to do it, but because the ceiling was so high he couldn't build the scaffolding from the floor up, so instead he made a special flat wooden platform that hung from bolts beside the windows. Painting the ceiling was a very uncomfortable business, as you can probably imagine, but it's a myth that Michelangelo had to lie flat on his back to do it. Instead he stood upright, with his head bent back, for four years. By the end of it, he was so sore that he wrote a poem about it:

> I've grown a goitre by dwelling in this den –
> As cats from stagnant streams in Lombardy,
> Or in what other land they hap to be –
> Which drives the belly close beneath the chin:
>
> My beard turns up to heaven; my nape falls in
> Fixed on my spine: my breast-bone visibly
> Grows like a harp: a rich embroidery
> Bedews my face from brush-drips, thick and thin.

And so on for a few more verses, which can be summarised basically as 'owww . . .'

Samuel's father had suggested that if Mr Armitage *had* been asked to paint the ceiling of the Sistine Chapel, he would have taken twenty years instead of four, and still would have left God without a beard. At that point, Mr Armitage had said a rude word and walked away, and Samuel's father had ended up finishing the ceiling and wall himself.

Badly.

Anyway, while Rodin's gates looked very impressive, they didn't seem to have a blue light around them, and Samuel read that they had been inspired by a writer named Dante, and his book *The Divine Comedy*. Samuel suspected that neither Dante nor Rodin had ever really seen the gates of Hell, and had just taken a guess.[17]

After that, Samuel found some dodgy heavy metal groups who either had songs named after the gates of Hell, or simply liked putting images of demons on their album covers in order to make themselves seem more terrifying than they really were, since most of them were just hairy

---

[17] *The Divine Comedy* is not funny, but it's not supposed to be, despite its name. In Dante's time, a comedy meant a work that reflected a belief in an ordered universe. Also, serious books were written in Latin, and Dante wrote in a new language: Italian. Some of Shakespeare's comedies *are* funny, though, but not if you're being forced to study them in school. In school, everything Shakespeare wrote starts to seem like a tragedy, even the ones that aren't tragedies, which is a bit unfortunate, but that's just because of the way they're taught. Stick with them. In later life, people will be impressed that you can quote Shakespeare, and you will sound very intelligent. It's harder to quote trigonometry, or quadratic equations, and not half as romantic.

chaps from nice families who had spent too much time alone in their bedrooms as teenagers. Samuel did discover that the Romans and Greeks believed the gates were guarded by a three-headed dog called Cerberus, who made sure that nobody who entered could ever leave, but they also believed a boatman took dead people across the River Styx, and Samuel had seen no sign of a river in the Abernathys' basement.

He tried 'doors of Hell', but didn't have any more luck. Finally, he just typed in 'Hell', and came up with lots of stuff. Some religions believed that Hell was hot and fiery, and others thought it was cold and gloomy. Samuel didn't think any of them could know for certain, since by the time someone found out the truth he would be dead and the information would probably be too late to be useful. What he did find interesting was that most of the world's religions believed in Hell, even if they didn't always call it that, and lots of them had names for whatever they believed ruled over it: Satan, Yanluo Wang, Yamaraj. The one thing everyone seemed to agree on was that Hell wasn't a very pleasant place, and was not somewhere that you wanted to end up.

After an hour, Samuel stopped searching. He was frustrated. He wanted answers. He wanted to know what to do next.

He wanted to stop Mrs Abernathy before she opened the gates.

Samuel's mother was trying to work out if two small cans of baked beans were better value than one big can when a figure appeared beside her. It was Mrs Abernathy.

'Hello, Mrs Johnson,' said Mrs Abernathy. 'How lovely to see you.'

Mrs Johnson didn't know why exactly it was lovely for Mrs Abernathy to see her. She and Mrs Abernathy barely knew each other, and had never exchanged more than a polite 'hello' in the past.[18]

'Well, it's lovely to see you too,' Mrs Johnson lied. Something about Mrs Abernathy was making her uneasy. In fact, now that she thought about it, there were lots of things not quite right about the woman standing next to her. She was wearing a lovely black velvet overcoat, which was far too nice to wear for shopping unless you were shopping for an even lovelier black overcoat and wanted to impress the salesperson. Her skin, although very pale, paler than Mrs Johnson remembered from their previous brief meetings, had a bluish tinge to it, and the veins beneath her skin were more obvious than before. Her eyes,

---

[18] Adults say lots of things that they don't quite mean, usually just to be polite, which is no bad thing. They also say things that are exactly the opposite of what they appear to mean, such as:

　1) 'To be perfectly honest . . .', which means 'I am lying through my teeth.'

　2) 'I hear what you're saying . . .', which means 'I hear it, but I'm not really listening, and I don't agree with you anyway.' and

　3) 'I don't mean to be rude . . .', which means, 'I mean to be rude.'

There are some people who use phrases like this more often than anyone else, and who become very good at using them to avoid answering questions or telling the entire truth. These people are known as 'politicians'.

too, were very blue. They seemed to burn with a faint flame, like a gas fire. Mrs Abernathy was wearing lots of strong perfume, but she still smelled a little funny, and not in a ho-ho way.

As Mrs Johnson looked at Mrs Abernathy, and inhaled her perfume, she felt herself growing sleepy. Those eyes drew her in, and the fire within them grew more intense.

'How is your delightful son?' Mrs Abernathy asked. 'Samuel, isn't it?'

'Yes,' said Mrs Johnson, who couldn't remember anyone calling Samuel 'delightful' before. 'Samuel.'

'I was wondering if he ever mentioned me to you?'

Mrs Johnson heard the words emerge from her mouth before she was even aware that she was thinking them.

'Why, yes,' she said. 'He was only talking about you this morning.'

Mrs Abernathy smiled, but the smile died somewhere around her nostrils.

'And what did he say?'

'He seemed to think . . .'

'Yes?'

'. . . that you were trying . . .'

'Go on.'

'. . . to open . . .'

By now, Mrs Abernathy was leaning in very close to Mrs Johnson. Mrs Abernathy's breath stank, and her teeth were yellow. Her lipstick was bright red, and slightly smeared. In fact, thought Mrs Johnson, it looked a little like blood. Mrs Abernathy's tongue flicked out, and for just a moment, Mrs Johnson could have sworn that it was forked, like a snake's tongue.

'. . . gates . . .'

'What gates?' said Mrs Abernathy. '*What* gates?' Her hand reached for Mrs Johnson, gripping her shoulder. Her nails dug into Mrs Johnson's arm, causing her to wince.

The pain was enough to bring Mrs Johnson out of her daze. She took a step back, and blinked. When she opened her eyes Mrs Abernathy was standing farther away from her, a strange, troubled look on her face.

Try as she might, Mrs Johnson couldn't remember what it was they had been talking about. Something about Samuel, she thought, but what?

'Are you all right, Mrs Johnson?' asked Mrs Abernathy. 'You look a little unwell.'

'No, I'm fine,' said Mrs Johnson, although she didn't feel fine. She could still smell Mrs Abernathy's perfume and, worse, whatever it was the perfume was being used to disguise. She wanted Mrs Abernathy to go away. In fact, she felt that it was very important to stay as far from Mrs Abernathy as possible.

'Well, take care,' said Mrs Abernathy. 'It was nice talking to you. We should do it more often.'

'Yes,' said Mrs Johnson, meaning 'No.'

No, no, no, no, no.

When she arrived home Samuel was sitting at the kitchen table, drawing on a sheet of paper using crayons. He hid it away when she entered, but she glimpsed a blue circle. Samuel looked at her with concern.

'Are you OK, Mum?'

'Yes, dear. Why?'

'You look sick.'

Mrs Johnson glanced in the mirror by the sink.

'Yes,' she said. 'I suppose I do.'

She turned to Samuel. 'I met—' She stopped. She couldn't remember whom she had met. A woman? Yes, a woman, but the name wouldn't come to her. Then she wasn't certain that it had been a woman at all, and seconds later she wasn't sure she'd met *anyone*. It was as though her brain was a big house, and someone was turning off the lights in every room, one by one.

'Met who, Mum?' asked Samuel.

'I . . . don't know,' said Mrs Johnson. 'I think I'm going to lie down for a while.'

Mrs Johnson was beginning to wonder if she might not be coming down with something. The day before, she could have sworn that she'd heard a voice coming from the cupboard beneath the stairs, just as she was putting away the vacuum cleaner.

She left the kitchen and Samuel heard her go upstairs. When he went to check on her minutes later, his mother was already asleep. Her lips were moving, and Samuel thought she might have been having bad dreams. He wondered if he should call one of her friends, maybe Auntie Betty from up the road, then decided that he would just keep a close eye on his mother. He would let her sleep for now.

Samuel went back downstairs, and finished his drawing. He worked very slowly and carefully, trying to capture exactly what he had seen in the Abernathys' basement. It was the third such drawing he had done. He had thrown the first two away because they weren't quite accurate, but this one was better. It was nearly right, or as close to it as he was going to get. From a distance it looked more like a photograph than a drawing, for if there was one thing that Samuel was good at, it was art.

When he was done, he hid it carefully in his big atlas. He would show it to someone. He just had to decide who that someone should be.

Mrs Johnson didn't get up until later that evening. Samuel stayed downstairs and watched television, reckoning that his mum wouldn't mind, despite what she had said earlier. After a time, he got bored and did something else he wasn't supposed to do.

He went out to the garage at the back of the house to sit in his dad's car.

The 1961 Aston Martin DB4 Coupe was his dad's pride and joy, and Samuel had been for only a handful of trips in it before his dad had left, and even then his dad had seemed to resent Samuel's presence slightly, like a child forced to allow another child to play with his favourite toy. Because his dad was living in a flat with no garage, he had decided to leave it in Biddlecombe for now. In a way Samuel was pleased, because he believed that meant his dad might return home at some point. If he took the car away permanently, though, there would be nothing of him left. It would be a sign, thought Samuel, a sign that the marriage was over and it was now just Samuel and his mum.

When Mrs Johnson rose they ordered takeaway pizza, but his mum couldn't finish hers and went back to bed. Every time she tried to recall what had happened at the supermarket her head began to hurt, and intermingled smells came to her, perfume and something else, something foul that the scent would be able to hide for only so long.

That night Mrs Johnson had bad dreams; but they were only dreams.

Samuel's nightmares, on the other hand, came alive.

Ten

In Which We Learn of the Difficulties Involved in Being a Monster Without a Clearly Defined Form

Samuel woke to find there was a monster under his bed. He didn't just *think* there was a monster under there, the way very small boys and girls sometimes do; Samuel was no longer a very small boy and had accustomed himself to believe that, in all probability, monsters did not inhabit the spaces under beds. They particularly did not occupy the space under Samuel's bed because there wasn't any, every spare inch being taken up by games, shoes, sweet wrappers, unfinished model aircraft, and a large box of toy soldiers with which Samuel no longer played but which he was most reluctant to get rid of, just in case.

Now many of those objects were scattered across his bedroom floor, and a sound was coming from beneath his bed that resembled pieces of jelly being tossed from hand to hand by a troupe of tiny jugglers. In addition, Boswell was standing on the bed, trembling and growling.

Samuel felt a sneeze coming on. He tried every trick he knew to stop it. He held his nose. He took deep breaths. He pressed the tip of his tongue against the top row of his teeth, the way that Japanese samurai used to do when they didn't want to reveal their presence to an enemy, all to no avail.

Samuel sneezed. It sounded like a rocket taking off. Instantly, all noise and movement from below his bed ceased.

Samuel held his breath and listened. He had the uncomfortable sense that a very squishy creature was also holding its breath, if it had any to hold. Even if it didn't, it was definitely listening.

Maybe I imagined it, thought Samuel, even though he knew that he hadn't. You didn't imagine something squishing under your bed. Either it squished, or it didn't, and something had definitely squished.

He looked around, and saw one of his socks lying at the end of his bed. As an experiment, he leaned forward to pick up the sock, then dangled it over the edge of the mattress before dropping it on the floor.

A long pink thing that might have been a tongue, or an arm, or even a leg, grabbed the sock, and pulled it under the bed. Samuel heard chewing, and then the sock being spat out and a voice saying, 'Ewwwww!'

'Hello?' said Samuel.

There was no reply.

'I know you're under there.'

Still no reply.

'Look, this is silly,' said Samuel. 'I'm not getting off this bed. You can stay there for as long as you like. It's just not going to happen.'

He counted to five in his head before he heard a sigh from beneath the mattress.

'How did you know?' said a voice.

'I heard you squish.'

'Oh. I'm new at this. Still getting the hang of it. You tricked me with that sock thing. Very clever, that. Tasted horrible.

You need to get something done about your feet, by the way. They must stink something awful.'

'It's a gym sock. I think it's been there for a while.'

'Well, I suppose that explains it, but still. You could knock someone dead with a sock like that. Lethal weapon, that sock. It's made me feel quite ill.'

'Serves you right,' said Samuel. 'You shouldn't be hanging around under people's beds.'

'Well, it's a job, innit?'

'Not much of a job.'

'Agreed, but you try being a demon of no set form in this day and age. It's not like I'm going to get work looking after puppies, or singing babies to sleep. Frankly, it's this or nothing.'

'What do you mean, "no set form"?'

The demon cleared its throat. 'Technically, I'm a free-roaming ectoplasmic entity . . .'

'Which is?' asked Samuel, a little impatiently.

'Which is,' said the demon huffily, 'if you'll wait for me to finish, a demon capable of assuming almost any shape or form, based on psychic vibrations given off by its victim.'

'You've lost me,' said Samuel.

'Oh look, it's not that complicated. I'm supposed to become whatever scares you. I just picked the whole tentacled slushy thing because, well, it's a classic, isn't it?'

'Is it?' asked Samuel. 'So you're a bit like an octopus, then?'

'A bit, I suppose,' admitted the demon.

'I quite like octopi.'

'Octopodes,' corrected the demon. 'Don't they teach you anything at school?'

'There's no need to be rude,' said Samuel.

'I'm a *demon*. What do you expect me to be? Pleasant? Tuck you in and read you a story? You're not very clever, are you?'

'No, you're not very clever, turning up here in the dead of night and being caught out by an old sock. *And* you haven't assumed a form that scares me. You're an octopus.'

'I'm *like* an octopus,' said the demon. 'But scarier. I think. It's hard to see under here.'

'Whatever,' said Samuel. 'If it's all about psychic vibrations, then why didn't you take the form of something else?'

The demon muttered something.

'I beg your pardon,' said Samuel. 'I didn't quite catch that.'

'I said, 'I can't do psychic vibrations.'' The demon sounded embarrassed.

'Why not?'

'They're hard, that's why not. You try it, see how much luck you have with it.'

'So you just take a form and hope that it will be scary? That all sounds a bit casual, to be honest.'

'Look, it's my first time,' said the demon. 'Are you happy now? It's. My. First. Time. And I have to say that you're being very hurtful. You're not making this easy, you know.'

'I'm not supposed to make it easy,' said Samuel. 'What would be the point in that?'

'Just saying, that's all,' said the demon. Samuel heard it sniff dismissively.

'OK,' said Samuel. 'I'm not very keen on spiders.'

'Really?' said the demon.

'Yes.'

'You're not just saying that?'

'No, I really don't like them very much at all. Why don't you start with that and see how you get along?'

'Oh, I will. Thanks very much. Very nice of you. Give me a minute, will you?'

'Take your time.'

'Right you are. Much appreciated. Don't go anywhere, now.'

'Wouldn't dream of it,' said Samuel.

He sat on the bed, humming to himself and patting Boswell. From under the mattress came various squelching sounds, and the occasional grunt of effort. Finally, there was silence.

'Er, a question,' said the demon.

'Yes?'

'Do spiders have ears?'

'Ears?'

'You know, huge big flappy things.'

'No. They feel vibrations with the hairs on their legs.'

'All right, all right, I didn't ask for a lecture. It was just a simple question.'

There was silence again.

'What are the things with big flappy ears, then?' said the demon.

Samuel thought. 'Elephants?' he suggested.

'Elephants! They're the ones. Right, are you scared of them?'

'No,' said Samuel.

'Awwww,' said the demon. 'I give up. Let's forget about the whole shape-shifting thing. Just climb off the bed and we'll get this over with.'

Samuel didn't move. 'What will you do if I climb off the bed?'

'Well, I can eat you, or I can drag you down to the depths of Hell, never to be seen or heard from again. Depends, really.'

'On what?'

'Lots of things: hygiene, for a start. After tasting that sock,

I don't fancy eating any part of you, to be honest, so it'll have to be the depths of Hell for you, I'm afraid.'

'But I don't want to go to the depths of Hell.'

'*Nobody* wants to go to the depths of Hell. I'm a demon, and even I don't want to go there. That's the point, isn't it? If I told you that I was going to take you for a nice holiday, or on a trip to the zoo, it wouldn't be much of a threat, would it?'

'But why do you have to drag me off to Hell?'

'Orders.'

'Whose orders?'

'Can't say.'

'Can't say, or won't?'

'Both.'

'Why not?'

'She wouldn't want me to.'

'Mrs Abernathy?'

The demon didn't reply.

'Oh come on, I know it's her,' said Samuel. 'You've already given most of it away.'

'Right then,' said the demon. 'It's her. Happy now?'

'Not really. I still don't want to be dragged off to Hell.'

'Then we have what's known as an impasse,' said the demon.

'How long can you stay down there?'

'First sign of daylight, I have to depart. Them's the rules, just like I can't get you unless you step on the floor.'

'So you can't touch me if I just stay up here?'

'I just said that, didn't I? I don't make the rules. I wish I did. This whole business would run a lot more smoothly, I can tell you.'

'Then I'll simply stay here.'

'Fine. You do that.'

Samuel folded his arms and stared at the far wall. From under the bed, he heard what sounded like tentacles being folded. Lots of tentacles.

'Not much point in you hanging around, though, is there, if I'm not going to set foot on the floor until you're gone?' said Samuel.

The demon thought about this. 'Suppose not,' it said.

'So why don't you just leave? It can't be very comfortable under there.'

'It's not. Smells funny, too. And there's something poking into me.'

Samuel heard scuffling from beneath the bed, and moments later a stray toy soldier was tossed against the wardrobe. 'You don't even want to know where that was,' said the demon.

'Whatever,' said Samuel. 'Are you going to leave?'

'Not much else I can do, really,' said the demon, 'not if you're going to be difficult about it.'

'Off you go, then,' said Samuel.

'Right. Bye.'

There was a great deal of squelching, then silence.

'You're still under there, aren't you?' said Samuel.

'No,' said a small voice, slightly ashamedly.

'Fibber.'

'Fine, I'll go. Don't know what I'm supposed to tell her, though.'

'Don't tell her anything. Just keep a low profile until dawn, then say that I didn't get up during the night.'

'Might work,' said the demon. 'Might work. You promise not to get up to use the bathroom or anything?'

'Cross my heart,' said Samuel.

'Can't ask for more than that,' said the demon. 'Well, pleasure doing business with you. Nothing personal about all this, you know. Just following orders.'

'You're not going to come back, are you?'

'Oh no, I shouldn't think so. Took a lot of power for her to summon me up. Can't imagine she'll try that one again. She has a lot on her mind, what with keeping the portal open and all. Very unstable, that portal. Someone could do themselves an injury in there if they're not careful. She might look for another way to get at you, though. Then again, she might not. Soon, it won't matter much either way.'

'Why not?' said Samuel.

'End of the world,' said the demon. 'Won't be any beds left to hide under.'

And with a squish and a pop, it was gone.

Eleven

In Which We Encounter the Scientists Again

No good ever comes of someone sticking his head round his boss's door, a worried expression on his face and a piece of paper in one hand that, if it could talk, would shout, very loudly: 'Bad! This is bad! Run away now!'

Thus it was that when Professor Stefan, CERN's head of particle physics, saw Professor Hilbert hovering on his doorstep with both a) a worried expression; and b) a piece of paper that, despite being white and bearing only a series of numbers and a small diagram, also managed to look worried, he began to feel worried too.

'What is it, Hilbert?' said Professor Stefan in the tones of one who would rather not know what 'it' is at all, thank you very much.

'It's the portal,' said Professor Hilbert. He had always liked the sound of that word, which fitted in with his theories of the Universe. Anyway, since they still didn't know for certain what it was, he could call it anything he liked.

'So you've found out what it is?'

'No, not exactly.'

'Do you know if it's ongoing?'

'We're not sure.'

'Have you even found out if that's actually what opened?'

'Oh, we know it opened,' said Professor Hilbert. 'That part's easy.'

'So you've *proved* that it exists.'

Professor Stefan liked things to be proved before he accepted the fact of their existence. This made him a good scientist, if not a very imaginative one.

'Er, no. But we strongly suspect that it exists. A portal has been opened, and it hasn't closed, not entirely.'

'How do you know, if you can't find it?'

A smile of immense satisfaction appeared on Professor Hilbert's face.

'Because we can hear it speak,' he said.

If you listen hard enough, there's almost no such thing as silence: there's just noise that isn't very loud yet. Oh yes, in space no one can hear you scream, or blow up a big spaceship, because space is a vacuum, and sound can't travel in a vacuum (although think how dull most science fiction films would be if there were no explosions, so pay no attention to grumps who criticise *Star Wars* because you can hear the Death Star explode at the end. Spoilsports.) but otherwise there is noise all around us, even if we can't hear it terribly well. But noises aren't the same as sounds: noises are random and disorganised, but sounds are *made*.

Deep in the LHC's command centre, a group of scientists was clustered round a screen. The screen displayed a visual representation of what had occurred on the night that the collider had apparently malfunctioned. The scientists had painstakingly re-created the circumstances of that evening, restoring lost and rewritten code, and had attempted to trace, without success, the trajectory of the unknown energy particle, which now expressed itself as a slowly revolving spiral.

'So this is what you think happened to our collider,' said Stefan.

'It's still happening,' said Hilbert.

'What? But we've shut down the collider.'

'I know, but I suppose you could say that the damage, if that's what it is, has been done. I think – and I stress "think" – that, somehow, enough energy was harnessed from the collider to blow a hole between our world and, well, somewhere else. When we shut down the collider, we took away that energy source. The portal collapsed, but not entirely. There's a pinhole where there used to be a tunnel, but it's there nonetheless. Listen.'

Beside the screen was a speaker, currently emitting what sounded like static.

'It's static,' said Professor Stefan. 'I don't hear anything.'

The static whooshed slightly, its pattern changing as though in response to the professor's words.

'We wanted you to hear the signal before we cleaned it up,' explained Hilbert.

'Signal?' said Stefan.

'Actually, a voice,' said Hilbert, flipping a switch, and instantly the static was replaced by something that Professor Stefan had to admit sounded a great deal like a low voice whispering. The professor didn't like the sound of that voice at all, even if he had no idea what it was saying. It was like listening to the mutterings of a madman in a foreign tongue, someone who had spent too long locked in a dark place feeling angry with all those responsible for putting him there. It gave the professor, who was, as we have already established, not an imaginative man, a distinct case of the collywobbles. Its effect on the other listeners was less

85

disturbing. Most of them looked excited. In fact, Dr Carruthers appeared to be having trouble keeping his teacup from rattling against its saucer, his excitement was so great.

Professor Stefan leaned in closer to the speaker, frowning. 'Whatever it is, it sounds like the same thing being said over and over. Are you sure it's not someone's idea of a joke? Perhaps there's a bug in the system.'

Hilbert shook his head. 'It's not in the system. We've checked.'

'Well, what's it saying?'

Professor Hilbert looked puzzled. 'That's the thing,' he said. 'It's a known language. We've had it examined. It's early Aramaic, probably from around one thousand BC. It's the same language that we found embedded in our code.'

'So it's coming from somewhere on Earth?'

'No,' said Professor Hilbert. He pointed at the image of the Event. 'It's definitely coming from somewhere on the other side of that. Professor, we may just have proved the existence of the multiverse.'

Stefan looked doubtful. 'But what's it saying?' he repeated.

Professor Hilbert swallowed. What might have been worry creased his face.

'We think it's saying, "Fear me . . ."'

Twelve

In Which We Encounter, Once Again, the Unfortunate Nurd, Who is About to Take Another Unexpected Trip

Nurd, the Scourge of Five Deities, had been devoting a lot of thought to his recent experiences. Given that he didn't have a whole lot else to think about beyond whether or not Wormwood was looking even mangier than usual, or, 'My, isn't it flat around here?' it was quite a welcome distraction.

Among the subjects under consideration was his size. Was he, Nurd wondered, very, very small, small enough to be crushed by what he now believed was a mechanism of some kind? He had never really speculated upon this before, since demons came in all shapes and sizes. Indeed some of them came in more than one shape or size all by themselves, such as O'Dear, the demon of People Who Look in Mirrors and Think They're Overweight, and his twin, O'Really, the demon of People Who Look in Mirrors and Think They're Slim When They're Not.

A great many demons were little more than ethereal beings, wisps of nastiness that floated around like bad thoughts in a dark mind. Some chose physical forms just so that they could hold on to things, which made tea breaks much more satisfying.

Others were given form by the Great Malevolence himself, for his own nefarious purposes.[19]

Nurd wasn't privy to the Great Malevolence's plans for the conquest of Earth. Few were, except those closest to him. The Great Malevolence had been stuck in Hell for an extraordinarily long time, marooned in that desolate place with only his fellow demons for company. He had managed to carve out a kingdom for himself, but it was a kingdom of rock and dirt and pain. He could hardly be blamed for wanting to get away from it.

The Great Malevolence was extremely angry, and unfathomably cruel, and what the Great Malevolence hated more than anything else was people. People had trees, and flowers, and dragonflies. They had dogs, and footballs, and summers. Most of all they were free to do pretty much whatever they liked where they liked and, as long as they didn't hurt anybody else along the way, or break the law, life wasn't bad. The Great Malevolence wanted nothing more than to bring that to an end, preferably an end that involved wailing and screaming, and big fires, and demons with pitchforks poking people where they didn't like being poked.

Even though Nurd was a demon, the Great Malevolence frightened him a lot. If Nurd had been the Great Malevolence, he would have been afraid to look at himself in a mirror, so frightening was the Great Malevolence. The Great

[19] 'Nefarious' means very wicked indeed, in a cunning way. If you plan on being nefarious, it pays to look the part: dress in black; wear a hat, preferably one with a wide brim and no flowers; and perhaps grow a moustache that you can twirl. It also helps to have a deep and sinister laugh, to indicate when you're being nefarious. You know the kind: 'BWAH-HA-HA-HA-HA!' That kind.

Malevolence probably didn't even *have* a reflection, Nurd thought. Any mirror would be too scared to show it.

Nurd stared out at the Wasteland. Anywhere had to be better than here. If he could make his way to the Place of People, then he could rule it in his own manner, and perhaps be a little nicer about it than the Great Malevolence, once he'd got some of the fireballs and general terrifying of the population out of his system.

But he would need to be ready for his journey, if it were to happen again. He tried to remember the sensations he had experienced as he was dragged from one world to the next, but couldn't. He had been so confused, and so terrified, that the journey was over before he'd realised what was happening, and then someone had dropped something on him, and that had been the end of that.

He did his best to recall whether he had been given any indication that he was about to pop out of existence in one place and pop up in another not very long afterwards, and remembered that the tips of his fingers had begun to itch something terrible in the seconds before he went off on his unanticipated trip.

Actually, just like they were itching now.

Oh.

Oh dear.

Nurd barely had time to concentrate on making himself very large indeed before there was a loud pop and he vanished from his throne.

As Professor Hilbert suspected, the Large Hadron Collider had, through only some fault of its own, managed to open a hole between our world and somewhere else entirely. It wasn't quite a *black* hole, since it obeyed only some of the rules of a black hole while rudely ignoring others, which would have greatly irritated Einstein and many other scientists like him. Neither was it quite a wormhole, although it obeyed some of the characteristics of a wormhole too. Nevertheless, it would do nicely until a black hole or wormhole came along.

Here are some things that are worth remembering about black holes, should it ever seem likely that you're going to encounter one. The first is that if, at some time in the future, a group of nice scientists in white coats suggest that you – yes, you! – have been chosen as the lucky candidate to enter a black hole and find out what's going on at the other side, it would be a good idea for you – yes, you! – to find something else to do, preferably far away and not involving, even peripherally, black holes, space suits, or scientists with an unsettling gleam in their eyes.

Perhaps you've already worked this out for yourself, being a clever young person. After all, if sticking a head, or any other part of oneself, into a black hole is such a great idea, then scientists would be queueing up to do it, instead of tapping someone else on the shoulder and inviting him to have a go.

Which brings us to the second thing worth noting about black holes: your life is likely to be very short, but spectacularly eventful, if you go messing about with one. There may well be something fascinating at the other side of a black hole, but you're unlikely to be able to tell anyone what it is. The gravitational force of a black hole is subject to quite dramatic changes, so just as you're thinking to yourself, 'Wow, a black hole. How interesting and swirly it is. Wait until I tell those nice scientists all about it!' your body will be ripped to shreds and then compacted to a point of infinite density.

Which will probably hurt a lot, although not for very long.

Figure 1: You in a black hole

A.   B.   C.

Then again, you might be lucky enough to plummet into a super-massive black hole, where the gravitational changes are a little gentler. In that case you'll still be torn apart, but more slowly, so you might have time to come to terms with what it feels like before once again you are crushed to a point of infinite density.

It all depends upon the sacrifices one is willing to make for the sake of science really. It's your choice. Frankly, I'd find a less risky job, if I were you, like being an accountant, or cleaning the teeth of great white sharks with a toothpick and some floss.

As it happened, Nurd, the Scourge of Five Deities, was learning a great deal about the nature of not-quite-black holes since he was, at that moment, plunging through one. He really didn't want to be, either, because he felt that no good was going to come of it. He was pretty certain that he was

falling, even though he had no sensation that he was doing
so, and he was rapidly approaching a point of light in the
distance that didn't seem to be getting any closer, which was
very confusing. He did his best to pull himself back in the
direction from which he had come, like a swimmer kicking
against a strong tide, but here is another interesting thing
about black holes: the more you struggle to escape the force
of one, the quicker you'll reach that whole part about infinite density, and crushing and stuff, due to time and space
being all muddled up.[20]

The sensation that, even though he was trying to move
away from whatever he was falling towards, he was still
approaching it with increasing rapidity, gave Nurd a
headache. Fortunately he was distracted from it by the
feeling that every atom of his demonic form was being
stretched on an infinite number of tiny racks, each of which
had also helpfully been fitted with a selection of very sharp
pins. Then that particular pain came to an end, to be

[20] If that sounds confusing, it isn't really. The equivalent effect can
be found on Earth, such as when you haven't studied for a test in
school and, the more you want that test to be put off, the faster the
time for the test seems to arrive. The same is true for painful dental
appointments, visiting that aunt you don't like at Christmas, and
waiting for your mum to come home while you try to stick back
together her favourite vase that you've just broken. The opposite
occurs for events to which you're rather looking forward, like
Christmas, your birthday, or the first snows of winter. Someday, a
very bright child will create an equation for all this in order to explain
it, and other, even brighter, children will look at him in a funny way
and wonder why he bothered, since everyone instinctively understood it anyway.

replaced by the way a banana might feel if someone peeled it, briefly balanced it upright on a table, and then dropped a rock on it.

Just as Nurd began to think that this was the end for him, all the pain stopped and he felt firm ground beneath his feet. His eyes were squeezed shut. He opened one of them carefully, then another, and then a third, which he kept for special occasions.

He was standing in the middle of a road, and around him metal objects were whizzing by at what seemed like great speeds. One of them, he noticed, was sleek, and red, and pretty.

I don't know what that is, said Nurd to himself, but I *want* one.

He heard a sound behind him. It was very loud, like the bellowing of some great beast.

Nurd turned just in time to be hit full in the face by a very large version of one of the metal objects.

Samuel was staring out of his bedroom window. He had not yet changed out of his pyjamas, and was reflecting on what had taken place during the night. The area beneath his bed had been a little slimy when he checked it once dawn came, but other than that there was no sign of the demon.

He was wondering if the demon might return, despite its protestations to the contrary, when a figure with greenish skin, a large head and pointed ears, wearing a red cloak and big boots, appeared briefly on the street below in a flash of blue light. The figure looked about, its attention caught by a passing car, and then was promptly hit by a truck. There was another flash of blue light and the figure was gone. The truck driver stopped, climbed out of his cab, tried to find a body and then quickly drove off.

Samuel considered telling his mum, but decided that it was probably better just to add it to the list of Things Nobody Was Likely to Believe.

At least, not until it was too late.

Back in the Wasteland, Wormwood was staring suspiciously at the throne, the crown, and the sceptre. Once again, all three tempted him, but after what had happened the last time he didn't want to be caught waving them around if, and when, Nurd returned. Say what you liked about Nurd (and Wormwood had said most things, under his breath), but he wasn't entirely stupid. It had not escaped his attention that he had rematerialised after his earlier disappearance to find a mangy demon waving his sceptre and wearing his crown. Once Nurd had recovered from the shock, Wormwood had earned an extra bump for each offence and one more between the eyes for good luck. Wormwood had now decided to bide his time, but he couldn't hide his disappointment when, not very long after he had vanished, Nurd reappeared, this time looking like an insect that had just been hit by the largest swatter ever created.

'So how did that go, Master?' asked Wormwood.

'Not terribly well, actually,' replied Nurd.

He was about to faint when his fingers and toes began to tingle again. 'Oh, no,' said Nurd, who was hurting in so many places that he was wondering if he'd somehow acquired new body parts just so they could ache. 'I've only just—'

And then he was gone again.

* * *

Samuel's bedroom was suddenly lit by a blue flash, which was followed by a loud pop and a smell like eggs burning. Dank mist filled the room. Samuel dived to the floor, closely followed by Boswell, and peered over the edge of his bed.

Slowly the mist began to clear, revealing a green-skinned figure in a red cloak. The figure had one leg raised, and his head covered with his hands, as if he were expecting to receive a nasty blow at any moment. When the blow didn't come, he peered out cautiously from between his fingers, then breathed a sigh of relief.

'Well, that makes a pleasant change,' he said, and started to relax. Unfortunately at that moment, Boswell decided to make his presence known, and gave a bark, causing the new arrival to leap on to a chair and cover his head again.

'What are you doing?' asked Samuel from behind the bed.

'I'm cowering,' said the figure.

'Why?'

'Because every time I shift into this world, I get hurt. Frankly, it's starting to become wearing.'

Samuel stood. Boswell, sensing that the figure on the chair wasn't half as threatening as it had at first seemed, experimented with a growl, and was pleased to see the green-skinned personage tremble.

'Didn't you just get run over by a truck?' asked Samuel.

'Is that what it was?' said Nurd. 'I didn't have time to exchange pleasantries with it before it knocked me into another dimension. The cheek!'

'What *are* you?'

'I'm a demon,' said Nurd. 'Nurd, the Scourge of Five Deities.'

'Really?' said Samuel sceptically. The demon's clothes looked tatty, and Samuel didn't think that demons climbed on chairs to get away from small dogs. 'Are you sure?'

'No, I'm a saucepan,' hissed Nurd testily. 'Of course I'm a demon.' He coughed. 'I'm actually a very *important* demon.'

He looked at Samuel, who arched an eyebrow at him.

'Oh, I give up,' said Nurd. 'No, I'm not important. I live in a wasteland with an irritating entity called Wormwood. Nobody likes me, and I have no power. Happy now?'

'I suppose,' said Samuel. 'Who sent you here?'

'Nobody sent me. I just got . . . dragged here. Very uncomfortably, I might add.'

Nurd glanced at Boswell. 'What's that?'

'It's my dog. His name is Boswell. And I'm Samuel.'

Boswell wagged his tail at the sound of his name then, remembering that he was supposed to be ferocious, showed some teeth and growled again.

'He doesn't seem very happy to see me,' said Nurd. 'Then again, nobody ever is.'

'Well, you did pop up a little unexpectedly.'

Nurd shrugged. 'Sorry about that. Not my fault. Would you mind if I stopped cowering now? I'm beginning to get a cramp.'

Samuel had a good instinct for people. He could tell a good person from a bad one, often before the person in question had even spoken. Although his experience of demons was rather more limited, something told him that if Nurd wasn't exactly good – and, being a demon, it was hardly part of the job description ('Wanted: demon. Must be good . . .') – he was not entirely bad either. Like most ordinary people, he was just . . . himself.

'All right,' said Samuel, then added, because he'd once

heard someone say it in a police movie, 'but no sudden movements.'

'Does shooting off into another dimension count?' asked Nurd.

'No.'

'Fine, then.' Nurd sat on the chair, and looked around the room. 'Nice place.'

'Thank you.'

'You decorate it yourself?'

'My dad did most of it.'

'Oh.'

They were silent for a time.

'If you don't mind me saying so, you don't look very happy,' said Samuel.

'I think I'm in shock,' said Nurd. 'You try being wrenched from one dimension to another, being hit by a truck, sent back home again for long enough to start hurting, and then have the whole thing begin all over. It's not conducive to a healthy outlook on life, let me tell you.'

Nurd put his large chin in his hands, and regarded Samuel. 'Anyway,' he said, 'it's not like you look overjoyed either.'

'I'm not,' said Samuel. 'My dad's left us, my mum cries in the evenings, and I think the woman down the road is trying to kill me. Are you sure she didn't send you?'

'Quite sure,' said Nurd, and for the first time in very many years he felt sorry for someone other than himself. 'That's not very nice of her.'

'No, it isn't.'

'Well, like I said, I live in a wasteland. There's nothing to see, nothing to do, and Wormwood and I have run out of things to talk about. In fact, this whole interdimensional thing has brightened up my days no end, or it would have if I didn't keep being injured by hard metal objects. This is such an *interesting* place.'

He moved to the window and gazed out. 'Look' he said, and there were aeons of longing and sadness in his voice. 'You have white, fluffy clouds, and sunshine. What I wouldn't give to be able to see sunshine every day.'

Samuel picked up a bag of wine gums from his bedside table.

'Would you like a sweet?'

'A what?'

'A sweet. They're wine gums.'

Tentatively Nurd reached into the bag, and came out with a long red sweetie.

'Oh, those ones are lovely,' said Samuel, popping an orange one into his mouth and chewing thoughtfully. Nurd followed his example, and seemed pleasantly surprised by the result.

'Ooooh, that's good,' he said. 'That's very good. Fluffy clouds. Wine gums. Big metal things that move fast. What a world you live in!'

Samuel sat down on his bed, and Nurd returned to his chair.

'You're not going to hurt me, are you?' asked Samuel.

Nurd looked shocked. 'Why would I do that?'

'Because you're a demon.'

'Just because I'm a demon doesn't mean that I'm bad,' said Nurd. A piece of wine gum had stuck to his teeth, and he worked at it with a long fingernail. 'I didn't ask to be a demon. It just happened that way. I opened my eyes one day, and there I was. Nurd. Ugly bloke. No friends. Even other demons don't care much for my company.'

'Why? You seem all right to me.'

'I suppose that's it, really. I've never been very demonic. I don't want to torture, or wreak havoc. I don't want to be frightening, or terrible. I just want to potter along, minding my own business. But they told me I had to do something destructive or I'd be in trouble, so I tried to find a role that wouldn't attract too much attention, or cause a lot of bother to people, but all those jobs were taken. You know, there's a demon who looks after the little bit of toothpaste that you can't squeeze out of the end of the tube, even though you know it's there and there's no other toothpaste in the house. There's even a demon of shyness, or there's supposed to be. Nobody's ever seen him, so it's hard to know for sure. I quite fancied a job like that.

'Eventually, some of the other demons just got irritated with me trying to muscle in on their action, and I was banished. It all seemed pretty hopeless, and then suddenly I started popping up here. I just feel like I could make something of myself in this world. There are so many opportunities.'

'This world is hard, too,' said Samuel, and there was something in the boy's voice that made Nurd want to reach out to him. The demon picked up the bag of wine gums, and offered one to Samuel. He picked a green one.

'You can have another too,' he said to Nurd.

'You're sure?'

'Absolutely.'

Nurd beamed. He tried a black one. It tasted a bit funny, but it was still better than anything else he had ever eaten, except for that first wine gum.

'Go on,' said Nurd. 'You were saying?'

'It doesn't matter,' said Samuel.

'No, it does. I want to know. Really.'

So Samuel told him. He spoke of his mother and his father, and of how his dad had left and maybe it was Samuel's fault, and maybe it wasn't. He spoke of how the world doesn't listen to children, even when it should. He spoke of Boswell, and of how he would be lost without the little dog for company.

And Nurd, who had never had a mother and father, and who had never loved or been loved, marvelled at the ways in which feeling so wonderful could also leave one open to so much pain. In a strange way, he envied Samuel even that. He wanted to care about someone so much that it could hurt.

Thus the boy and the demon passed the hours. The day grew brighter, and they drew closer, talking of places seen and unseen, of hopes and fears. The only shadow cast upon their conversation was Samuel's description of the events in the Abernathys' basement, which made Nurd uneasy, even as he struggled to understand what they might mean. It sounded to him as though there might be other demons in this world, demons with a plan. Well, Nurd had plans of his own, assuming he could find a way to stay in the world of men permanently and not simply spend the rest of his existence whizzing painfully between dimensions.

At last, Nurd's fingers began to tingle again.

'I have to go,' he said, with regret. He smiled, a movement so unfamiliar that at first his muscles struggled with it. 'It really has been very nice talking to you. When I work out how to rule this world, I'll make sure that you're well looked after.'

Just as Nurd was about to vanish, Samuel thrust the bag of wine gums into his hand, so that when Nurd arrived back in the Wasteland he might have something with which to cheer himself and Wormwood up a little.

Nurd reappeared on his throne. He opened his eyes to find Wormwood staring anxiously at him.

'What's wrong with your face?' asked Wormwood.

Nurd tested his mouth with his fingers.

'Wormwood,' he said, 'I appear to be smiling. Here, have a wine gum . . .'

Thirteen

In Which Samuel Decides to Consult an Expert on Demons and Hell, but Doesn't Get Anywhere

Reverend Ussher, the vicar, and Mr Berkeley, the verger, were standing outside the Church of St Timidus, greeting the congregation as its members filed out on that bright Sunday morning.

The church was named after St Timidus of Biddlecombe, a very holy man who died in 1380 AD at the age of 38. St Timidus became famous when, in 1378 AD, he decided to go and live in a cave outside Biddlecombe so that he would not be tempted to do bad things. It wasn't a very large cave, and when people came to bring him food Timidus would sometimes be able to see them coming, or hear what they were saying. He decided to dig himself another cave next to the one in which he was living, so that there would be absolutely no chance of seeing or hearing someone and being tempted to sin. (It's not entirely clear what sins Timidus was afraid of committing, since he never said, but it probably had something to do with ladies. It often does in such cases.)

Unfortunately, while he was digging the second cave Timidus caused the first cave to fall in on him, and he was buried alive under a large pile of rocks. It was decided that Timidus should be made a saint because of his commitment to avoiding bad things, and also because Biddlecombe didn't have any saints at the time, and there's nothing like a good, old-fashioned saint to bring believers to a place and encourage them to spend money. So it was that plain old Timidus became St Timidus of Biddlecombe.

Now you and I might wonder if Timidus might not have been better off leaving his cave and doing nice things for other people, such as helping old ladies across the road or feeding the poor, instead of hiding himself away and not talking to anyone. After all, not doing bad things is not the same as doing good things, but that is why you and I will never become saints. On the other hand, you and I are unlikely to be buried under a big pile of stones as a result of bad engineering practices, so these things even themselves out in the end.

The bishop of Biddlecombe at the time was named Bernard, but he was known far and wide as Bishop Bernard the Bad. Obviously this wasn't what his parents named him, as that would have been a bit foolish. I mean, if you name someone 'the Bad' then, really, you're just asking for trouble. It would have led to conversations like the following:

Bernard's parents: Hello, this is our son Bernard the Bad. We hope he'll become a bishop some day. A nice one, of course. Not a bad one.

Not Bernard's parents: Er, then why did you name him 'the Bad'?

Bernard's parents: Oh dear . . .[21]

---

[21] There are lots of people throughout history with the word 'the' somewhere in their names. Some of these people were rather pleasant, such as Richard the Lionheart (1157–1199 AD), the English king (even if he didn't speak much English, oddly enough, although he

Bishop Bernard the Bad was given his nickname because he was very nasty. Bishop Bernard didn't like people who disagreed with him, especially if they disagreed with his decisions to steal lots of money, kill people who had anything that he might want, and have children, even if he wasn't supposed to have children because he was a bishop. In fact, he wasn't supposed to do *any* of those things, but that didn't stop Bishop Bernard. Bishop Bernard also believed there were few problems in life that couldn't be solved by sticking a hot poker up somebody's bottom. If that didn't work, which was rare, he would put his enemies on a rack and stretch them until they said, 'Ow!' very loudly, or just kill them, often in a slow and painful way. Bishop Bernard knew that people called him Bernard the Bad behind his back, but he didn't care. He rather liked the idea that people were terrified of him.

---

was very good at French) who commanded an army by the age of 16, fought in the Crusades, and forgave the young boy who shot the arrow that fatally wounded him; and Alfred the Great (849–899 AD), who defended his Saxon kingdom of Wessex against the Danish invaders and was, well, great.

On the other hand, there were some people with 'the' in their names who were very unpleasant indeed. Vlad the Impaler (1431–1476 AD) of Wallachia, who was also known as Dracula and inspired the name of the famous vampire, liked to stick his enemies on big spikes. Ivan the Terrible of Russia (1530–1584 AD) was a tyrant and a bully who died while playing chess. It wasn't the excitement of the game, though: he was probably poisoned with mercury. Finally, certain historical figures with 'the' in their names were just a bit lame. I give you Hencage the Dismal (1621–1682 AD), Hugh the Dull (1294–1342 AD), Charles the Silly (1368–1422 AD), Childeric the Stupid (died 755 AD), and Wenceslas the Worthless (1361–1419 AD), who once cooked his chef alive for serving a bad ragout.

By the time St Timidus of Biddlecombe, who wasn't bad at all, just a little confused, died in his cave, Bishop Bernard the Bad was getting old. He decided that a church should be built and named after St Timidus, and when he died, Bishop Bernard would be buried in a special vault in that church. That way, Bishop Bernard could pretend that he had something in common with the saint and perhaps, over time, people might forget that he was bad, as he would be the one buried in the church.

People aren't that stupid.

Instead, when he died, Bishop Bernard was buried beneath a little room at the side of the church, the only sign that he was there a stone in the floor with his name on it. Thereafter, he was only ever mentioned when visitors were brought on tours of the old church, and they were only told of the bad things that he had done, mainly because he had never done anything good.

So there you have it: the history of the Church of St Timidus. Why all that is so important we shall discover later. For now, it is enough to know that Reverend Ussher and Mr Berkeley were standing outside its doors, being very polite, when Mr Berkeley saw Samuel approaching and nudged the vicar.

'Look out, Vicar,' he said, 'it's that strange Johnson boy.'

The vicar looked alarmed. Samuel Johnson was only eleven years old, but he sometimes asked the kinds of questions that would challenge elderly philosophers. Most recently, the vicar recalled, there had been a lengthy discussion about angels and pins, which was something to do with a school project, although he couldn't imagine what kind of school, other than a theology college, might require its students to debate the size and nature of the angelic host. To be frank it had made Reverend Ussher's head spin. He thought that Samuel Johnson might possibly be some kind of child prodigy or genius. Then again, he might simply be a rather annoying small boy, of which, in Reverend Ussher's experience, there were already too many in the world.

Now here Samuel was again, his brow furrowed in the kind of concentration that suggested the vicar's knowledge of matters divine and angelic was about to be severely tested.

'Hello, Samuel,' said the vicar, composing his face into some semblance of goodwill. 'And what's on your mind this morning?'

'Do you believe in Hell, Vicar?' asked Samuel.

'Um, well.' Reverend Ussher paused. 'Why are you asking about Hell, Samuel? You're not worried about going there, are you? I can't imagine that a young man like you could have much cause to fear, er, eternal damnation. Or even temporary damnation, come to that.'

Beside him Mr Berkeley stifled a cough, suggesting that he would be quite happy to see Samuel Johnson suffer in a hot, fiery place, if only for long enough to discourage him from asking the vicar awkward questions.

'It's not so much that I'm afraid of ending up there,' said Samuel. 'It's more that I'm afraid of *it* ending up *here*.'

The vicar looked confused. He'd known that he was likely to become confused at some point in the conversation; he just hadn't imagined that it would happen quite so fast.

'I'm not sure that I follow you.'

'I mean, is there a chance that Hell could come here?'

'Come here?' said the verger, intervening. 'It's Hell, not the number forty-seven bus.'

106

Samuel ignored him. He'd never thought much of Mr Berkeley, who always seemed to be scowling, even on Christmas morning when nobody had any business to be scowling at all.

The vicar quieted Mr Berkeley with a wave of his hand.

'No, Samuel. Even if Hell does exist, and I'm not entirely convinced that it does, it has nothing to do with this earthly realm. It is distinct and of itself. People may end up there, but I can say with some confidence that it will never end up here.'

He beamed beatifically at Samuel. Samuel did not beam back. Instead he seemed about to offer some further argument, but Mr Berkeley had had enough. He gripped the vicar by the elbow and steered him towards less challenging company, namely Mr and Mrs Billingsgate, who ran the local fish-and-chip shop and rarely asked anything more awkward than whether or not one might require vinegar with that.

Samuel stared glumly as the two men walked away. He'd wanted to say much more to the vicar, but it didn't look like that was going to happen. The vicar seemed very certain about things he couldn't possibly know for sure, but Samuel supposed that was all part of being a vicar. After all, it wouldn't have done for the vicar to stand up before the congregation in church on Sunday and ask if there was any point in their being there. As a vicar, you had to learn to take some things on trust.

As Samuel returned to his mum, who was chatting with friends, he saw Mrs Abernathy by the church wall, watching him. He noticed that she was careful to remain outside the church grounds. She hadn't been at the service either.

She beckoned to Samuel, but Samuel merely shook his head, trying to ignore her.

Samuel.

He heard her voice in his head, as clearly as if she were standing next to him. He glanced at her again. She hadn't moved but a small smile was playing on her face.

Samuel, her voice came again. *We need to talk. If you don't come to me, I'm going to find your little dog, and I'm going to kill him. What do you think of that, clever Samuel Johnson? Would you sacrifice your dog's life because you're too frightened to face me?*

Samuel swallowed. Mrs Abernathy was like the witch in *The Wizard of Oz*, threatening Toto to get back at Dorothy. He left his mother, and approached the woman at the wall.

'How are you, Samuel?' she asked, as though they were friends who had just happened to meet on a pleasant Sunday morning.

'I'm fine,' he answered.

'I'm disapppointed to hear that,' said Mrs Abernathy. 'In fact, I was hoping you wouldn't be here at all.'

Samuel shrugged. Mrs Abernathy's eyes, already blue, seemed to brighten a shade, drawing his gaze towards them.

'You sent the monster who hid under my bed,' said Samuel.

'Yes, and I'm going to have words with him, when I find him. I expended rather a lot of energy bringing him here. The least he could have done was eat you alive.'

'Well, he didn't,' said Samuel. 'He seemed quite decent, actually.'

Mrs Abernathy's calm expression altered for an instant. She might have been a demon but, in common with most of the human adults who had encountered Samuel Johnson, she wasn't sure if he was being deliberately cheeky, or was just a very unusual child.

'I'm here to seek a truce. I don't know what you saw, or

thought you saw, in our basement that night, but you're mistaken. There's nothing for you to be concerned about. We're just . . . *visiting* for a time.'

Samuel shook his head. There was something strangely insistent about Mrs Abernathy's voice. Samuel recalled a play that they had read about in school, one in which a king was murdered by having poison poured into his ear. Listening to Mrs Abernathy, he felt just as he imagined the king must have felt as he started to die.

'I—'

'I don't want to hear it, Samuel. You must learn to keep your mouth shut. If you don't interfere with me then I'll leave you in peace, but if you cross me you won't even live long enough to regret it. Do you understand?'

Samuel nodded, even as he knew that what Mrs Abernathy was saying was a lie. There would be no peace for him, or for anyone, if she succeeded with her plans. But her voice was so sweet and hypnotic, and his eyelids were starting to feel so very heavy.

'Come closer, Samuel,' whispered Mrs Abernathy. 'Come closer, and let me whisper in your ear . . .'

Whisper. Ear. Poison.

At that instant, Samuel sensed the danger he was in. With a great effort of will he pinched himself hard on the hand, using his nails so that the pain was sharp and he drew blood. He took a step back from Mrs Abernathy, his head clearing, and he saw her face cloud with rage. One of her hands reached for him, almost as though it had a will of its own.

'You nasty child!' she said. 'Don't think you can escape me that easily. You'd better be careful, unless—'

'Unless what?' said Samuel, goading her now. 'Unless I want something bad to happen to me, is that it? What could be worse than a monster under my bed waiting to eat me?'

Mrs Abernathy got her anger under control. She smiled almost sweetly.

'Oh, you have no idea,' she said. 'Well then, here it is. Something bad is going to happen to you no matter what you do. The question is: how bad will that something be? When the time comes, I can make it so that you simply fall asleep and never wake up again. But if I choose, I can ensure instead that you never sleep again, and that every moment of your wretched existence is spent in searing agony, gasping for breath and begging for the pain to stop!'

'It sounds like gym class,' said Samuel, with considerable feeling. He was happy that his voice didn't tremble. It made him appear braver than he was.

Mrs Abernathy looked past Samuel. He risked a glance in the same direction and saw his mother approaching.

'Very funny, Samuel,' said Mrs Abernathy, beginning to move away. 'When my master comes we'll see if he finds you quite so amusing. In the meantime, you keep your mouth shut. Remember when I said I'd kill your dog? Well, if you speak of this to your mother, then I'll kill her instead. I'll smother her in her sleep, and no one will ever know except you and I. I met her in the supermarket yesterday. I know you've been talking about my affairs. Remember this, Samuel: careless talk costs lives . . .'

With that she headed off in the direction of town, trailing strong perfume and a faint whiff of burning.

'What did she want?' asked Mrs Johnson. She was staring at Mrs Abernathy's back with ill-concealed distaste. She couldn't remember why she disliked Mrs Abernathy so much, just that she did.

'Nothing, Mum,' said Samuel resignedly. 'She was simply saying hello . . .'

That evening Samuel decided that there was no point in telling any grown-up in Biddlecombe of what he knew. They simply wouldn't believe him. But perhaps someone his own age might. He could no longer deal with all this alone. Tomorrow, at the risk of being laughed at, he would call upon his friends for help.

Fourteen

*In Which We Learn That it is Sometimes Wise to Be
Afraid of the Dark*

Samuel's dad called the house that night to speak to his
son. Samuel tried to tell his dad about the Abernathys' basement, but his dad only said 'Really?' and 'How interesting',
and asked Samuel how he was enjoying his half-term break,
and if his mum was OK.

Samuel made one final effort.

'Dad,' he said, 'this is serious. I'm not making it up.'

'You think these people, the Abernathys, are carrying out
experiments in their basement?' said Mr Johnson.

'Not experiments,' said Samuel. 'I think they were messing
about with something that they shouldn't have been messing
about with, and it all went wrong. Now they've opened a kind
of doorway.'

'Into Hell?'

'Yes, except it's not working right yet. The door is open,
but the gates aren't.'

'Don't you usually have to open the gates before the door?'
said Mr Johnson.

'Yes,' said Samuel, 'but—'

He stopped.

'You're making fun of me, aren't you?' he said. 'You don't believe me.'

'Have you been playing those computer games again, those ones where you have to kill demons? Samuel, put your mum on the phone.'

Samuel did, and heard one side of a conversation that seemed to revolve around whether or not Samuel knew the difference between reality and fantasy, and if this was some kind of reaction to the difficulties in their marriage, and if Samuel should see a psychiatrist. The conversation moved on to other matters, and Samuel drifted away.

His mum had a troubled expression on her face when she hung up the phone, as though she realised that she was supposed to remember something important, but couldn't quite recall what it was.

'Samuel, go to bed early tonight,' said Mrs Johnson. 'Read something that doesn't involve demons, or ghosts, or monsters, hmmm? For me. And, darling, be careful what you say to people.'

Then she started crying.

'Your dad's buying a house with that woman, Samuel,' said his mum, through her tears. 'He says he wants a divorce, Samuel. And he wants to come down and collect that stupid bloody car of his!'

Samuel held his mum, and didn't speak. After a while she told him that it was time for bed. He went up to his room and spent a long time staring out of the window, but he didn't cry. Suddenly, monsters and demons didn't seem so important any more. His dad wasn't coming home again. Meanwhile, he was just a small boy, and nobody – not his mum, not his dad – listened to small boys, not ever. Shortly after nine he changed into his pyjamas and climbed into bed.

Eventually he fell asleep.

It was Boswell who first sensed the coming of the Darkness. He woke at the end of Samuel's bed, where he had now decided to sleep permanently after the nasty slimy thing had briefly taken up residence on the floor beneath. Boswell's nose twitched, and his hair stood on end.

Although he was a very intelligent animal, Boswell, like most dogs, divided the world into things that were Good to eat and things that were Bad to eat, with a small space in the middle for things that might potentially be either, or just Good or Bad generally, but about which he wasn't entirely certain as yet.

Thus Boswell's first impression, upon waking up, was that something was Bad, but he wasn't sure exactly what. He couldn't hear or smell anything out of the ordinary. Neither could he see anything out of the ordinary, although his eyesight wasn't very good at the best of times, so that a whole army of Very Bad Things could have been standing a few feet away and, unless they smelled Bad, or sounded Bad, he would have had no idea that they were there.

He leapt off the bed and sniffed around, then trotted to the window and put his front paws on the sill so that he could peer out. All seemed to be perfectly normal. The road was empty. Nothing was moving.

The streetlight at the nearest corner flickered and went out, creating a pool of darkness that stretched halfway to the next light. Boswell put his head to one side and whined softly. Then the next streetlight went out and, seconds later, the first light came back on again. Even with his weak eyesight, Boswell caught something slipping from one pool of darkness to the next. The third streetlight, the one directly in front of their house, buzzed and then extinguished itself, and this time it stayed out. Boswell stared at the pool of blackness, and a figure in the shadows seemed to stare back at him.

Boswell growled.

And then the pool of blackness began to change. It extended itself, like oil running down a hill, rivulets of it flowing from the base of the streetlight towards the garden gate of number 501. It slid beneath the gate and oozed along the path until it reached the front door and Boswell could no longer mark its progress.

Boswell dropped down from the window, padded to the half-closed bedroom door and edged his body through the gap. He stood at the top of the stairs and watched as the Darkness slipped under the door, seemed to pause for a second to find its bearings, and then, its speed increasing, flowed to the first step and began to climb, the edge of the Darkness forming fingers that seemed to pull the rest of its mass along. Boswell heard a soft *pop* as the far end of the Darkness slipped beneath the front door, so that now he was staring at a puddle perhaps three feet long making its way inexorably towards him.

Boswell began to bark, but nobody came. Mrs Johnson's bedroom door remained firmly closed, and Boswell could hear her snoring softly. The Darkness was now halfway up the stairs and, at the sound of Boswell's barks, it began to increase its progress. With no other option, Boswell beat a retreat to Samuel's bedroom door, pushing his way in and then nudging the door closed with his nose. He backed away, still growling. He could see a thin line of illumination between the door and the carpet, and deep in his clever dog mind he sensed that this gap was not a Good thing.

Slowly the light disappeared, diminishing from left to right until nothing of it remained. For a couple of seconds, all was still. There was only the sound of Samuel's breathing and the distant buzz of Mrs Johnson's snores to disturb the silence.

Boswell jumped onto the bed and barked in Samuel's ear.

'Mwff,' said Samuel. 'Argle.'

Boswell tried licking him, while at the same time keeping an eye on the door. Samuel just pushed him away, not even waking up properly to do so.

''S early,' he mumbled. 'No school.'

Just then, with a speed that caused Boswell to jump backwards in fright, the Darkness poured under the door, moving swiftly towards where Samuel lay. It found the leg of the bed and climbed it like a snake, winding its way round the wood before sliding across the blankets. Boswell could smell it now. It reeked of old clothes, and stagnant water, and dead things. It did not shine like oil, even though it moved with the same relentless viscosity. It was absence made solid, nothingness given form and purpose.

And as it moved to smother Samuel, Boswell knew what he had to do.

Standing near the edge of the bed he gripped one end of the Darkness with his teeth, and pulled. He felt it stretch like rubber in his mouth. His tongue grew cold, and his teeth began to hurt, but he did not release his grip. Instead he dug his paws into the blanket and began working his way back to the end of the bed. The Darkness extended towards Samuel, by now almost within reach of his neck. Boswell's paws tore at the blanket as he tried to maintain his position, his teeth tugging with all his might, even as he felt his back legs begin to slide and he fell off the edge of the bed, his bite still hard upon the Darkness.

The impact of Boswell hitting the floor, combined with the sensation of the blanket slipping away from him, finally woke Samuel up.

'What's happening?' he asked, rubbing his eyes.

From the floor came the sound of a struggle, and he heard Boswell whimper.

'Boswell?'

Samuel sat up and looked over the edge of the bed. He saw what appeared to be a blanket of blackness, and beneath it the shape of a small, struggling dog. The Darkness, or whatever was controlling it, had at last recognised the threat posed by the little dachshund, and was doing its level best to extinguish it.

'Boswell!' shouted Samuel.

He reached down and began to pull at the shadow, but even as he did so it froze his fingers and, as he watched in horror, it began to flow up his arms.

'Ugh!' said Samuel.

Meanwhile, Boswell, now freed from the suffocating force, was catching his breath. Seeing his master in trouble, he recommenced his attack, digging his aching teeth in once again. Simultaneously, Samuel began to move backwards, until, at last, the Darkness was stretched between them.

'Don't let go, Boswell,' said Samuel. He pulled the Darkness and Boswell in the direction of the small bathroom that lay to the right of his bedroom. It contained only a toilet and a basin, but it was enough for what Samuel had in mind.

'Stay, Boswell!' he said, as he reached the toilet and Boswell was almost at the door. Holding on to the Darkness with one hand, so that it remained at full stretch, Samuel lifted the toilet seat and, taking a deep breath, told Boswell to open his mouth.

The Darkness sprang from Boswell's mouth, the force sending its bulk flying in Samuel's direction. As quickly as he could, Samuel released his own grip. The Darkness struck the cistern, then fell into the bowl. Immediately tendrils of it extended upwards as it tried to pull itself out, but Samuel was too quick for it. He hit the flush and watched with satisfaction as the Darkness swirled around the bowl for a time and then was swept into the sewers.

Breathing heavily, Samuel leaned back against the sink.

'I'm never using that toilet again,' he said to Boswell, but Boswell was no longer at the door. Instead he had returned to the bedroom window, where Samuel now joined him. Together they watched as the streetlight across from the house came on once more, and the next one extinguished itself, and so on until at last the corner was plunged into darkness for a moment, and something fled away into Stoker Lane.

Before it disappeared, Samuel and Boswell caught a glimpse of it.

It looked like a woman.

In fact, it looked very much like Mrs Abernathy.

Fifteen

In Which Samuel Johnson Begins to Fight Back

Samuel didn't say much at breakfast the next morning. His mother noticed how subdued her son was.

'Is everything all right, dear?' she asked.

Samuel just nodded, and ate his cornflakes. He wanted to tell his mother what had happened the night before with the pool of Darkness, but he couldn't. She wouldn't believe him, and he had no proof. He had no idea where the Darkness had ended up, and was at first a little worried that it might be stuck in one of the household pipes, waiting for a chance to emerge. Once he had thought about it for a while, though, he realised that it was probably lost in a smelly old sewer which was just fine by Samuel. Still, he had taken the precaution of gluing the toilet seat closed using super-strong adhesive. He was the only one who ever used the little bathroom anyway, and as long as he was careful nobody would discover for a while what he had done.

But Samuel was also very frightened, for his mother and for himself. He remembered Mrs Abernathy's threat to kill his mother if he continued to try to convince her of what he knew. The demon under the bed had been bad enough, but at least that could be reasoned with. The Darkness had been something else entirely. He had been lucky last night;

Boswell's bravery had saved him, but Boswell might not be able to save him, or his mum, from whatever came next.

Because Samuel was sure of one thing: Mrs Abernathy wasn't going to give up. The Darkness had simply been her latest attempt to silence Samuel. Others would follow, and eventually she would succeed.

Samuel didn't want to die. He quite liked being alive. But as he tried to come to terms with how scared he was, he began to feel angry. Mrs Abernathy was evil. She wanted to do something awful, so awful that the world would never be the same after it, if there was even any world left once the gates were opened. She had to be stopped, and Samuel was determined to fight her until his last breath.

It was at that moment that fortune began to turn in Samuel's favour.

There was a small portable television in the corner of the kitchen. Samuel's mother sometimes liked to watch it while she was having breakfast. The volume was turned down low, and the news was on. Samuel glanced up and saw a man in a white coat talking. Behind him was what looked like an enormous series of pipelines. Samuel knew what it was: the Large Hadron Collider in Switzerland. He had watched a documentary about it earlier in the year and, although he hadn't understood everything that had been discussed, he thought it all sounded like pretty fascinating stuff. He reached for the remote control and turned up the volume.

The scientist, whose name was Professor Stefan, looked a bit embarrassed. It became clear that he was trying to explain why the collider had been shut down. Samuel knew the collider hadn't worked properly the first time it was turned on, and the scientists had been forced to tinker with it for a while before it began running to their satisfaction. Now, after all the money that had been spent on it, it still didn't appear to be working the way that it should.

'Well,' said Professor Stefan, when the reporter pointed this fact out to him, 'that's not entirely true. It was working perfectly, but then there was an, um, unanticipated release of unknown energy.'

'What does that mean, exactly?' asked the reporter.

'Well, to put it in layman's terms, a bit flew off, and now we're trying to find out what it was.'

'A bit?' said the reporter.

'A particle of energy,' said Professor Stefan, 'but one that has not been encountered before, and appears to show unusual characteristics.'

'What kind of characteristics?' said the reporter.

'Well, the collider is a vacuum, and therefore it's sealed. It simply should not be possible for anything to find its way out of there.'

'But now you think that something has?'

'We believe so. It may just be a leak, so we're checking every inch of the collider for possible breaches. As you can imagine, that's a time-consuming procedure. In the meantime, we're going back over our systems in an effort to determine precisely what we're dealing with.'

The reporter thought over what he had just been told.

'Is there any possibility that this "energy" might be dangerous?'

'Oh, none whatsoever,' said Professor Stefan.

Samuel thought that he seemed very sure of this for someone who didn't know what exactly the energy was.

'And when precisely did you become aware of this energy leak?'

'At precisely seven thirty p.m. on October the twenty-eighth,' said Professor Stefan. 'The collider was shut down shortly afterwards.'

Samuel paused, a spoonful of cornflakes suspended between the bowl and his mouth. Seven thirty p.m. on October 28th. At 7.30 p.m. on October 28th Samuel and Boswell had been sitting on the Abernathys' wall when they'd heard the bang from the Abernathys' basement, and they'd seen the blue light and smelled that nasty smell. It might be a coincidence, of course, but for the first time Samuel sensed that there could be someone out there who might be prepared to listen to him.

Samuel sat at his computer and examined the website for CERN. He couldn't find a telephone number, but there was a section entitled 'Ask an Expert'. Samuel didn't know how long an expert might take to answer his question, or even if what he had to say counted as a question at all. He thought very hard, then composed his message to CERN:

Dear CERN,

My name is Samuel Johnson, and I am 11 years old. I have reason to believe that I may have found your missing energy particle, or know where it ended up. I think it is in the basement of number 666, Crowley Avenue in the town of Biddlecombe, England. It is owned by a couple named the Abernathys. It is very blue, and smells of rotten eggs. The energy, that is, not Biddlecombe. It materialised there at precisely 7.30 p.m.

on October 28th. I enclose a drawing of what I saw in the basement, scanned into the computer for your information.

Yours sincerely,
Samuel Johnson

PS I believe Mr and Mrs Abernathy have become possessed by demons, and may be using the energy to open the gates of Hell.

When he was finished, Samuel checked his spelling and went over the letter once again to make sure that he had included all the important details. He had considered leaving out the bit about Hell, but thought it might add a sense of urgency to his message. After all, he didn't know how many people wrote to 'Ask an Expert' every day, or if there was just one expert answering the questions or a whole team. In any case, he thought it was important to attract CERN's attention and, if nothing else, the mention of demons and Hell was likely to make his message stand out.

He pressed Send, and his missive shot off into cyberspace. He considered staying at his computer and waiting for a reply, but he suspected that, even if someone read his message very soon, a certain amount of discussion would still be required before it was answered.

Samuel was not about to sit around doing nothing. It was Halloween, and he had heard Mrs Abernathy say that she and her fellow demons had four days to prepare the way. Samuel didn't know precisely what 'preparing the way' meant, but by any calculation four days from October 28th led to November 1st. He had a terrible feeling that, at some time the next day, the gates of Hell would begin to open.

So Samuel went to the telephone and began making some calls.

It would not be true to say that Samuel was unpopular at school. There were some boys and girls in his class who looked at him a little oddly, especially when he began talking about angels and pins, but for the most part he got on well with nearly everyone. He was also quite happy to spend time by himself, though, and after sharing the same small schoolroom with a bunch of kids his own age for two months, he had rather been enjoying being by himself during half-term. His closest friends were Tom Hobbes and Maria Mayer. Tom's father delivered milk for the local dairy, where his mum also worked, and Maria's dad worked for the telephone company. Samuel, Tom, and Maria had planned to go trick or treating that evening, and Tom and Maria had been a little surprised to hear from Samuel so early in the day.

When Samuel said he had something important to tell them, they were both intrigued. They agreed to meet outside the pie shop in the town centre, and Samuel, with Boswell in tow, was already waiting for Tom and Maria when they arrived together shortly after one p.m. The pie shop was called Pete's Pies, even though Pete had died many years before and his son Nigel now made all the pies, but Nigel's Pies didn't sound right and, anyway, everyone would have just kept calling it Pete's Pies even if Nigel had changed the name. People in small towns are funny that way.

There were always tables and chairs outside Pete's Pies, even in winter, which made it a popular place for people to meet. Pete, and then Nigel, never objected to people taking a seat there. Even if they didn't come along with the intention of buying a pie, the smell from the pie shop would cause their mouths to water and, usually in less than a minute, they would be inside buying a pie 'for later'. About one minute after that they would be eating the pie and considering having another, maybe the apple and raspberry, for dessert.

It was one of these same apple and raspberry pies that Samuel was eating when Tom and Maria strolled up to his table. Tom was taller than Samuel by a couple of inches, and never really seemed to have bad days. He was always in good spirits, except when the school cricket team, of which he was one of the star batsmen, lost. Tom didn't mind losing at most things, but he drew the line at cricket. Tom and Samuel only ever argued on the cricket pitch. Samuel was a good bowler, with a strong right arm, but his eyesight was poor, and he had trouble catching balls when fielding. This meant that he was both an asset and a liability on the cricket pitch, and more than one match had ended with him and Tom shouting at each other at the tops of their voices. Still, they remained friends, and Tom was secretly a little in awe of Samuel, whose mind worked in ways that Tom admired, even if he did not fully understand.

Maria, meanwhile, was smaller than both of them, and had very long hair that she tied in a ponytail each day with one of a selection of bows. She sometimes seemed shy and quiet to those who didn't know her well, but Samuel knew she was very clever and very funny. She just didn't like showing off. Maria wanted to be a scientist when she grew up, and was the only person Samuel and Tom knew who did homework for pleasure.

Boswell wagged his tail in greeting at the two new arrivals, then returned his attention to the pie on the table. He knew that Samuel would share some with him eventually. Samuel shared nearly all of his food with Boswell, except chocolate, because that wasn't good for Boswell and gave him wind, and Boswell could be a smelly dog if he was fed the wrong things.

'All right, then,' said Tom, once he and Maria had bought pies of their own and settled down on their seats. 'What's the big mystery?'

Boswell finished the piece of pie that Samuel had fed to him, licked up the last of the crumbs, and began drooling over Tom's shoe instead. Tom decided to give him some pie to distract him before Boswell's spit started to soak through to his socks.

'Well, it's like this,' said Samuel. 'You're probably going to have trouble believing me, and I'm not sure how I'm going to prove that what I have to say is true. All I'm asking is that you listen to me, because I really need your help.'

He was so serious that Tom stopped eating for a moment and Tom, like Boswell, didn't like to stop eating for no good reason.

'Wow, that sounds serious,' he said. 'Off you go, then. I'm listening.'

He looked at Maria, who nodded. 'We both are.'

So Samuel told them everything, right up to the point at which he'd sent off his message to CERN. When he was finished nobody spoke for a time, then Tom said:

'You're barmy.'

'Tom!' Maria scolded him.

'No, really. You're trying to tell us that this Mrs Abernathy isn't really Mrs Abernathy but a thing with tentacles, and that in her basement is a blue hole that somehow is a tunnel to Hell, and tomorrow some gates are going to open in that tunnel and – what? Demons are going to come out?'

'Something like that,' said Samuel calmly.

'You *are* barmy,' repeated Tom.

Samuel turned to Maria. 'And you?' he asked her. 'What do you think?'

'It is a little hard to believe,' said Maria gently.

'I'm not lying,' said Samuel. He looked at them both, his face serious. 'On my life, I promise you I'm not lying. And . . .'

He paused.

'What?' said Maria.

'I'm scared,' said Samuel. 'I'm really scared.'

And they both believed him when he said it.

'Well,' said Tom. 'There's only one thing for it.'

'What's that?' asked Maria, but she already knew the answer.

Tom grinned.

'We'll just have to take a look at the Abernathys' house.'

Meanwhile, at CERN, the technician who had been monitoring the 'Ask An Expert' section of the website approached Professor Hilbert holding a printed message at the bottom of which was a drawing of a blue spiral.

'Professor,' he said, nervously, 'this may be nothing, but . . .'

Sixteen

In Which We Visit the Abernathy House, and Decide That We Wouldn't Want to Live There

It was determined that they should leave the visit to the Abernathys' house until the light had begun to fade, so Samuel and Maria spent the early part of the afternoon helping Tom to practise his batting. When it began to grow dark they paid a brief visit to Samuel's house to check his e-mail, but there was no reply to his message from CERN.

'Maybe they're very busy,' said Tom, 'what with their big collider thing being broken.'

'It's not broken,' said Samuel. 'Well, not exactly. They've shut it down while they investigate the energy leak.'

'The one that you say has turned up in the Abernathys' basement,' said Tom. 'That's a long way from Switzerland. They're not Swiss, are they?'

Samuel thought about it. 'No, I don't think so. Mr Abernathy didn't sound Swiss when I spoke to him. Mrs Abernathy just smells funny.'

Then again, Samuel had never, to his knowledge, spoken to a Swiss person. He just suspected that Swiss people didn't sound like Mr Abernathy, who spoke with a gruff northern accent, or Mrs Abernathy, who seemed quite posh.

Maria looked out of Samuel's bedroom window. 'It's getting dark now,' she said. 'Are you sure we should be doing this? It doesn't seem right, creeping around somebody's garden in the dark. I mean, what is it that you hope we'll see?'

Samuel shrugged. 'Just . . . something. Something that will make you believe me.'

'And if we do believe you?' asked Maria. 'What then?'

'Well, you'll know I'm not mad,' said Samuel. 'Or a liar.'

Maria smiled fondly. 'I know you'd never lie to us, Samuel,' she said.

'Although you might still be mad,' added Tom, but he too was smiling. 'Well, come on, then. I have to get home for tea, or I'll catch hell from my mum.' He realised what he had just said. 'Catch hell? Get it? See, I'm funny even when I'm not trying to be.'

Maria and Samuel rolled their eyes.

'Oh, please yourselves,' said Tom. 'Some people have no sense of humour . . .'

The Abernathys' house appeared to be empty when they reached it, Boswell somewhat reluctantly in tow.

'Doesn't seem like there's anybody home,' said Tom.

'It looks creepy,' said Maria 'I know it's just a normal house, but maybe it's because of what you've told us about the people who live there . . .'

'No,' said Tom, his tone subdued. 'You're right. I can feel it. The hairs on the back of my neck are standing up. There's something wrong here.'

'Boswell feels it too,' said Samuel, and, indeed, Boswell was whimpering. The dog planted his small bottom firmly on the ground outside the garden gate, as if to say, 'Right, this is as far as I go. If you want me to go any farther, you'll have to drag me.'

Samuel tied Boswell's lead to the garden gate. 'We'd best leave him here,' he said.

'Can I stay with him?' asked Tom, only half joking.

'Come on, silly,' said Maria taking Tom by the arm and pulling him into the garden, Samuel close behind them.

'Weren't you scared just a minute ago?' whispered Tom.

'I'm still scared,' said Maria, 'but this is *interesting.*'

The expression on Maria's face had changed. She looked excited. Mr Hume had once said that she had the perfect brain for a scientist. She was both curious and careful, and once she got the scent of something that intrigued her, she would pursue it right to the end.

Samuel led them to the basement window. A bare bulb glowed orange in the ceiling, casting a dim light on the room. They crouched down and peered inside, but apart from the usual junk that accumulated in people's basements, there was nothing out of the ordinary to be seen.

'That's where it happened,' said Samuel. 'The blue circle, the big clawed hand, all of it.'

'Well, it's quiet now,' said Tom. 'Mind you, it smells nasty here.'

He was right. A stink of rotten eggs hung around the basement and the area of the garden nearest to it. A concentrated breeze was blowing, carrying the stench on it, as though a hole had been bored in a great wall behind which a wind was blowing.

'Do you feel that?' said Maria. She raised her hand so that it was very close to the glass. The two boys did likewise.

'It feels like static electricity,' said Tom. He moved his hand farther forward, as though to touch the glass, but Maria reached out to stop him.

'No,' she said. 'I don't think that's a good idea.'

'It's just static,' said Tom.

'No,' said Maria, 'it's not.'

She pointed at the frame of the window. There, barely visible to the naked eye, was the faintest blue glow.

Maria moved on, following the wall of the house.

'Where's she off to?' said Tom.

Samuel didn't know, but he decided to follow Maria nonetheless. Tom, not wanting to be left alone, was soon trotting along behind.

The Abernathys' house stood in the centre of a large garden, so that there was nothing to stop someone circling from the front of the house to the back. Maria was pointing at the windows as she went.

'There!' she said softly. 'And there!'

If they concentrated hard, each time they looked they saw that faint blue glow around every window frame.

'I think it might be a kind of alarm,' said Maria. 'They've secured the place, somehow.'

By this time they had reached the back of the house. To the left of the back door was a kitchen, which was empty. To the right was a living room, with a TV, some couches, and a pair of armchairs. A lamp was lit in the room, casting a square of light upon the back lawn.

Together, the three children made their way to the window and peered inside.

Boswell was very unhappy at having his lead tied to a garden gate. Like most dogs, he didn't like being tied to anything. If you were tied to something, it was hard to fight if a bigger dog came along, and impossible to run away if fighting wasn't an option. Boswell was not much of a fighter. To be honest, he wasn't even very good at running away, given his short legs and long body.

But if there was anything worse than having his lead tied to a garden gate it was having it tied to this particular one. The big house smelled wrong to Boswell. It wasn't just the stink that the children had also picked up. Boswell's sense of smell was far more sensitive than that of any human. He had 25 times more smell receptors than a person, and he could sense odours at concentrations 100 million times lower than a human could. As he sniffed the air around the big house, drawing it deep down to the receptors at the back of his snout, he picked up hints of tainted meat, of disease, of dead things that shouldn't be touched, or tasted, or even sniffed for very long for fear of being sick. Lurking behind them all was one smell in particular, one that every animal hated and feared.

It was the smell of burning.

Suddenly Boswell stood up. He had heard something, the sound of footsteps approaching. One of the bad smells started to grow stronger, although it was mixed up with another that wasn't quite so bad, as though the not-so-bad smell was being used to hide the really bad one. The not-so-bad smell was familiar to Boswell, although that didn't mean he liked it. It was too strong and sweet and sickly. It reminded him of the scent that sometimes came from Mrs Johnson, the scent that emerged from some of the little bottles she kept in her bedroom. It smelled of too many flowers.

Even with his poor eyesight Boswell was able to identify the woman as soon as she turned the corner. He had already built up a picture of her using his nose, and now his worst fears were confirmed.

It was the nasty lady, the one who had brought the Darkness. Boswell began to whine.

There were three people, two men and a woman, sitting in the living room, the walls of which were covered with a strange orange mould that was spreading from the carpet and extending towards the ceiling. The mould covered the chairs on which the three people were sitting, as though they were rotting and their decay was slowly infecting the room. They were not moving, or speaking, but they all had strange, fixed smiles on their faces, like people who had seen something that only someone with a very strange sense of humour would think was funny. Samuel recognised the men as Mr Abernathy and his friend, Mr Renfield. The woman was Mrs Renfield.

They had changed since last he had seen them. He thought that they appeared fatter; bloated somehow, as if by a great internal swelling. He could see Mr Abernathy the most clearly. Mr Abernathy's skin was a grey-green colour, and there were blisters on it. He looked sick. In fact, he looked so sick that Samuel wondered if Mr Abernathy might actually be worse than sick. Despite the time of year the room was filled with flies, and Samuel knew immediately that the people in the room stank very badly. Samuel thought he saw a fly land on one of Mr Abernathy's eyeballs and crawl across it, a black speck against the milky white of the eye. Mr Abernathy didn't even blink.

It was Tom who voiced what Samuel had been thinking. 'Are they . . . dead?' he asked.

As he spoke, the fly buzzed away from Mr Abernathy's

eyeball. At the same instant a long tongue unrolled from Mr Abernathy's mouth, like a party favour. It was pink, and covered with little spines that looked sharp and sticky. It plucked the fly from mid-air, then rolled back in Mr Abernathy's mouth. He chewed on the fly for a moment before swallowing it down.

'Oh, I think I'm going to be sick,' said Maria.

'Was that a tongue?' asked Tom. 'That was a tongue! People don't have tongues that long. *Things* have tongues that long.'

Then they heard the sound of frantic barking from the front of the house, and knew that they were in trouble.

As soon as Boswell saw Mrs Abernathy, he began trying to wriggle out of his collar. It was never kept very tight, mainly because Boswell's neck was so thin that no collar fitted him right. He tugged hard against the lead, and felt the collar begin to rise up against the back of his head. It hurt his ears, but he didn't stop. He knew that if he was still tied to the gate when the bad lady came she would hurt him, and then she would hurt Samuel. Nobody was going to hurt Samuel, not if Boswell had anything to do with it.

The collar was halfway over his ears when the sound of the nasty lady's footsteps started to come faster.

Mrs Abernathy spotted the dog as soon as she rounded the corner. It took her only a moment to identify it as Samuel Johnson's pet.

'Oh, you naughty boy!' she whispered. 'You naughty, *naughty* little boy.'

She began to run.

Boswell risked a glance to his left, and saw the nasty lady drawing nearer. He gave a final hard tug against the collar, and felt it pull free, almost taking his ears with it. He barked, alternating glances between the path leading into the garden of the big house and the bad lady. He kept hoping that Samuel and his friends would come, yet they didn't.

Run! he barked. Nasty lady! Run!

But still there was no sign of them. He looked to his left, and saw the nasty lady's shape begin to change. There were things moving beneath her coat. Suddenly, the material began to tear, and long pink feelers burst through the holes, each one ending in sharp pincers that snapped at the cold air. One extended itself towards him, the pincers making a clicking sound and dripping foul-smelling liquid on the ground. Instinctively he snapped back at it, and it withdrew, but only for a moment. It rose up, like a snake about to strike. Boswell sensed the danger.

With no other choice, he put his tail between his legs and ran as fast as his little legs would carry him. He thought he felt something graze his coat; but he didn't look back, not until he had reached the corner. He hid behind a car and peered out from behind the wheels. The nasty lady stood for a moment at the garden gate, the long pink tentacles waving against the night sky, then turned away and headed into the garden. Seconds later Boswell heard a terrible sound, one so sharp and piercing that it hurt his ears. It was too high-pitched for a human to detect, but Mrs Abernathy wasn't trying to contact any human.

She was alerting her fellow demons.

Seventeen

In Which Mrs Abernathy Changes Her Plans

Tom peered round the corner of the house, and saw Mrs Abernathy enter the garden and close the gate carefully behind her. The tentacles moved in the still evening air, the moonlight catching the fluid that dripped from their pincers. Tom counted twelve of them. On the ground at Mrs Abernathy's feet lay Boswell's empty collar. Mrs Abernathy took three steps forward, then stopped. She cocked her head to one side, as though listening for something, but she did not move any closer to the house.

She was waiting, guarding the gate.

Tom ran back to where Samuel and Maria were waiting beneath the window.

'We're in trouble,' he said. 'There's a woman in the garden with tentacles sticking out of her back.'

'Mrs Abernathy,' said Samuel. 'What about Boswell?'

'There's no sign of him. His collar is there, but it's empty.'

Samuel looked worried. 'She couldn't have . . . ?' he began to say, then trailed off. He didn't want to think about what Mrs Abernathy might have done to his dog.

Seconds later, he heard Boswell's bark. It sounded farther away than before, but it was definitely him.

'He's OK!' said Samuel.

'Yeah, but we're not,' said Tom. 'If she recognised Boswell, she'll know that you're here.'

Samuel swallowed hard. 'She doesn't know you and Maria are with me. I could distract her, so you two can get away.'

Tom looked at Samuel with something approaching admiration, then hit him hard on the arm.

'Ow!' said Samuel. 'What was that for?'

'For being stupid,' said Tom. 'We're not going to leave you here alone.'

Suddenly Maria's hand was pushed against his mouth, silencing him. She put a finger to her lips, then withdrew it and pointed at the rectangle of light from the window. The shadow of a man could now be seen against it. They remained very still, hardly daring to breathe. The shadow began to alter. As they watched, eight spiny limbs, like spider legs, emerged from it. Then the shadow turned and began to recede, as whoever, or whatever, it was moved away from the window.

'We have to make a run for it,' said Samuel.

'We can't go out the way we came in,' said Tom. 'That woman's guarding the gate.'

'And we can't go over the garden wall,' said Maria. 'It's too high.'

Now noises were coming from inside the house. They heard a vase break, and then shambling footsteps, as though someone who was having trouble walking was approaching the back door.

To their left, Tom saw two plastic boxes filled with empty wine bottles, ready for recycling.

'Do you think you could hit those wine bottles with a stone?' he asked Samuel.

'If I had a stone,' said Samuel.

Tom gestured to Samuel's right, where there was a small rockery dotted with plants. Samuel immediately reached for a stone roughly the size of a cricket ball, took a breath, and threw it overarm at the boxes of bottles. The stone landed slap bang in the middle of them, breaking the necks of the longest and scattering glass on the ground.

'Now!' said Samuel.

They ran to the right, past the rockery and along the side of the house. From behind them came the sound of the back door opening, but by then they were already at the corner of the house, the front gate before them. Mrs Abernathy was gone, and when Maria risked a look round the corner she saw the shape of a woman moving quickly away from them and towards the other end of the house.

They took their chance and sprinted for the gate, leaping over the flowerbeds and the bushes that had been carefully tended by Mr Abernathy before he was taken over by a thing with no appreciation for the finer points of gardening. Tom was bringing up the rear when his foot caught on a length of trailing ivy and he stumbled, then fell. Samuel and Maria stopped at the gate, Maria preparing to go back and help Tom when Mrs Abernathy, alerted by the noise, appeared at the side of the house.

'Bad children!' she said. 'You shouldn't trespass on other people's property.'

Two of the tentacles grew longer than the rest, then shot at speed towards Tom as he tried to get to his feet. He could see how sharp their pincers were, and could smell the stuff that dripped like spittle from them as they came. He was raising his hand to protect himself when something slashed through the air before him. It was a garden rake, which caught the tentacles a hard blow and drove them to the ground. They remained pinned there beneath the rake's teeth, writhing feebly and spraying thick black blood on the lawn. Mrs Abernathy screamed in shock and pain as Maria let go of the rake and pulled Tom to his feet.

'Come on,' she said and the three children, accompanied by a happy and very relieved Boswell, disappeared into the dusk.

Mrs Abernathy walked across the lawn, her face contorted with rage and agony. The tentacles had retreated into her body, except for the two that the horrid girl had pierced with the rake. Mrs Abernathy knelt down and pulled the rake free, then tossed it away. Slowly, like wounded animals, the tentacles grew smaller, withdrawing into her flesh where they left a series of small holes that bled black against her ruined coat.

Mr Renfield shuffled towards her, eight spiny legs now withdrawing into his body, and what looked like mandibles disappearing back into his mouth. The same bland, humourless smile was still on his face. Behind him, Mrs Renfield and Mr Abernathy appeared, followed by a cloud of flies.

Mr Abernathy stopped beside his wife. He turned to look blankly at her, and she hit him so hard across the face with the back of her hand that his neck broke and his head hung at a strange angle upon his shoulders. He raised his hands and tried to put his head back into place, but it wouldn't stay. Eventually he gave up and left it hanging. It didn't seem to cause him any great discomfort, and his smile remained unchanged.

'You fool,' said Mrs Abernathy. 'Now *three* of them know about us.'

Mrs Renfield joined her. 'What shall we do?' she asked. 'Kill them?'

'We can't wait any longer,' said Mrs Abernathy. 'We have to begin.'

'But all is not ready.'

'Enough will have gathered,' said Mrs Abernathy. 'The gates will open, and the first will pour through. They will prepare the way for the Great Malevolence, and he will finish what they have begun. Go! I will join you in a moment.'

Mr and Mrs Renfield moved away, followed by Mr Abernathy and his wobbling head. Mrs Abernathy strolled to the garden gate and looked to the direction in which the three children and the dog had run. She saw the ghosts of them still hanging in the air before they drifted away like fog.

Perhaps the others were right, she thought. It was not yet time. The Great Malevolence had wanted to enter this new world in glory, provoking awe and terror as he came, his demonic army arrayed behind him. Instead, their attack upon the world of men would begin more slowly. As the demons began to pour through, the portal would grow larger. They would draw the energy that they needed from the collider. It would only be a matter of hours before the gates would melt away, and the Great Malevolence would be unleashed upon the Earth.

A small figure wearing a devil's horns and mask appeared before her.

'Trick or treat,' said a voice from behind the mask.

Mrs Abernathy regarded him curiously, then began to smile. The smile turned to a fearsome, terrible laughter. She put the back of her hand to her mouth, and said: 'How delightful! Oh, this is just perfect!'

Like small boys the world over, the small boy behind the mask, whose name was Michael, didn't care much for things that were 'delightful', or grown-ups who seemed to find things funny when they weren't funny at all.

'Look, are you going to give me something or aren't you?' he asked impatiently.

'Oh, I'll give you something,' she said. 'I'll give you all something, and it will be the last thing you will ever receive. I'll give you death.'

'No sweets, then,' said the small boy.

Mrs Abernathy's laughter faded, and she knelt down before the little boy. He saw a faint blue glow to her eyes. It grew brighter and brighter, until there was nothing in the woman's eye sockets but cold blue light that made him wince with pain. When she opened her mouth, he smelt the foulness of her insides.

'No sweets,' said Mrs Abernathy. 'No sweets ever again.'

She watched the small boy run away, and thought:

Flee! Flee while you can, but there will be no escape, not from me.

And not from my master.

Eighteen

In Which the Portal Opens Wide

Mrs Johnson sat on the couch, smiling awkwardly at her visitor, whose name was Dr Planck. Dr Planck was small and dark, with a pointed beard, and black-rimmed glasses. Mrs Johnson had made him tea, and offered him a biscuit. Now she was trying to understand why he was with her in the first place. All she knew was that it had something to do with Samuel. These things always did.

Dr Planck worked at the local university as part of the experimental particle physics research programme, and had been involved with CERN for a number of years. When the message from Switzerland about Samuel's e-mail had come through to him, he had rushed to Biddlecombe. He wasn't certain that a small boy could be entirely helpful to them, but there was something about his drawing, and the description of the rotten egg smell, that had caught the attention of the scientists at CERN. Now here he was, drinking tea and eating Bourbon cream biscuits, and trying to establish if Mrs Johnson's son might just have given them the help they had been seeking.

'Samuel hasn't done anything wrong, has he?' said Mrs Johnson.

'No, not at all,' said Dr Planck. 'He just sent us a very interesting e-mail, and we'd like to talk to him about it.'

'By "us", you mean the CERN people,' said Mrs Johnson. 'That's right.'

'Has Samuel solved one of the mysteries of the Universe, then?'

Dr Planck smiled politely, and nibbled on his Bourbon cream. 'Not exactly,' he said. 'Tell me, what do you know about the people at number six-six-six . . . ?'

Mrs Abernathy stood in the basement, Mr Abernathy and the Renfields behind her. A pinpoint of blue light hung in the air, pulsing softly. Mrs Renfield growled in disapproval.

'It was there all along,' she said to Mrs Abernathy, 'and yet you hid it from us.'

'You did not need to know,' said Mrs Abernathy.

'Who are you to decide such things?'

Mrs Abernathy turned on her. For an instant, her mouth grew so large that it threatened to engulf her entire head, revealing row upon row of jagged teeth. The huge jaws snapped at Mrs Renfield, who staggered backwards in alarm. Then, almost as soon as it had revealed itself, the monstrous mouth was gone, and Mrs Abernathy was restored to her former beauty.

'You will keep a civil tongue in your head, or you will find yourself deprived of both,' warned Mrs Abernathy. 'Remember to whom you are speaking. I have the ear of our master, and I am his emissary here on Earth. Any disrespect shown to me will be communicated to him, and the punishment will be great.'

Mrs Renfield hung her head, quaking at the thought of what punishments might befall her. She belonged to a lower order of demons than Mrs Abernathy,[22] yet she was envious of Mrs Abernathy's power and her closeness to the Great Malevolence, for that which is evil is always jealous, and seeks constantly to advance itself. Now her display of anger had left open the possibility of retribution from their master, because Mrs Abernathy would surely tell him of Mrs Renfield's impertinence. But if she could overcome Mrs Abernathy and take her place, if she, and not Mrs Abernathy, could pave the way for their master, then she would be rewarded, not punished.

And so she made her move. Her jaws widened, and from between her lips her spider chelicerae emerged, two appendages ending in hollow points, each loaded with poison. She approached Mrs Abernathy from behind, her eyes fixed on the pale skin at the base of Mrs Abernathy's neck.

Suddenly Mrs Renfield froze, unable to advance. She felt her throat tighten, as though a hand had gripped it and was slowly choking her. Mrs Abernathy turned, her eyes ablaze with blue fire.

'You foolish creature,' she said. 'Now you will suffer.'

Mrs Abernathy waved her fingers in front of Mrs Renfield's face. The chelicerae continued to grow from Mrs Renfield's mouth, but now they began to curl down towards her own neck. Mrs Renfield's eyes widened in panic, but she could do

---

[22] A book named *Le Dragon Rouge* (*The Red Dragon*), possibly written in the sixteenth century, classified the demons of hell in three orders, from officers to generals. Books like this are known as 'grimoires', and to have power they must be written in red ink and, some say, bound in human skin.

nothing to stop what was about to occur. The twin points pierced her skin and she began to pump poison into her own system. Her eyes bulged, and her face blackened, until at last she fell to the floor. Her body jerked once before it turned to dust.

Mrs Abernathy returned her attention to the blue light.

'Master,' said Mrs Abernathy. 'Your servant calls.'

The blue light grew larger, and the basement became colder. Mrs Abernathy's breath plumed whitely. Her fingertips were so chilled that they began to hurt.

And then a voice spoke. It seemed to come at once from everywhere and nowhere, echoing around the basement. It was deep and sibilant, like the hissing of a giant snake in a dank cave.

'*Yessssss*,' it said. '*Speak.*'

'Master,' said Mrs Abernathy again, and her voice trembled. Even now, after she had spent so long in the presence of this great evil, so close to an eternity that the difference hardly mattered, it still had the power to terrify her. 'We must act now. We can wait no longer.'

'*Why?*'

'There has been a . . . difficulty,' said Mrs Abernathy, choosing her words carefully. 'Our presence has become known.'

'*To whom?*'

'A child.'

'*Why was this child not dealt with?*'

'We tried. He was lucky. Now he has shared his knowledge with others.'

There was silence. Mrs Abernathy could almost feel her master's rage building.

'*You disappoint me,*' he said at last. '*There will be a reckoning for this.*'

'Yes, Master.' Mrs Abernathy bowed her head, as though the Great Malevolence were standing before her, ready to visit his wrath upon her.

'*So be it,*' said the voice. '*Let it begin.*'

But before they could proceed any further, the doorbell rang.

Deep in the bowels of CERN, the chief scientists were gathered in Professor Stefan's office.

'Is there any word yet from Doctor Planck?' asked Professor Stefan.

Professor Hilbert glanced at his watch. 'He should be with the boy by now,' he said.

'If it's some kind of joke, I'll have that child's hide,' said Professor Stefan.

He reached for his pen, if only to give him something to do with his hands. The pen lay close to the edge of his desk, but before he could get his fingers to it the pen dropped to the floor.

Professor Stefan looked at it curiously. 'That's odd,' he said, just as he began to feel the vibrations running through his desk. A great humming filled the entire facility, and all the lights dimmed for a moment. Computer screens throughout the facility began displaying huge amounts of data, Aramaic mixed with binary code.

'What's happening?' said Professor Stefan.

But he already knew.

Somehow, the collider had started up again.

*   *   *

Mrs Abernathy answered the door. Standing on the step was a small man with a pointed beard. He was sucking on the frame of a pair of dark-rimmed glasses.

'Mrs Abernathy?' he said.

'Yes?'

'I'm Doctor Planck. I'd like to talk with you for a moment, if it's convenient.'

'Actually,' said Mrs Abernathy, 'I'm rather busy right now.'

Dr Planck sniffed the air. He smelled rotten eggs. Then he noticed a faint blue glow coming from the basement, a light that also seemed to be flickering on the window frames of the house, and around the door. A wind blew in his face, its force increasing. As it did so, the blue glow became brighter.

'What are you doing?' said Dr Planck. 'This isn't right.'

'Run,' said Mrs Abernathy.

'What?'

'I said, "Run".'

Her eyes filled with cold fire. Her mouth opened, and the light shone like a beam from it. It felt like ice on Dr Planck's skin.

He ran.

The basement of number 666 was filled with a vast swirling mass of light and dark, of blue beams and a blackness that was so thick as to be almost tangible. Little tendrils of electricity flickered deep within it like bolts of lightning against the night sky, then shot out to strike Mr Abernathy and Mr Renfield. They began to change shape, shedding their human skins and assuming once again their true demonic forms. Mr Abernathy looked like a grey toad, with unblinking eyes that protruded from his head on long stalks. Mr Renfield became spiderlike, his body covered with spiny hairs, eight black eyes appearing on his head: two large ones at the front, two smaller ones on either side, then four more behind. Eight long, jointed legs burst from his torso, each ending in a sharp claw, yet he remained standing on his human legs, which were stronger and thicker than the rest. Pointed fangs burst from his jaws, their tips glistening with poison.

Mrs Abernathy joined them, but she remained unchanged, the blue fire in her eyes aside. She did not want to assume her true shape, not yet. Although she was restricted by this human body, it had its uses. If necessary it would allow her to move freely through the world of men during the early stages of the attack. Only when victory was secured did she intend to reveal herself as she really was.

The walls of the house began to shudder. Dust fell from the ceiling of the basement, and old paint cans and boxes of nails dropped from shelves and spilled their contents on the floor. The mortar between the bricks crumbled, and the bricks started to float away. As the house came apart more tendrils of blue light appeared, shooting through the gaps and disappearing into the ground. The wind grew stronger, blowing from one universe into another across the portal that was now opening. Mrs Abernathy watched as the gates, those hated prison, began to glow white hot, dripping molten metal as her master harnessed the power of the collider to begin to free himself.

Now the first of the demons appeared. They were simple entities, little more than skulls with black wings. Their mouths appeared to have too many teeth, so that the top and bottom rows were snagged and uneven, yet sharp as needles. There were four of them, and they hovered in the air before Mrs Abernathy, their jaws snapping and their wings flapping.

'I have work for you,' she said. She reached out to touch the nearest one, imparting through her fingers knowledge of the three children, the ones who had hurt her and forced her to appear weak before her master, and the little man with the beard, who she sensed meant her harm.

'Find them,' she said. 'Find them all and tear them apart.'

Samuel, Maria and Tom were in Samuel's bedroom, sitting in front of Samuel's computer and staring at the e-mail message that Samuel had accessed through his Google account. Samuel's mother stood over them. The message from Dr Planck read:

VERY INTERESTED IN YOUR E-MAIL. I WILL COME TO YOUR HOUSE THIS EVENING AT FIVE THIRTY TO DISCUSS IT. HOPE THIS IS CONVENIENT. IF THERE IS A PROBLEM, I CAN BE CONTACTED AT THE NUMBER BELOW.

'He waited here for a while, then said he wanted to take a look at the Abernathys' house,' said Mrs Johnson. 'What have you been telling people, Samuel?'

'What I've been trying to explain to you all along,' said Samuel. 'The Abernathys are about to do something terrible, and they have to be stopped.'

This time his mother didn't contradict him. Listening to Dr Planck, she had begun to remember her encounter with Mrs Abernathy at the supermarket, and about how frightened she had been to see Samuel talking to her by the churchyard, even if she hadn't understood why at the time. Now she knew that Samuel was telling the truth. Mrs Abernathy was bad. Mrs Abernathy was, in fact, quite horrid.

There was a mobile phone number with the message. Using his home phone, Samuel dialled the number. The phone was answered on the second ring.

'Hello?' said a man's voice. He sounded out of breath.

'Is that Doctor Planck?' asked Samuel.

'Indeed it is. Is that Samuel?'

'Yes. I got your e-mail.'

'Samuel, I'm rather busy right now.'

'Oh.'

'Yes. It appears that I'm being chased by a flying skull.'

Before Samuel could say anything more, they were cut off.

Mrs Johnson looked worried.

'Is everything all right?' she asked.

Samuel tried redialling the number, but there was no tone. He handed the phone to Tom.

'It's gone dead.'

'What did he say?'

'That he was being chased by a flying skull.'

'Oh,' said Tom. 'That's not good.'

But before he could say anything else, they heard the sound of glass breaking from somewhere downstairs.

'What was that?' said Mrs Johnson.

'It sounded like one of your windows breaking,' said Tom. He grabbed Samuel's cricket bat from beside the bedroom door. They listened, but could hear no further noise. Slowly they advanced down the hallway towards the stairs, Tom in the lead.

'Careful,' said Mrs Johnson. 'Oh, Samuel, I wish your dad was here.'

They were halfway to the stairs when a white object flew round the corner and then stopped in mid-air, its wings flapping just hard enough to keep it from falling to the floor. Its jaws never stopped snapping, opening wide enough for a moment to take a man's fist before its twin rows of sharp teeth closed on each other again. Two unblinking black eyes were set like dark jewels in its bony sockets.

'What. Is. *That*?' said Mrs Johnson.

'It looks like a skull. With wings,' said Samuel.

'What's it doing in our house?' said Mrs Johnson.

It was Maria who spoke. 'I think it's looking for us.'

As if in response, the wings of the chattering skull began to beat faster. It changed its position slightly, then shot forward so fast that it was almost a blur. Samuel, Maria and Mrs Johnson dived to the floor, but Tom remained standing. Instinctively he drew back his bat and struck the flying skull when it was about two feet from his face. There was a loud *crack*! and the skull fell to the floor, its jaws still moving but with most of its teeth now knocked out. One wing had broken off, while the other was beating feebly against the carpet. Tom stood over it and hit it once again with the bat. The skull broke into fragments, the jaws ceased snapping, and its eyes went from black to a milky grey.

'Tom!' shouted Maria. 'Look out!'

A second skull appeared at the end of the hallway, followed by a third. The three children and Mrs Johnson backed away until they came to the wall. Tom took a few steps forward, tapped his bat on the carpet, and then took up a stance that would have been frowned upon on a cricket field, the bat raised to shoulder level, ready to strike.

'Tom,' said Mrs Johnson, pulling Samuel and Maria into the nearest bedroom. 'Please be careful!'

'I know what I'm doing,' said Tom. 'Right, then,' he shouted at the skulls. 'Come and have a go, if you think you're hard enough.'

The two skulls flew towards him at the same moment, one travelling slightly faster and lower than the other. Tom crouched and caught the lead skull with a perfect swing, the bat striking so hard that the skull immediately shattered into three pieces, but Tom wasn't quick enough to hit the second skull as well. He was forced to drop to the floor as it zoomed over his head and hit the wall, leaving a mark on the paintwork and dislodging a chunk of plaster. It seemed a little dazed by the contact, but recovered quickly and was preparing to attack again when Samuel flung a blue towel over it, blinding it.

'Now, Tom!' shouted Samuel.

Tom brought the bat down as hard as he could on the top of the skull. It dropped to the floor, still covered by the towel, and he struck at it until he had virtually flattened it.

Samuel, Maria and Mrs Johnson joined him, and all four of them stared at the remains of the skulls that now littered the hallway.

'Well,' said Samuel. 'I think it's begun.'

Nineteen

In Which Assorted Foul Things Begin to Arrive, and Nurd Discovers the Joys of Motoring

Nurd felt his fingertips begin to tingle again, but this time he was ready. He was wearing an assortment of rusty armour, some of the few possessions he had been permitted to retain in exile, to protect himself from any unseen eventualities. Given that he was about to be torn out of one world and hurled into another, this meant just about every possible eventuality was unseen. Only his head remained uncovered because the helmet no longer fitted correctly.

'Maybe your head has swollen,' Wormwood had suggested somewhat unhelpfully as he tried for the third and last time to force the helmet over Nurd's ears.

Nurd had responded by hitting Wormwood with his sceptre.

'Now *your* head is swollen,' Nurd had replied. 'Leave the helmet. It must have taken a dent.'

The tingling spread to the rest of his body. It was time. Nurd wondered if he would get to see Samuel again. He hoped so. Samuel was the only creature who had ever been truly kind to Nurd, and the memory of the boy's company made the demon smile. He was determined to become friends with Samuel, if he could avoid being crushed by household appliances or hit by trucks.

'Goodbye, Wormwood,' said Nurd. 'I'd like to say that I'll miss you, but I won't.'

With that he blinked out of existence, leaving Wormwood alone once again.

'Good riddance,' said Wormwood. 'I never liked you anyway.'

He looked around at the great Wasteland, which stretched emptily in every direction. He felt very lonely.

At CERN, the collider was generating impacts at a startling rate, creating a constant stream of explosions. As the collisions released their energy, the collider filled with more blue light.

In the main control room, Professor Hilbert and his team were frantically trying to turn the collider off, to no avail.

'We're not in control of it,' he told Professor Stefan, who was pacing anxiously in the manner of someone who sees his job about to go up in smoke. Given the amount of energy being given off by the collider, it wasn't the only thing in danger of doing so.

'If we aren't, then who is?' asked Professor Stefan.

Professor Hilbert reached for the volume control on the nearest computer, and turned it up to full. The control room filled with the sound of whispering: many voices speaking in an assortment of ancient tongues. Despite their panic, all activity ceased as the scientists listened, their faces betraying confusion, yet also curiosity. After all, this was fascinating! Dangerous, and very possibly fatal to all of mankind, but undoubtedly fascinating.

Then a single voice rose above the babble, a deep voice filled with aeons of loneliness and jealousy and rage. It spoke just two words.

'*It begins.*'

'I think,' said Professor Hilbert, his face pale, 'that *he* is.'

Nurd popped into existence again in the world of men just at the point where his body felt as though it were about to be crushed to the size of a pea. He immediately began running, wary of standing still for too long after what had happened to him on his previous visits. He got three steps before the ground disappeared beneath him, and he fell down an open manhole into a sewer.

There was a wail, then a splash, followed by a long, smelly silence.

Finally, Nurd's voice spoke from the darkness. He said, somewhat unhappily, 'I appear to be covered in poo.'

The portal in the Abernathys' basement was growing larger with every minute. The flying skulls had been followed by more demonic forms. Most were still primitive, and not very clever, but some of them were big and strong, and all of them were frightening to look at. Mrs Abernathy watched them stumble forth into the Halloween night to sow terror: a pair of pig demons, their snouts moist with mucus, great boar tusks on either side, their little eyes glinting with menace; three winged creatures with the bodies of lizards and the heads of beautiful women, their fingers tipped with nails of steel; and a quartet of horned devils, their bodies entirely black from shovelling coals into the fires of Hell, their eyes transformed into red orbs from centuries of staring into the flames. There were creatures that looked like fossils come to life, their insides protected by hard exoskeletons, carried along on short, plated legs. Others were warped versions of earthly animals, as though the things emerging had once caught a brief but imperfect glimpse of life on this planet: goat-headed men with long, curved horns; beasts with the heads of dinosaurs and the torsos of mammals; and winged crocodiles with the tails of lions.

And then there were those that bore no resemblance to any living thing that had ever existed, pale, nightmarish visions consisting of little more than legs and claws and teeth, with no urge other than to consume.

'Go,' said Mrs Abernathy. 'Begin our master's work. Kill and destroy until there is no building left standing, and nothing left alive. Turn this world to blood and ash. Make it smell of death.'[23]

They lumbered away, and Mrs Abernathy resumed her vigil at the portal. Through the mists she could see more forms approaching, more demons sent to prepare the way for the Great Malevolence. Soon the gates would disintegrate entirely, and their master would be free at last, free to lead his great army into this world.

Nurd climbed from the sewer, unpleasant substances dripping from his armour. He had also managed to hurt his head,

---

[23] Mrs Abernathy did not like the smell of Earth. Her demonic senses made her acutely sensitive to all nice scents, so that she was even aware that the Milky Way itself smelled bad to her. Actually, astronomers who were recently sifting through thousands of signals from Sagittarius B2, a big dust cloud at the centre of our galaxy, found a substance there called ethyl formate, which is the chemical responsible for the flavour of raspberries, and the smell of rum, the drink popular with pirates. Therefore, our galaxy tastes a bit of raspberries and smells of rum, which is nice.

and there was a large lump behind his left ear, but at least he was still in one piece.

He looked to his right and instantly forgot his aches, and the nasty smells that were troubling his nostrils, and his plans to take over this place and rule it. In front of him was a sign that read BIDDLECOMBE CAR SALES. It stood on the roof of a building filled with a number of the small, fast metal things that ran on wheels. One of them, a blue one with stripes along the sides, was particularly lovely.

Nurd ran towards it with great joy, and smacked his face hard against the glass of the showroom. He stumbled back, his hand pressed to his nose. It was bleeding. The pain made his eyes water.

'Right,' said Nurd. 'That's it. No more Mr Nice Demon.'

Using an iron-booted foot, he smashed the glass. Somewhere a bell began to sound, but Nurd ignored it. He laid his hand on the fast blue stripy thing and stroked it lovingly, concentrating hard, trying to come to an understanding of what he was touching.

Car, he thought. Engine. Fuel. Keys.

Porsche.

He explored its workings in his mind until they became clear to him. There was a locked box in a small office at the back of the dealership. When he touched it, he knew that it held the keys to the cars. He ripped the door from it and instantly found the ones he wanted.

Porsche. Mine.

Minutes later, with a screech of tyres and the smell of burning rubber, Nurd was in car heaven.

Twenty

In Which It Becomes Increasingly Clear That the Demons Are Not Going to Have Things All Their Own Way

All across the town, some very strange things were starting to happen.

While Tom used flying skulls for cricket practice, a pair of old ladies were called rude names by a dark-eyed entity that appeared to be living in a drain. One of the old ladies poked at it with her umbrella until it gave up and went away, still calling out rude names, some of which she had never heard before but which, she was certain, were meant to be offensive. In her statement to local police some time later, she claimed that it 'looked and smelled like a big, diseased fish'.

Two men on their way to a Halloween party dressed as schoolboys – only grown-ups think that it's fun to dress up in school uniforms; young people, who have no choice in the matter, don't think it's fun at all – reported that a hunched shape resembling a lump of frog spawn, albeit frog spawn with arms like trumpets, was squatting on the roof of the hardware shop and 'absorbing pigeons'.

A taxi, or something that had taken the form of a taxi, stopped to pick up a young lady on Benson Road and subsequently tried to eat her. She escaped by spraying perfume into its mouth. 'At least,' she told a puzzled streetsweeper, 'I *think* it was its mouth.'

Meanwhile, in a house in Blackwood Grove, Stephanie, the babysitter so unbeloved of Samuel, heard noises coming from the wardrobe in her bedroom She approached it warily, wondering if a mouse might have become trapped inside, but when she opened the door she saw, not a mouse, but a very long, very thick snake. The snake, oddly, had elephant ears.

'Boo!' said the snake. 'Er, I mean, hiss.'

Stephanie promptly fainted. For a moment the snake looked pleased, or as pleased as a demon in the form of a snake can look, until it noticed that the girl had not been alone. There was now a large young man staring angrily into the wardrobe. The demon tried to discover some creature of which the young man was frightened in order to transform itself into the relevant animals, but the young man didn't appear to be afraid of anything. Instead he reached out and grabbed the demon by the neck.

'It's the ears, isn't it?' said the demon. 'I just can't seem to get those right.'

The young man leaned forward and whispered something threateningly into one of the ears in question.

'You know,' said the demon in reply, 'I don't think you can flush something all the way to China from here.'

As it turned out the demon was right: you couldn't flush something all the way from Biddlecombe to China.

Still, he had to give the young man credit.

He certainly tried.

Over in Lovercraft Grove, Mrs Mayer, Maria's mum, was washing the teatime dishes when she saw movement among the rose bushes in her back garden. The rose bushes were her husband's pride and joy. Mr Mayer was not a man with very green fingers. In fact he was the kind of man who, by and large, couldn't even grow weeds and yet something strange and wonderful had happened as soon as he put his mind to the cultivation of roses. When he and Mrs Mayer had bought the house in Lovecraft Grove, there had been a solitary, sad-looking rose bush at the end of the front garden. Somehow it had survived neglect, bad weather, and the deaths of the other rose bushes that had, judging by the rotting stumps surrounding it, once grown there. Mr Mayer seemed to find a soul mate in that rose bush, and was determined to save it. Mrs Mayer didn't hold out much hope, given her husband's previous forays into horticulture, but she held her tongue and did not suggest that he try a cactus instead.

So Mr Mayer had bought every book on the cultivation of roses that he could find. He consulted experts, and haunted garden centres, and lavished the little rose bush, Mrs Mayer sometimes felt, with more care and attention than he did his wife and children.

And in time the rose bush began to flourish. Mrs Mayer could still recall the morning when they had woken to find the first bud poking tentatively from its branches, soon to be followed by others that burst into bright red bloom. It was the only time she had ever seen her husband cry. His eyes shone, and a pair of big, salty tears rolled down his cheeks, and she believed that she had loved him more in that moment than ever before.

Over the years, other bushes had been added to the garden. Mr Mayer had even begun hybridising, creating strange new flowers of his own. Now it was the experts who came to

Mr Mayer, and he would make them mugs of strong tea and they would spend hours in the garden, in all weathers, examining the rose bushes. Mr Mayer was generous with both his expertise and the flowers themselves, and rarely did a visitor leave the garden without a cutting from one of the roses in his hand. Mr Mayer would watch them go, happy in the knowledge that the sisters and brothers of his roses would soon flourish in strange new gardens.

Only one bush was not permitted to be touched, the original one that Mr Mayer had found in the garden. Now big and strong, its flowers were the brightest and prettiest in the beds. It was Mr Mayer's pride and joy. If he could have taken it to bed with him each night to keep it warm in winter, then he would have, even if it meant being pricked occasionally by its thorns. That was how much Mr Mayer loved the rose bush.

Now there were shapes moving through the beds. It was foggy out, so Mrs Mayer could not discern precise forms, but they looked big. Teenage trick-or-treaters, she thought, pretending to be monsters. Silly sods. Her husband would have their hides.

'Barry!' she shouted. 'Bar-*eeeeee!*'

Oooh, he'd teach them a lesson, make no mistake about that.

Upstairs the Mayers' son, Christopher, was putting together a model aircraft at the desk by his bedroom window. Actually, he was sort of putting it together. He had been distracted by a message from his sister on his phone. It had been a bit garbled, but a few words had stood out. Those words had been 'monsters', 'Hell', 'demonic horde', and 'warn Mum and Dad'.

Christopher had not, of course, warned his mum and dad. He might have been younger than his sister, but he wasn't stupid. If he started babbling about demons and Hell to his dad he'd be locked up, or at the very least given a sound telling-off. Still, Maria had seemed very serious about it all. If it was a joke, she'd clearly been doing her best to convince her brother otherwise.

He was mulling over all this, and wondering how he was going to separate two parts of a tank that had accidentally stuck to each other, when he caught sight of the figures in the rose garden. Christopher's eyesight was very keen and, aided by a brief break in the fog, he had a different impression from his mum of the beings currently trampling his father's beloved bushes. They weren't trick-or-treaters, not unless trick or treaters had somehow found a way to grow seven feet tall, add spectacular horns to their heads, and contrive to make their eyes glow a deep, disturbing red.

'Crikey,' he said aloud. He *knew* that Maria hadn't been lying. Maria never lied.

It was the demonic horde. There really were demons here.

'Bar-*eeeeeeeeeeeee!*' Mrs Mayer called for the third time, just as her son burst into the kitchen.

'Mum!' he said. 'It's—'

'Not now, Christopher,' said Mrs Mayer. 'There are people trampling around in your dad's rose garden.' She walked to the end of the stairs and shouted: 'Barry! I'm talking to you.'

'What is it?' came an irritated voice from upstairs. 'I'm in the bathroom.'

'There's someone in your rose garden.'

'I said—'

'It's not people, Mum,' Christopher interrupted. 'It's things. It's the demonic horde.'

'The what?'

'The demonic *horde*.'

'Oh.' She walked to the kitchen door. 'Barry! Christopher says the demonic horde are in your rose garden. They must be a band or something.'

'What? In my rose garden?'

They heard scuffling from above, and a toilet flushing. Seconds later, Mr Mayer appeared at the top of the stairs, fixing the belt on his trousers.

'I hope you washed your hands,' said Mrs Mayer.

'Washed my hands?' said Mr Mayer. 'I know what I'll do with my hands.'

Christopher's dad was a big man who had boxed at amateur level until he started to be knocked down too often for his liking. He now worked for the telephone company, and Christopher and his mum had once passed in the car while his father and another man who was nearly as big as him were together lifting wooden telephone poles, unaided by machinery. It was one of the most impressive sights Christopher had ever seen.

Unfortunately, while Mr Mayer might have been the equal of most men, and was still pretty good with his fists, Christopher didn't believe that he was fully aware of the threat currently making its way towards the house from the direction of the rose garden.

'Dad,' he said. 'I think you should hang on for a moment.'

'Hang on?' said his father incredulously. 'Hang on? There are roses at stake, son. Nobody, and I mean nobody, messes with my roses.'

'That's just it,' said Christopher, his frustration growing. Didn't anyone in this family listen? 'It's not a "body", it's a—'

But it was too late. His dad had flung open the back door, and was preparing to unleash the full force of his rage upon the unfortunates who had trespassed on the most sacred patch of his little empire. His face was bright red, and his mouth was open, but no sound was coming out. Instead he was staring at the enormous demon standing five feet away from him. It looked like a hairy black yak that had managed to stand up on its hind legs and replace its hooves with hooked claws. Along the way it had clearly decided that chewing grass was infinitely less fun than chewing something much meatier, so its blunt vegetarian molars had been replaced with sharp, white, tearing teeth. Its eyes were bright red, and smoke was pouring from its nostrils. It drew back its lips and growled at Mr Mayer.

'Right,' said Mr Mayer. 'Well, we'll say no more about it, then.'

He closed the door and said, in a very small voice: 'Run.'

'Sorry, Barry?' said Mrs Mayer, whose view of what lay on the other side of the door had been blocked by her husband, and who was still under the impression that something needed to be done about the trick-or-treaters in their back garden.

'Run,' said Mr Mayer, in a slightly louder voice, then: 'RUN!'

A heavy body hit the back door very hard, rattling it in its frame. Mr Mayer grabbed his wife with one hand, his son with the other, and dragged them into the hallway just as the door burst from its hinges and landed on the kitchen floor. Mrs Mayer looked over her shoulder and screamed, but her scream was drowned out by a bellowing from behind them.

'It's OK, love,' said Mr Mayer, slamming the kitchen door, although he wasn't entirely sure how much good that would do, given what had just happened to the back door. 'Don't be frightened.' He didn't know why he was telling his wife not to be frightened, as there seemed a perfectly good reason to be very frightened, but that was what one did at times like this.

'Frightened?' said Mrs Mayer, yanking herself free from her husband's grasp and storming into the living room. 'I'm not frightened. That's a new kitchen, that is. I'm not just going to stand by while some bull *thing* destroys it.'

She moved with determination to the fireplace and picked up a poker.

'Mum,' said Christopher. 'It's a demon. I don't think a poker will hurt it.'

'It will where I'm going to put it,' said Mrs Mayer.

Mr Mayer looked at Christopher, and shrugged.

'You have to stop her, Dad,' said Christopher.

'I think I'd rather face the demon,' said Mr Mayer, as his wife pushed past him. 'You know your mum when she has her mind set on something.'

He grabbed a pair of coal tongs and followed his wife. From behind the kitchen door came another bellow, and the sound of dishes smashing on the tiled floor. Mrs Mayer entered the kitchen to find the demon standing amid the wreckage of her second-best crockery.

'Right, you!' said Mrs Mayer. 'That's quite enough of that.'

The demon turned, bared its teeth, and caught a poker straight between the eyes. It staggered slightly, then seemed about to recover itself when the next blow sent it to its knees. Meanwhile a second demon, smaller than the first, had just entered through the back door. Mr Mayer caught it by the snout with the coal tongs and twisted hard. The demon let out a pained howl as Mr Mayer forced it backwards and then, holding on to the tongs with his left hand, began to bang the demon across the head with a dustbin lid.

'That's.' *Crash!* 'For.' *Smash!* 'Messing.' *Thud!* 'Around.' *Whack!* 'With.' *Thump!* 'My.' *Whomp!* 'Roses!'

When he had finished, the demon lay unmoving upon the ground. The red light faded from its eyes before disappearing entirely. In the kitchen, Mrs Mayer was growing tired of hitting the demon with the poker, which was just as well as it had stopped moving some time before, and its eyes had also gone dark.

Mr Mayer stood in the yard, the tongs in one hand, the dustbin lid in the other, like a knight of old, albeit one who couldn't afford proper weapons. From the rose garden, two more demons watched him warily as their fallen comrades began to disappear in wisps of foul-smelling purple smoke.

'Now listen here,' said Mr Mayer. 'I'm going to count to five, and by then you'd better be off those roses, or you'll get what your friends got. One.'

While the demons had no idea what Mr Mayer was *saying*, they were smart enough to understand what he *meant*.

'Two.'

He began moving in their direction. Mrs Mayer appeared behind him, brandishing the poker. The demons exchanged a look, and the universal nod of those who have decided that it would be a smart thing to make themselves very scarce as soon as demonically possible. They squatted down and with a single leap propelled themselves over the six-foot-high garden wall then, not to put too fine a point on it, scarpered.

Mr Mayer walked to the rose garden where he stared down upon his beloved bushes, now trampled into the dirt. Only one remained standing: the original bush. It had survived everything that man and nature could throw at it, and it wasn't about to be crushed by any horde, demonic or otherwise.

Mr Mayer lay down his tong sword and dustbin-lid shield and patted its bare branches fondly.

'It's all right, little one,' he said. 'We'll start again come spring . . .'

Twenty-one

In Which The Verger Is Assaulted, and a Very Unpleasant Person Comes Back to Life

The vicar and verger were preparing the Church of St Timidus for the following day's early-morning service when they heard what sounded like a brick dislodging from the stonework high above their heads and falling to the ground outside. Both men looked a little concerned, as well they might. The church was very old, and in a poor state of repair. Reverend Ussher was always worried about the roof falling in, or the brickwork collapsing. Now it seemed that his worst fears were coming true.

'What was that?' he asked the verger. 'A slate falling?'

'It sounded a bit heavier than a slate,' said Mr Berkeley, who was a fat little man. Both the vicar and the verger were fat little men. They had played Tweedledum and Tweedledee in the local drama society's version of *Alice in Wonderland* earlier that year, and very good they were too.

The two men went to the front door of the church and unlocked it. They were about to step outside when a small, stunned stone gargoyle staggered from a nearby holly bush, its heavy wings beating slowly. It was a most ugly creature, more so even than the average gargoyle. Bishop Bernard the Bad had supervised its creation, just as he had every other detail of the church's construction. This explained why it was a dark, gloomy building, and why all of the faces and creatures carved on its stonework were hideous and scary.

The vicar and verger watched, open-mouthed, as the gargoyle rubbed its head. Small streaks of blue lightning flashed across its body. It coughed once, and spat out what looked like old pigeon feathers.

The gargoyle was very confused. It had wings, but it didn't seem able to fly. When it had come to life, the first thing it had done was attempt to soar elegantly into the air. Unfortunately, things made out of stone don't tend to soar terribly well, so the gargoyle had simply dropped off its perch. Even though it wasn't very intelligent, it knew the difference between flying and falling. It now also knew the difference between landing and just hitting the ground very hard.

More gargoyles, each one uglier than the last, began to descend upon the church lawns. One of them struck a tree and broke on impact, but most seemed to survive the drop more or less intact. Once they had recovered from their shock, they began to converge on the main door of the church where Reverend Ussher and Mr Berkeley were standing, rooted to the spot in amazement. They might have remained that way too, had the verger not been hit on the side of the head with a sharp piece of masonry.

'Oh, you're in trouble now,' said a voice. Mr Berkeley looked to his left and saw that the faces carved into the stonework of the church had also come to life, and the head of a monk, with a pair of hands supporting his chin, was talking to him. At least the hands should have been supporting his chin, but one of them had clearly just thrown a piece of brickwork at the verger's head.

The verger tapped the vicar's shoulder.

'The monk on the wall is talking to us,' he said.

'Oh,' said the vicar. He tried to sound surprised, but couldn't quite manage it.

'Oi,' said the stone monk. 'Fatties! I said, "You're in trouble now."'

'Why would that be?' asked the vicar, tearing his eyes away from the approaching gargoyles.

'End of the world,' said the stone monk. 'Hell is opening up. The Big Bad is coming. The Great Malevolence. Wouldn't want to be in your shoes. He doesn't like humans.'

The stone monk seemed to consider something for a moment.

'Actually he doesn't like anyone, but especially not humans.'

'I say,' said the vicar, 'you're part of the church's stonework. Aren't you supposed to be on our side?'

'Nah,' said the stone monk. 'Infused with the bishop's evil, we are. Couldn't be nice if we tried.'

'The bishop's evil?' said Reverend Ussher. He thought about that for a moment, until another piece of masonry was picked from the church and thrown hard at the verger, who did a little skip in order to avoid it.

'Oooh,' said the monk. 'Tubby's a dancer.'

'You're a nasty piece of stonework!' said the verger.

The monk stuck its fingers in its ears and blew a raspberry at him.

'Sticks and stones, Tubby,' it said. 'Sticks and stones . . .'

One of the gargoyles reached the vicar's foot, opened its mouth, and bit down hard. Fortunately the vicar had been working in his garden that afternoon, and was still wearing his favourite steel-toed work boots. The gargoyle lost its fangs and immediately looked a bit sorry for itself.

'Inside,' said Reverend Ussher. 'Quickly!'

He and the verger retreated into the church and locked the door. Outside they could hear gargoyles beating against the wood and scratching at the lock, but the door was very old and very thick, and it would take more than a bunch of foot-high stone monsters to break it down.

'What do we do now?' asked the verger.

'We'll call the police,' said the vicar.

'And what'll we tell them?'

'That the church is under siege from gargoyles,' said the vicar, as if this was the most obvious thing in the world.

'Right,' said the verger. 'That'll work.'

But before he could say anything else he was distracted by another sound, like one stone rubbing against another, coming from the little room to the right of the main altar, used mainly to store old candlesticks, spare chairs, and the verger's broken bicycle. The room was kept unlocked, since there was little in it that anyone would be bothered to steal. The floor was made entirely of stone, but one of the slabs had a name on it, and this slab was now moving up and down, as though something was pushing at it from beneath.

After almost 900 years, Bishop Bernard the Bad had woken up.

Twenty-two

In Which the Forces of Law and Order
Take an Interest in Nurd

Nurd was alternating between jubilation and absolute terror. He had discovered a crucial detail about fast cars: they can go fast. When he touched a foot to the accelerator the Porsche shot off like a speeding bullet and Nurd's braking technique, like his driving, left a lot to be desired. The first time Nurd braked, he bashed his face against the windscreen, since he had neglected to fasten his seat belt. Now his already injured nose had swollen painfully, and there was blood on his hands where he had tried to wipe it. He had thus confirmed an interesting, if alarming, fact about this world: while he was an immortal being, theoretically incapable of being killed, he could experience pain here. Pain and, if he wasn't careful, something a bit like death, except without the nice long rest afterwards. Still, he was having the time of his very long life, and the Wasteland and Wormwood seemed to belong to another, far-off era.

Not for the first time, a pair of red lights whizzed by on either side of the road. Sometimes those lights were green, or even amber, but Nurd liked the red ones best. They reminded him of the fires of Hell, fires that he might never have to see again if he could terrify this world, or even a little part of it, into submission. But before that there was more driving to be done.

A pair of flashing blue lights appeared in Nurd's rear-view mirror, accompanied by a howling noise. Despite his speed, they appeared to be drawing closer and closer. Hmmm, thought Nurd, I wonder what they are. Then the blue lights came near enough for him to see that they were stuck on the top of another car. Nurd wondered if the lights came in red. If they did, he might try to find some and stick them on the top of his car as well. They would look splendid.

The car with the flashing blue lights pulled alongside Nurd. It was white, with writing on the side, and wasn't even half as pretty as Nurd's car. There were two men in uniform in the car, one of whom was waving at Nurd. Not wishing to seem impolite, even if he was a demon, Nurd waved back. The men in the other car looked quite annoyed at this. Nurd suspected that perhaps he had given them the wrong wave, but he didn't know enough about the habits of this world to be sure of what might be the *right* variety.

The white car pulled ahead of him, and then braked, forcing Nurd to slam his foot down hard on his own brake pedal. If his seat belt hadn't been fastened this time, Nurd would probably have gone through the windscreen. Instead the belt pulled him up short, winding him.

Now Nurd didn't know a lot about driving, but he could tell that the men in the white car had just performed a distinctly dangerous manoeuvre, and he had half a mind to tell them what he thought of them and their little blue lights. Then the two men got out of the car and put hats on, and a warning signal went off in Nurd's brain. He knew Authority when he saw it. His lips moved as he tried to read the word on the back of the car.

Po-lice.

One of the police tapped on Nurd's window while the other walked round the car, holding a notebook and still looking annoyed. Nurd found the button that rolled the window down.

'Evening, sir,' said the man at the window, wrinkling his nose at the unpleasant odour emerging from the vicinity of Nurd. Nurd saw that the man had three stripes on his shoulder. Nurd thought they looked very fetching.

'Hello,' said Nurd. 'Are you a police?'

'I prefer policeman, sir,' came the reply. 'That's quite the costume. Off to a fancy dress party, are we?'

Nurd didn't know what a fancy dress party was, but the policeman's tone of voice suggested that 'yes' might be a good answer.

'Yes,' said Nurd. 'A fancy dress party.'

'Any idea how fast you were going back there, sir?'

Oh, Nurd knew the answer to this one. He could tell from the little red numbers on the dashboard.

'One hundred and twelve miles per hour,' he said proudly. 'Very fast.'

'Oh, yes, very fast, sir. *Too* fast, one might say.'

Nurd thought about this. In his current mood, it didn't seem possible that one could go 'too fast'. There was just 'slow' and 'very fast'.

'No,' said Nurd. 'I don't think so.'

One of the policeman's eyebrows shot up like a startled crow.

'Can I see your licence, please, sir?'

174

'Licence?'

'Licence. Little piece of paper with a photograph of you on it without your Halloween mask, says you can drive a car, although in your case it might have a picture of a rocket ship on it as well.'

'I don't have a licence,' said Nurd. He frowned. He liked the sound of a piece of paper that said he could drive, although he couldn't imagine to whom he might show it, policemen aside. Wormwood might have been impressed by it, but Wormwood wasn't here.

'Oh dear, sir,' said the policeman, who had just been joined by his colleague. 'That's not good, is it?'

'No,' said Nurd. 'I'd like a licence.' He composed his monstrous features into something resembling a smile. 'You wouldn't have one that you could give me, would you? Even if it doesn't have my picture on, it would still be lovely to have.'

The policeman's face went very still.

'What's your name, sir?'

'Nurd,' said Nurd, then added, 'the Scourge of Five Deities.'

'Scourge of Five Motorways, more like,' said the second policeman.

'Very witty, Constable Peel,' said the first policeman. 'Very witty indeed.'

He returned his attention to Nurd. 'A foreign gentleman, are we, sir?' he said. 'Visiting, perhaps?'

'Yes,' said Nurd. 'Visiting.'

'From where, sir?'

'The Great Wasteland,' said Nurd.

'He's from the Midlands, then, Sarge,' said Constable Peel.

The one called Sarge hid a smile. 'That's enough, Constable. Don't want to offend anyone, do we?'

175

'Not only does he not have a licence, Sarge, he doesn't appear to have any licence plates,' said Peel.

Sarge frowned. 'Is this a new car, sir?'

'I think so,' said Nurd. 'It smells new.'

'Is it *your* car, sir?'

'It is now,' Nurd said.

Sarge took a step back. 'Right you are, sir. Step out of the car, please.'

Nurd did as he was told. He towered at least a foot above the two policemen.

'He's a big lad, Sarge,' said Peel. 'Don't know how he managed to fit in there in the first place. Mind you, he smells a bit funny.'

Nurd had to admit that it had been a bit of a squeeze getting into the Porsche, but he was quite a squishy demon. Some demons were all hard bone, or thick shells. Nurd was softer, mainly because he hadn't taken any exercise in centuries.

'That's quite a costume you have there, sir,' said Sarge. 'What exactly are you supposed to be, then?'

'Nurd,' said Nurd. 'The Scourge of—'

'We got all that the first time,' said Sarge. 'Do you have *any* form of identification?'

Nurd concentrated. On his forehead, a mark began to glow a deep, fiery red. It looked like a capital 'B' that had been drawn by a very drunk person. Its appearance on his skin was accompanied by a faint smell of burning flesh.

'You don't see that very often, Sarge,' said Constable Peel. He looked quite impressed.

'No, you don't,' said Sarge. 'What exactly is that supposed to be, sir?'

'It is the mark of Nurd,' said Nurd.

'He's a nutter, Sarge,' said Constable Peel. 'Nurd the Nutter.'

Sarge sighed. 'We'd like you to come along with us, sir, if you don't mind.'

'Can I bring my car?' said Nurd.

'We'll leave, er, *your* car here for the moment, sir. You can come along with us in ours.'

'It's got pretty lights on the top,' explained Constable Peel helpfully. 'And it makes a noise.'

Nurd looked at the policemen's car. It still wasn't as nice as his, not by a long shot, but it was different, and Nurd felt that he should be open to new experiences, especially having spent so long in the Wasteland with no new experiences at all, some curious noises from Wormwood apart.

'All right,' he said. 'I will travel in your car.'

'There's a good Nurd,' said Constable Peel, opening one of the rear doors. Nurd got the uncomfortable feeling that Constable Peel was making fun of him. Constable Peel also made sure to keep the windows rolled down in order to let the smell out of the car.

'When I assume my throne,' said Nurd, 'and I rule this world, you shall be my slave, and your life will be one of pain and misery until I choose to end it by turning you to a small mass of red jelly that I will crush beneath my heel.'

Constable Peel looked hurt as he closed the door behind Nurd. 'That's not very nice,' he said. 'Sarge, Mr Nurd here is threatening to turn me to jelly.'

'Really?' said Sarge. 'What flavour?'

Then, with Nurd squashed in the back, they began the drive back to the station.

Twenty-three

In Which We Learn That One Should Be Careful About Accepting Anything That Is Offered For Nothing

The Fig and Parrot pub was well known in the village for its Halloween celebrations. The owners, Meg and Billy, decorated it with cobwebs, skeletons, and other ghoulish oddities. The grass square outside the pub's main doors was dotted with polystyrene tombstones, and a noose dangled from the thickest branch of the old oak tree at its centre, the rope tight round the neck of a scarecrow.

Inside the festivities were in full swing, as Meg and Billy had arranged for the local brewery, Spiggit's, to offer free pints to those who arrived in fancy dress, and there was nothing that the regulars at the Fig and Parrot appreciated more than free pints. Hence, everyone had made an effort at dressing up, even if, in the case of Mangy Old Bob (as he was known to most people except Mangy Old Bob himself), it consisted of nothing more than sticking a sprig of holly on his hat and claiming to be the Spirit of Christmas. For the most part, the villagers in attendance favoured the old reliables, and had come dressed as vampires, ghosts, mummies wrapped in bandages and toilet paper, and the odd French maid. The French maids were not, it must be said, terribly frightening, except for Mrs Minsky, who was a very large lady,

178

and who had not been constructed to occupy anything as small and frilly as a French maid's outfit.

The two demons who approached the Fig and Parrot that night were not intellectually gifted. This was true of most of the demons that had so far poured through the interdimensional doorway into the village. They were foot soldiers, nothing more. The real horrors had yet to come. This was not to say that the demons who were already in place were not terrifying. Seen in the right light, and at an unexpected moment, they might have proved bed-wettingly frightening. Unfortunately, as Nurd had recently discovered, they had arrived on the one evening of the year when lots of people were doing their utmost to look as frightening as possible, and therefore a great many of the demons were simply blending in.

The two demons in question were called Shan and Gath. Facially they resembled warthogs, although their bodies were those of men, albeit rather overweight ones whose leather clothing was a couple of sizes too small for them. Their eyes, like those of a great number of the other minor hellish entities currently exploring the village and its environs, glowed a deep red from exposure to the fiery pits of Hades. Large tusks jutted over their snouts from their bottom jaws, and their heads and faces were covered in short, rough hair. They had two thick fingers on each hand, but no thumbs. They were clumsy, vicious creatures, intent only on doing harm to whomever happened to come their way.

The girl employed by Spiggit's to hand out the free-beer vouchers, a young lady named Melody Prossett, was currently dressed as a pink fairy, and wearing a very short dress, a disguise that did little to hide the fact that Melody was jolly lovely. Melody was studying the history of art at the local university, which made few demands upon her time or, it must be said, her intelligence, which was probably just as well. Melody was as sweet and beautiful as – oh, all right then – as a melody, but she was by no means the brightest bulb in the box. In fact, even a box of very dark bulbs buried in a windowless coal shed might have given Melody some competition in the brightness stakes.

Thus it was that, when Shan and Gath entered the Fig and Parrot, the first person they encountered was Melody Prossett.

'Guys, what great outfits!' Melody shouted. Shan and Gath looked as confused as only a pair of destruction-bent demons can look when faced by a leggy fairy with a cardboard wand. Admittedly, thought Melody, the new arrivals smelled a bit odd (even worse than Mangy Old Bob, who could kill flies with his breath and had mould in his armpits) but perhaps it had something to do with whatever they had used to make their costumes. Then again, those hog heads were very realistic. Melody wondered if they had somehow managed to hollow out real hog heads and fit them over their own. If so, she admired their efforts, although it wasn't something that she would have been inclined to do, not for all the beer in Spiggit's brewery.

Somewhat awkwardly, she managed to fit six vouchers into the demons' cloven hands.

'I'm only supposed to give you one each,' she whispered conspiratorially, 'but you've gone to such trouble . . .'

Shan raised the vouchers to his snout and sniffed them warily.

'Urk?' he said.

'Oh, I expect you're having trouble seeing through your mask,' said Melody. 'The bar's over here. Let me give you a hand.'

She took each demon by an arm and began to steer them

towards the bar. Along the way Shan and Gath passed an assortment of beings – vampires, ghouls and the like – that looked vaguely familiar from the depths of Hell. Somewhere in their tiny minds they began to wonder if they might, possibly, have been better employed elsewhere, given that this place seemed to have plenty of foul creatures to be getting along with. Unfortunately they were now firmly in the grip of Melody Prossett, who was determined to be as helpful as possible, because that was the kind of girl she was. Melody Prossett was so helpful that people, even quite elderly people, often ran fast in the opposite direction when they saw her coming, just to avoid Melody's irritating helpfulness.

'Now, each voucher entitles you to a free pint of Spiggit's Old Peculiar,' Melody explained. 'It's new! I've tasted it, and it's wonderful.'

This was not entirely true. Spiggit's Old Peculiar was indeed very new, but Melody had not, in fact, tasted it. She had put it close to her nose and decided that it smelled like something a cat might have done; a cat, furthermore, that wasn't feeling at all well. It had also scorched her nasal hairs, and when a drop fell on her hand it had turned her skin a funny colour.[24]

---

[24] Be wary of anything that is offered to you for nothing, especially if it is a new product that the makers are anxious to test. Usually, they will have discovered that the bunny rabbits, dogs, or iron-stomached employees who have already tried it have not died or gone blind as a result, and therefore it's about time to try it on people who might, at some point, be expected to pay for it. Unless you've always wanted to be a human guinea pig, it might be wise to think twice before saying yes to something that a stranger hands to you with a smile, free of charge, especially if there is a doctor or a lawyer hovering nervously nearby.

Spiggit's Old Peculiar was an aptly named beer. Even those at the brewery who rather liked it took the view that something needed to be done about its nose (the technical term for its smell) and, while the brewers were about it, perhaps its taste, which veered somewhere between 'not very nice' and 'quite nasty', and the fact that, if left too long on the skin, it tended to burn. It was, though, quite amazingly strong, and after the first sip issues of flavour tended to be forgotten, since Spiggit's Old Peculiar managed temporarily to deaden the drinker's taste buds, leaving only the sensation that he had just accidentally consumed a naked flame. Fortunately that sensation was quickly replaced by one of complete intoxication and a sense of goodwill towards anyone within hugging distance until, after a second pint, he fell over and went to sleep.

Shan and Gath had never tasted alcohol of any kind. Given that they were demons, and therefore not troubled by normal appetites, they had never eaten anything other than the odd chunk of coal or grit, and occasionally other, smaller demons, although mostly they just tended to chew them and spit them out. So, when Meg handed them their first free pints, carefully removing two vouchers from their misshapen fists along the way, they just stared at them suspiciously to begin with. Gath was about to shatter the glasses and start being properly demonic when Shan noticed a vampire take a long drink from a similar glass. For a moment the vampire looked as though he had just been hit through the heart with a large stake, as the unusual taste of Spiggit's Old Peculiar seared his mouth and erased a few memories. Then a strange, happy smile appeared on his face, and he hugged the nearest mummy.

Shan lifted the glass to his snout and sniffed. Shan was

used to the stench of Hell itself, but whatever was in the glass still smelled a bit odd, even to him. He took a tentative sip.

Something exploded in Shan's head, and he looked around to see who had hit him and then poked him in the eyes. As his vision began to return, and he found there was nobody nearby, Shan realised that it was the stuff in the glass that had somehow managed to hit him. He was considering throwing it at the wall and laying waste to all around him when he began to feel very mellow. He took another sip, longer this time. Now Gath raised his glass and drank. He staggered a bit when the beer began knocking out brain cells, and almost fell over.

'Hurh, hurh,' said Shan. It was a sound that he had never made before, and it took him a while to recognise it as laughter.

'Hurh, hurh,' said Gath, as he too began to recover.

They drank some more. Someone began playing the piano. Meg and Billy began dispensing free chips, and Shan and Gath got their first taste of greasy, deep-fried potato. Gath put an arm round Shan. Shan was his best mate. He loved Shan. No, he *really* loved Shan.

They moved on to their second pints of Spiggit's Old Peculiar, and all thoughts of world domination faded away.

Meanwhile, back at Crowley Avenue, Mrs Abernathy was unhappy. The destruction of the flying skulls she had sent after Samuel Johnson and his friends had not gone unnoticed, for each demon that passed through the portal was linked to Mrs Abernathy's consciousness, so she could see through their eyes and assess the progress of the invasion. She was also aware that two hellbulls had been beaten into non-existence with household implements over what appeared to be some trampled rose bushes, but that was not a primary concern. Increasingly, she found herself infuriated by the Johnson boy. Why couldn't he simply die? After all, he was just a child. His continued refusal to accept his fate was like a splinter under one of her fingernails.

She recalled something she had learned from her interrogation, and subsequent torture, of the demon that had so unsuccessfully occupied the space under Samuel Johnson's bed, and her unhappiness began to ease.

Oh yes, she thought, I know what frightens you, little boy.

She closed her eyes, and her lips moved as she issued her summons.

Twenty-four

*In Which Nurd Puts On an Unexpected
Show For the Police*

The call came through on the police car's radio while
Nurd, Constable Peel, and the Sarge, whose name Nurd
had now learned was Rowan, were still some way from the
station.

'Base to Tango One, Base to Tango One. Over,' said a
male voice. It sounded somewhat panicked.

'This is Tango One,' said Sergeant Rowan. 'Everything all
right back there, Constable Wayne? Over.'

'Er, not exactly, Sarge,' said Constable Wayne. 'Over,' he
added, with a tremor in his voice.

'Clarify the situation, Constable, there's a good lad,' said
Sergeant Rowan. 'Over.'

'Well, Sarge, we're under attack. Over.'

Sergeant Rowan and Constable Peel exchanged a look.
'What do you mean, attack? Over.'

'We're being attacked by flying women, Sarge. With the
bodies of lizards . . .'

Biddlecombe's police station was a small building set in a
field on the outskirts of the town. It had replaced an older
building on the main street that had become infested with

rats, and which was now a chip shop that nobody frequented unless they were very drunk, or very hungry, or rats visiting their relatives. The station consisted of a small waiting area and a large desk, behind which was an open-plan office and a single cell that was rarely used for prisoners; currently it was filled with Christmas decorations and an artificial tree.

The village had only six policemen, two of whom would usually be on duty at any one time. On this particular night four were on duty, as it was Halloween and people tended to get up to all sorts of mischief involving fireworks and, occasionally, fires.

PC Wayne and WPC Hay were currently holding the fort at the station. 'Holding the fort' is usually a turn of phrase, a bit like 'manning the barricades' or 'fighting a losing battle'. In other words, people use it to describe perfectly mundane situations, like staying at home on a cold night, or keeping an eye on the local shop while the shopkeeper goes for a wee.

Unfortunately PCs Wayne and Hay were now *literally* holding the fort, *literally* manning the barricades, and also *literally* fighting a losing battle. The first of the flying lizard women had appeared in the station car park while PC Wayne was having a crafty smoke outside, almost causing him to swallow his cigarette in shock. The woman had a green saurian body and long black nails. Her wings were like those of a bat, with curved talons in the middle and at the ends, and she had a long tail that terminated in a vicious-looking spike. Her hair was dark and flowing, and for a moment Constable Wayne thought that she wasn't bad-looking, the whole lizard body and wings thing excepted. Then she opened her mouth and a forked black tongue flicked at the air between the kind of jagged yellow teeth that crop up in dentists' nightmares, and any thoughts of dating her vanished from Constable Wayne's mind.

At that point Constable Wayne decided that the best course of action would be to head back inside and lock the door, which is precisely what he did. There was a large bolt, and he pulled that across as well, just to be sure.

'What are you doing that for?' asked Constable Hay. 'The sarge will spit nails if he comes back and finds that you've locked the front door.'

Constable Hay was small and blonde, and Constable Wayne was a little in love with her. He had always thought she was very pretty, but now, after being confronted with a woman who appeared to be made up of bits of other creatures that really didn't belong together, he decided that Constable Hay was quite possibly the loveliest girl in the world.

'There's a woman outside,' said Constable Wayne. 'With wings. And a tail.'

'It's Halloween,' said Constable Hay slowly, as though she were talking to an idiot. She liked Constable Wayne, but he really could be very thick sometimes. 'On my way here, I saw a man dressed as a toadstool.'

'No, this isn't a woman dressed up to look like she has wings and a tail. She *does* have wings and a tail.'

There was a massive *thud* on the door. Constable Wayne backed away from it.

'That's her,' he said. 'The lizard lady.'

'Lizard lady,' said Constable Hay dismissively. 'You'll be telling me she can fly next.'

A woman's face appeared at the barred window to the right

of the door. Constable Hay walked determinedly towards it, her finger wagging.

'Now listen here, miss, it may be Halloween but we'll have no more nonsense or . . .'

She stopped talking when she noticed that the woman was hovering two feet from the ground, her huge wings flapping hard to keep her in place. Then, bracing her feet against the outside wall, the flying woman gripped two of the bars with her claws and tried to pull them from the wall.

'See?' said Constable Wayne. 'I told you so.'

From above their heads came the sound of something landing on the roof. Seconds later the first of the slates began to fall into the car park as whatever it was tried to force its way into the station.

'Call the sarge,' said Constable Hay.

Constable Wayne ran to the radio. 'Where are you going?' he asked, as Constable Hay ran past him.

'To lock the back door!'

Inside the police car there was a long pause followed Constable Wayne's description of the attackers. Constable Peel made a gesture of someone drinking from a bottle, followed by an imitation of that same someone being very drunk. Then they heard the sound of glass breaking.

'Constable, what's that noise? Have you been drinking?' said Sergeant Rowan. 'Over.'

'I wish I had,' said Constable Wayne. 'One of them has broken the front window, and there's another on the roof. Oh, crikey: the back door. Get here, Sarge, quickly. Please! We need help. Er, over. Over and out.'

* * *

The woman at the window had injured herself breaking the glass, and black blood now covered the shattered pane, but the bars had held. The woman appeared to give up, and flew upwards. Constable Wayne heard her land on the roof and then followed the sound of her footsteps as she ran across it in the direction of the rear of the station. There, Constable Hay was using the full force of her body to try to force the back door closed when Constable Wayne joined her. The problem quickly became apparent: a claw was clutching at the door as the thing outside tried to push its way in. The gap widened slightly, and a gnarled foot appeared, and then Constable Wayne saw one of those terrible female faces pressed against the wood, its teeth bared.

'Help me!' cried Constable Hay. 'I can't hold it much longer.'

Constable Wayne reached for his truncheon and began using it to smack the creature on the knuckles. It screeched in pain and withdrew the claw, but its foot remained in place. Constable Wayne tried stamping on it with his size 11 shoes. Its claw appeared again, slashing at him.

'Hold the door!' said Constable Hay, and suddenly Constable Wayne was alone, with only his weight to keep the creature at bay.

'Where are you going?' he cried.

'Just hold it. I have an idea.'

It had better be a good one, thought Constable Wayne, as he heard more footsteps above his head, followed by the sound of flapping wings as a second creature flew down to aid the first.

'Oh no,' said Constable Wayne to himself. 'That's not good. That's not good at—'

The door was struck with such force that Constable Wayne

was flung head first across the room. He scrambled to his feet in time to see two of the lizard women trying to force their way through the narrow door at the same time, and getting tangled up in each other's wings along the way. Then the larger of the pair pushed aside her smaller sister and stalked inside, her claws raised and her mouth open wide as she advanced on Constable Wayne.

Constable Hay appeared beside the demon, her arm outstretched and a small bottle in her hand.

'Hey!' she said. 'Over here.'

The winged woman turned, and Constable Hay sprayed perfume straight into her eyes. She screeched and tried to rub at the irritant, but that just made things worse. At the same time Constable Wayne picked up a hatstand and swung it at the second demon, which was trying to sneak round her sister. The hatstand caught the demon a vicious blow on the side of the head. She reeled away, stunned but still dangerous. Constable Wayne, now using the hatstand like a spear, began poking at her, forcing her back outside. Meanwhile Constable Hay continued to spray perfume mercilessly into the first demon's face until she stumbled blindly towards the door. Constable Wayne helped her on her way with a sharp kick to the behind, then slammed the door closed.

A series of loud shrieks came from outside and the two coppers watched through a window as the lizard women ascended into the night sky, off to seek easier prey.

'Great,' said Constable Wayne. 'The sarge will never believe us now . . .'

Sergeant Rowan had just hit the lights and Constable Peel was about to put his foot on the accelerator when Nurd

tapped on the sheet of toughened plastic that partially separated him from the men in the front seats. He had heard the
exchange over the radio, and he had also noticed some things
that the policemen had not. The first were the little tendrils
of blue energy that were shooting across a field in the direction of what looked like a nearby church.

The second was a small being about two feet in height that
appeared to be little more than a yellow ball on legs, although
most yellow balls didn't have two mouths and a multitude of
eyeballs. The yellow ball was chasing a rabbit, which jumped
down a burrow, the ball in hot pursuit. Unfortunately for the
ball, the hole was smaller than it was, and now it seemed to
be stuck, its stumpy legs waving wildly.

This isn't a positive development, thought Nurd. He recalled
what Samuel had told him about the woman in the basement,
and about her friends who no longer seemed to be human.
Nurd had been hoping that Samuel was mistaken, or that the
four people, or demons, or whatever they were, might just
have conveniently vanished, or returned home. Now there
were yellow balls with eyes chasing rabbits, which disturbed
him greatly. It's all very well if I'm the only demon here, he
mused, but if there are lots of demons, then there could be
problems. And that blue energy, that wasn't just regular old
electricity, or even average transdimensional residue. No, it
was energy of a very particular kind . . .

Nurd had once glimpsed the Great Malevolence. It was
shortly before Nurd's banishment, and he had been
summoned to the Great Malevolence's lair to be dealt with
by his most trusted lieutenant, the ferocious demon named
Ba'al. In the darkness behind Ba'al a huge shape had lurked,
taller than the tallest building, wider than the greatest chasm,

and for an instant Nurd had seen his face: eyes so red that they were almost black, great fanged jaws, and a horned crown upon his head that seemed to have grown out from his skull. The sight had so frightened Nurd that he had almost welcomed his banishment, for there could have been worse punishments. He could have been taken by the Great Malevolence himself deep into his lair, there to be slowly torn apart for eternity, always suffering and never dying. Compared to that prospect, banishment was a doddle.

But there was one other thing that he recalled about the Great Malevolence: the contours of his body had rippled with blue energy. It was his power made visible, and now it was here. On Earth. Where Nurd was and, most certainly, was not supposed to be.

'Hello?' he said, knocking on the glass again. 'I think there's been some mistake.'

'Not now, sir,' said Sergeant Rowan. 'We're a bit busy.'

'You don't understand,' said Nurd. 'I'd really like to go home. You can forget about the car. Actually you can have it. I don't want it.'

'I'm not sure that it's yours to give away, sir. Now you'll have to be quiet. We're a little concerned about our colleagues at the station.'

Nurd sat back in his seat. 'This isn't a disguise,' he said softly.

The two policemen ignored him.

Nurd said it again, louder this time. 'This isn't a disguise!'

'Beg your pardon, sir?' said the sergeant.

'Look, I'm not wearing a costume. This isn't "fancy dress." This is me.'

'Very droll, sir,' said the sergeant.

'If it was a costume,' said Nurd patiently, 'could I do this?'

Nurd's head split evenly in half down the centre, exposing his skull. His eyes popped from their sockets, extended themselves on lengths of pink flesh, and examined Sergeant Rowan very intently. Then Nurd's skull separated, revealing his brain. It was held in place by twelve curved purple muscles, which immediately stood upright and wiggled. Finally Nurd stuck out his tongue, which was three feet long at its fullest extension. The top of the tongue had a hole in it, through which Nurd played a short fanfare before restoring his head to its regular form.

Constable Peel drove off the road. He braked suddenly, and both he and Sergeant Rowan jumped from the car and backed away from it.

'Sarge,' stammered Constable Peel. 'He's a m –, he's a mo –, he's a mons—'

'Yes, he is, Constable,' said Sergeant Rowan, trying to sound calmer than he felt.

'Demon, actually,' said Nurd, shouting to make himself heard. 'Don't mean to be fussy about it, but there's a big difference.'

'What are you –?'

'– doing here?' Nurd finished for him. 'Well, I was going to try to conquer your world and rule it for eternity, but I don't think that'll happen now.'

'Why not?' asked Sergeant Rowan, carefully drawing a little closer to the car once more.

'Funny you should ask, but someone else has his eye on this place, and I don't think he'll fancy any competition. I'd really prefer not to be around when he gets here, so if you could see your way clear to letting me out, I'll be on my way.'

Sergeant Rowan stared at Nurd. Nurd smiled back politely.

'What exactly is happening?' asked Sergeant Rowan.

'Well, it's just a guess,' said Nurd, 'but I think it's the end of the world as you know it . . .'

Twenty-five

*In Which Bishop Bernard the Bad Makes His Presence
Felt, and the Dead Rise From Their Graves,
But Only the Nasty Ones*

Maria, Tom, Samuel, and Samuel's mother watched from the darkened house as all manner of infernal creatures slid, jumped, flew or crawled from the direction of 666 Crowley Avenue, where a blue light hung over the adjoining rooftops. They had already been forced to fend off two further attacks, the first from a pair of foot-long slug demons with mosquito-like proboscises for sucking blood, which had oozed through the letter box, the slime trail behind them eating away at the carpet as they approached their intended victims. The judicious use of a container of table salt had caused them to dry up into withered husks before disappearing in a puff of smoke.

The second attack was still ongoing, as the house was being buzzed by a pair of giant flies with jaws in their bellies. They struck the windows occasionally, the hooked teeth in their abdomens leaving marks upon the glass, and their pink saliva staining it like watery blood. Mrs Johnson monitored their attempts to gain entry, a can of fly spray in each hand. All things considered, Samuel thought she was coping very well with being confronted by demons, but he also felt angry at something she had said earlier. She had wished his dad was with them and, for a moment, when he first saw the flying skulls, Samuel had wished that too, but now he no longer felt the same way. He had suggested using salt on the slugs, he had found the fly spray hidden away in the back of a cupboard. With Tom's help, he had secured all the doors and windows, and set up a system of watches so that, between the three children and Samuel's mother, they were able to keep an eye on all the approaches to the house. For the first time since his dad had left, Samuel was starting to feel that if necessary he could look after both his mother and himself.

What he couldn't do, it seemed, was stop Mrs Abernathy. They were trapped inside the house, and they had heard nothing further from Dr Planck.

Soon, Samuel feared, all would be lost.

Back at the parish church of St Timidus, the thumping sounds continued from what should have been the final resting place of Bishop Bernard the Bad but clearly wasn't, since the last thing Bishop Bernard the Bad appeared to be doing was resting. Clouds of dust rose from the stone bearing his name, and the dates of his birth and death. One end lifted from the floor. It hung in the air, and the vicar and verger could almost feel the dead man below straining to move it higher, but then the stone fell down again and all was quiet.

'He's very strong,' said the verger, as he and Reverend Ussher peered through the small window in the door. He was quite surprised. After all, Bishop Bernard couldn't have been much more than a collection of old bones, and old bones tended to break easily. They shouldn't have been able to move huge slabs of stone. It just wasn't right.

'Limestone,' said the vicar.

'Beg your pardon?'

'The rock beneath the church is limestone,' said the vicar. 'Limestone preserves bodies. Not just that: it mummifies them. Bishop Bernard has been down there for a long, long time. I suspect that, if you were to touch him, his bones would feel as hard as rock.'

'I don't want to touch him,' said Mr Berkeley. 'I really don't.'

The burial slab began to move again, but this time it rose and didn't fall. A skeletal hand emerged from the crack and tried to get a grip on the edge of the stone.

'You may not want to touch him,' said the vicar, 'but I suspect that he would very much like to get his hands on you.'

Reverend Ussher opened the door of the little room and threw himself on the stone, hoping that his weight would push it back down. His right hand reached out and found the verger's bicycle pump, and with it he began hitting Bishop Bernard on the fingers. It took four or five strikes, but eventually the bishop was forced to release his grip. The stone slammed back down, and there was silence once more.

'Quick!' said the vicar. 'Give me some help here.'

Reluctantly Mr Berkeley joined him. In one corner of the room was an old stone statue of St Timidus. It had fallen from its plinth beside the front door of the church the previous winter, and its right hand had dropped off. There hadn't been enough money to repair it, or the plinth, so it had joined the old bicycle and the chairs in the storage room. With some difficulty, the vicar and the verger together managed to move the statue onto Bishop Bernard's marker stone.

'There,' said the vicar. 'That should keep him occupied for a while.'

The verger leaned against the wall as he tried to get his breath back.

'But why is all this happening now?' he asked.

'I don't know,' said the vicar. 'I don't even know what all "this" is.'

'Do you really think it's like the monk said: the end of the world?'

'I think the end of the world is some way off yet, Mr Berkeley,' said the vicar. He tried to sound confident, but he didn't feel it. This was all very disturbing: gargoyles running about on the church lawn; Bishop Bernard the Bad attempting to escape from his tomb. If it wasn't quite the end of the world, it might well be the *beginning* of the end.

Bishop Bernard began pounding on the floor once again.

'Oh, I do wish he'd stop that,' said the verger. 'He's giving me a headache.'

He knelt on the floor then put his mouth near the stone.

'Now, Bishop Bernard, Your Excellency, be a nice bishop and go to sleep,' he said. 'There's been a bit of a misunderstanding, but we'll get everything sorted out and you can go back to being dead. That sounds lovely, doesn't it? You don't want to be up here in the land of the living. It's all changed since your time. There's pop music, and computers, and, you know, you won't be able to go around sticking hot pokers up people, because that's not allowed any more, not even for bishops. No, you're much better off where you are, believe you me.'

The verger looked at the vicar, then nodded and smiled.

'See,' said the verger. 'All he needed was for someone to have a quiet word with him.'

There came a muffled roar of rage, and then the thud of stone upon stone as Bishop Bernard flung himself, hard, upwards. The statue of St Timidus shifted slightly.

'Oh, wonderful, Mr Berkeley,' said the vicar. 'That was most helpful!'

Bishop Bernard attacked the stone again, and the statue moved a little more. The verger tried to hold on to it, but it was no use. He gave up and retreated to the window.

'We should make a break for it,' said the vicar. 'Those gargoyles seemed rather clumsy and slow. We can easily outrun them, and my car is parked round the back.'

But the verger didn't appear to be listening. Instead, he was looking out of a small side window.

'I say, Mr Berkeley,' said the vicar. 'Did you hear what I said? I think we should run for it.'

'I don't think that would be a good idea, Vicar,' said the verger.

'And why is that?' asked the vicar, now quite annoyed that his plan had been shot down without even a discussion.

The verger turned to him, his face white.

'Because I think the dead are coming back to life,' he said. 'And not the nice ones . . .'

The Church of St Timidus had been in its present location for centuries. Much of its grounds were taken up with old gravestones because, for many generations, the people of the town had been buried beside the church when they died.

Unfortunately, not *everybody* had been buried under the church lawn. Church grounds were known as 'consecrated', which meant that they had been set aside for holy use. But people who committed serious crimes, and were executed for them, were not allowed to be buried on consecrated ground. For that reason a second graveyard existed not far from the old church, though beyond its walls. No gravestones were placed there, and no markers, but everybody knew of it. The townspeople called it the Dead Field, and nobody built houses on it, or walked their dogs there, or had picnics on its grass during the summer. Even birds didn't nest in its bushes and trees. It was, everybody felt, a Bad Place.

Now, as the vicar and verger watched, shambling shapes began to emerge from the Dead Field, their progress lit by the lights of the church grounds. Some still wore the tattered remains of old clothing, although there was precious little of it left. Thankfully, their modesty was preserved by the fact that most of them were just bones. The verger saw one skeleton with part of a rope round its neck, and knew that here was someone who had been hanged. The end of the rope dangled at its chest, a bit like a necktie. Another skeleton appeared to have lost both its arms. It tripped on a stone and couldn't get back up, so instead began to wriggle its way along the ground, like a bony worm with legs. Occasionally, flashes of blue light were visible in otherwise empty eye sockets.

'I wonder what that blue light is?' said the vicar.

'Maybe they've stuck candles in there,' said the verger sarcastically. 'After all, it is Halloween.'

'Well, we can't go outside now,' said the vicar, ignoring him.

'No, we can't,' said the verger.

And from beneath their feet came what sounded like laughter.

Twenty-six

In Which Constable Peel Wishes He Had Pursued Some Other Profession, and Dr Planck Reappears

Constable Peel and Sergeant Rowan were debating their options. They could a) let Nurd go, which didn't seem like a very good idea given that he was, quite clearly, not a human being and also, if he was to be believed, a demon; b) take Nurd back to the police station and wait for someone with a little more authority to decide what should be done with him; or c), and this was Constable Peel's suggestion, run away, because Constable Peel didn't want to see Nurd do that thing with his head again. It had made him feel quite ill.

'He's a demon, Sarge, and he doesn't half smell bad,' said Constable Peel. 'I'm not sure I want to be driving around with a stinky demon in the back of the car.'

'Hello,' said Nurd through the open car window. 'I can hear you. Less of the stinky, please. I fell down a hole.'

'You *have* been driving around with a stinky demon in the back of the car,' Sergeant Rowan replied, trying to ignore Nurd. 'Nothing happened.'

'"Nothing *happened*?"' said Constable Peel. 'His head split open, Sarge. His tongue played a *tune*. I don't know how you usually spend your evenings, but in my book that counts as "something" happening.'

'Careful now, son, you're getting worked up over . . .'

He almost said 'nothing', then realised this might not be entirely helpful given Constable Peel's current mood.

'. . . over, um . . .'

Constable Peel folded his arms and waited, then said, 'Over what, exactly, Sarge?'

'. . . over . . .'

'. . . over . . . a, let me see, demon in the back of the car?' finished Constable Peel. 'That about covers it, I think. Oh, and he says the world is coming to an end. That qualifies as "something" too.'

'Well, there you have it, then,' said Sergeant Rowan. 'We can't just sit around doing nothing while the world is coming to an end.'

'So what are we going to do, Sarge?'

'We're going to put a stop to it, Constable,' said Sergeant Rowan, with the kind of assurance that had kept the British Empire running for a lot longer than it probably should have.

The sergeant walked over to the car and leaned in close to the window, where Nurd waited expectantly.

'Now look here, sir,' he began, 'what's all this stuff about the world coming to an end?'

'Well,' said Nurd, 'I thought I was the only one who'd come through.'

'Through from where, sir?'

'From Hell.'

'*The* Hell?'

'That's the one.'

'What's it like, then?' asked Constable Peel, who had reluctantly joined them.

'Not very nice,' said Nurd. 'You wouldn't like it.'

'There's a surprise,' said Sergeant Rowan. 'What did you think he'd say, Constable? That it was pleasant on a sunny day? It's not the beach at Eastbourne, you know.'

'I was just asking,' said Constable Peel.

'Anyway, back to the issue at hand,' said Sergeant Rowan. 'So, you've come from Hell, and you thought you were alone, but you're not.'

'No, I'm not.'

'And these, er, "ladies" who may have attacked our police station, friends of yours, are they?'

'No, they came some other way.'

'How, exactly?'

'I don't know how!' said Nurd. 'Someone must have opened a portal, and now they're spilling through.'

'This portal, sir? What would it look like?'

Nurd considered the question. 'I think it would be sort of *bluish*,' he said, finally. 'It probably started off quite small, but now it's getting bigger and bigger. And when it gets big enough, well . . .'

'Well what?'

'Well, *he'll* come through. Our master. The Source of All Evil. The Great Malevolence, along with his army. And that'll be that, really. Hell on Earth.'

'Do you think you could find this portal, sir?'

Nurd nodded. He thought that he could already sense it. He'd felt the presence of the blue energy; it made the hairs on the back of his neck tingle. He knew that the closer he got to its source, the more he'd be aware of it. He was like a walking Evil Energy Detector. Now his hope was that, if he could get near enough, he might be able to sneak back to the Wasteland unobserved. Better yet, if Hell was empty, because all the demons had moved here, he might find a way to leave the Wasteland altogether. He could go and live somewhere else, perhaps in a cosy cave with a nice view of some burning lakes.

'That's decided then,' said Sergeant Rowan. 'This gentleman will show us where the portal is, and we can set about stopping all this nonsense. Get on the radio, Constable. Make sure everything is fine back at the station, and then tell WPC Hay to alert the army. We'll need all the help we can get.'

Constable Peel prepared to do as he was told. Before he could make the call, WPC Hay came on the radio herself.

'Base to Tango One, over.'

'This is Tango One,' said Constable Peel. 'Is everything all right, Liz? Over.'

'Those flying women have gone, and we've got the doors locked, but now we're getting calls left, right, and centre. People's houses are being attacked, there are monsters crawling and flying all over the place. And there's some trouble over at the church. Over.'

'What kind of trouble? Over.'

'According to the verger, the dead have started to rise. Over.'

Constable Peel, who already looked unhappy, now looked very, *very* unhappy. He'd joined the police to stop bank robberies, and solve the odd murder, neither of which he had yet managed to do as Biddlecombe was rather quiet, and so far the combined total of bank robberies and murders in the town was precisely nil.[25] Constable Peel had most certainly

[25] This is unlike the small towns in television detective shows, where so many people die that it's a wonder there's anyone left in the town to kill by the end of the first series. You'd imagine that some of the residents might wonder about this and think, 'Hmmm, our town appears to be populated entirely by murderers, or people who are

not joined the police to fight demons, not unless he was going to be paid overtime, and danger money, and given a great big gun.

He was about to ask another question, and possibly begin shouting at Sergeant Rowan to call out the air force, the US marines, the Swiss Guard, and perhaps the Pope, vampire hunters, and anyone else who might be able to sort out dead people popping up from the ground, when a bolt of blue lightning shot across the radio. Seconds later the radio exploded in a shower of sparks and went dead. He looked up and saw that the telephone lines along the road were also glowing blue and sparking at their connections. He reached for his mobile phone, but it too was dead.

Constable Peel banged his forehead against the steering wheel. A very bad situation had just got much worse.

Mrs Abernathy stood in the garden of 666 Crowley Avenue, her arms outstretched, blue energy flying from the tips of her fingers and out of her eyes. She was smiling as she brought down all communications within a ten-mile radius of Biddlecombe. She felt the power surge through her as she set about creating a barrier around the town, invisible to the naked eye but completely impenetrable. It would remain in place until the Great Malevolence himself emerged, and then he would unleash himself upon this miserable planet. Behind her, what was left of the walls of the house expanded, as though the whole structure had taken a deep breath, and then

---

about to be murdered, and since we're not murderers then we must be potential victims. Marjorie, grab the kids and the dog. We're going to live in New Zealand . . .'

most of it fell to pieces, to be replaced by a great tunnel of blue light twenty feet across from which more and more creatures began to pour: imps and small dragons, hooded serpents and hunched gnome-like figures armed with axes and blades. And those were just the ones that could be described in recognisable terms: there were other things that bore no resemblance to anything ever seen or imagined on earth, monstrous things that had lived so long in total darkness they struggled to accommodate themselves to their new environment, creatures that had never had a form because it would have been too dark to see them. Now they were trying to construct shapes for themselves, resembling balls of fleshy dough from which arms and claws and tails and legs occasionally emerged before retreating again, accompanied by the odd eyeball to enable them to see what they were becoming.

Mrs Abernathy turned to face them as they streamed past. She stared into the portal and saw the gates were now almost half gone, a huge hole gaping at the heart of them.

Soon. Soon he would be here, and then she would receive her reward. But first, there was one small matter to attend to. She turned to Mr Abernathy, now a toad, and the spider demon by his side, the one that had, until recently, been crammed into Mr Renfield's skin, and instructed them to find Samuel Johnson.

To find the interfering boy who was frightened of spiders and suck his insides dry.

Tom was keeping watch on the street and Maria and Samuel the back when Dr Planck appeared at the front gate.

'Mrs Johnson,' called Tom, 'there's a man coming up the garden path.'

'Are you sure he's a man?' asked Mrs Johnson.

'Pretty sure,' said Tom.

Dr Planck hadn't seen the huge flies, but the flies had seen him. With a loud buzzing they descended upon the scientist, but so intent were they that they didn't notice the front door opening, and Maria and Tom emerging, each with a can of fly spray. Before the flies could get within chomping distance of Dr Planck they had fallen to the ground, writhing and spitting, then had ceased moving entirely before they, like the other demons who had run afoul of their intended victims, vanished.

Samuel joined Mrs Johnson as she approached the front door, clutching a broom handle. Tom waited at the living-room door, Samuel's cricket bat at the ready.

'Hurry up,' Mrs Johnson told Dr Planck. 'We don't know what else is out here.'

As if to confirm her worst suspicions, a batlike shadow flew over the house. Seconds later a creature the size of an eagle, but with spines instead of feathers and a head that consisted of dozens of wriggling worms with a single eye at the end of each, got tangled up in the telephone lines and fell crashing to the ground. Boswell, who had been watching it suspiciously, barked with delight.

Dr Planck looked upon its demise with relief until the door slammed shut, cutting off his view and almost cutting off his nose as well.

'Thank goodness,' he said. 'That thing has been chasing me ever since I locked the skull in a shed.'

'Right,' said Mrs Johnson, waving the broom handle in a threatening manner. 'What's going on? None of your scientific nonsense, now. Keep it simple.'

Dr Planck kept it very simple indeed. 'I don't know.'

'Well, fat lot of good you are, then,' said Mrs Johnson.

'Actually, I was hoping Samuel might be able to help me in that regard,' said Dr Planck.

Samuel stepped forward. 'I'm Samuel.'

At that moment all the lights went out, as Mrs Abernathy deprived the town of its power. Samuel and Dr Planck sat at the kitchen table while Mrs Johnson lit candles and Samuel told him of almost everything that had happened, from the time that Samuel had gone trick or treating at the Abernathys' house to the battle with the flying skulls. Dr Planck said nothing until Samuel was finished, although he did raise his eyebrow when Samuel described Mrs Abernathy's tentacles, then sat back and tapped an index finger against his lip.

'It's incredible,' he said at last. 'Somehow, the power of the collider has been harnessed to create a rip in the fabric of time and space. I mean, on one level it's wonderful. We've proved the existence of other dimensions, even if it was by accident, and we've discovered a way to travel between them. On the other hand, if this Mrs Abernathy creature is right, and it is a gateway between this world and, for want of a better word, "Hell", then we're in a lot of trouble.'

'A lot of trouble' seemed like an understatement to Samuel, but then he wasn't a scientist. Mrs Johnson didn't look very impressed with this description either.

'So all this is your fault?' she said.

'Not exactly,' said Dr Planck. 'We were trying to discover something of the truth about the nature of the Universe.'

'Well, now something has discovered you instead, and the truth is that it doesn't like any of us. I hope you're happy.'

'What can we do?' asked Samuel.

'If the phones were working, or I had access to a computer,

I could contact CERN,' said Dr Planck. 'Unfortunately, the last I heard they were having troubles of their own.'

'What do you mean?' asked Samuel.

'I got a call on my way to the Abernathys' house. It seemed that the collider had started up again, and they couldn't shut it down.'

'Could Mrs Abernathy have done that?'

'Mrs Abernathy, or whatever this thing is whose will she is obeying,' Dr Planck said. 'Assuming the two events are linked, then if they can shut the collider down, it should close the portal as well.'

'So all we can do is wait?' asked Mrs Johnson.

'I'm afraid so.'

'What if they don't manage to shut it down in time?'

'We'll just have to hope that they do.'

By now Maria had joined them, and it was she who spoke next.

'It can't be very stable, though, can it?'

'What?' asked Dr Planck.

'The portal,' said Maria.

'It's not,' said Samuel. 'The monster under the bed told me as much. He said that Mrs Abernathy was expending a lot of power keeping it open.'

'Monster under the bed?' said Dr Planck.

'It's a long story,' said Samuel.

'I mean, there are only so many possibilities,' Maria continued. 'It could be an Einstein-Rosen bridge, but that doesn't sound likely given its size and duration, or a worm-hole of some kind, or even a combination of both. Either way, its stability is dependent on the energy resulting from the explosions in the collider. And there was that wind we felt when we spied on the Abernathy house . . .'

'Wind,' said Dr Planck thoughtfully. 'Yes, I felt it too. It smelt of . . . elsewhere.'

'So perhaps it was coming from the other side of the portal,' said Maria. 'But its force wasn't very strong. You're the expert, Dr Planck, but isn't it true that, in theory, a portal like that would allow only a one-way trip?'

'Well, according to some theories, yes, and assuming the portal was sufficiently stable. It's to do with the force of gravity,' Dr Planck added, to a confused-looking Mrs Johnson, and an even more confused-looking Tom.

'But that kind of force would hurl the travellers out the far side, wouldn't it?' said Maria. 'There should be a howling gale tearing this town apart, but there isn't.'

'You may be right,' said Dr Planck. 'I mean, this is all speculative.'

'So there isn't that force of gravity,' said Maria.

'It appears not. There's some, but not sufficient to suggest a perfect balance between gravity and centrifugal force.'

'Then suppose that we collapse it.'

'But how?' Even as he asked the question, Dr Planck seemed to come up with an answer, for his face cleared for the first time since he had arrived at the house. Nevertheless, it was Maria who was left to make the suggestion.

'By sending something in the opposite direction.'

'Like two cars meeting on a narrow bridge and destroying themselves *and* the bridge,' said Samuel.

'Two cars meeting on a narrow, *unstable* bridge,' said Maria.

'You know,' said Dr Planck, 'that just might work. The questions are, where do we find our car, and who will drive it?'

Twenty-seven

In Which We Meet Bishop Bernard the Bad At Last,
and Constable Peel Enjoys Himself Immensely

Over at the Fig and Parrot, Shan and Gath were having a rare old time. Someone had started playing the piano, and Shan and Gath were doing their best to grunt along to 'My Old Man's a Dustman'. Earlier, someone had sung 'Danny Boy', which, although they had never heard it before, Shan and Gath sensed was a very sad song. It had caused a tear to well up in Gath's eyes, leading Shan to give him a consoling hug.

'One more for the road?' asked someone, waving a handful of beer vouchers in their faces.

Why, Shan and Gath thought, spying the vouchers, we don't mind if we do . . .

Reverend Ussher and Mr Berkeley were in real trouble. In the first place the risen dead were proving to be a great deal cleverer than skeletons whose brains had rotted and turned to mush centuries before had any right to be. The windows of the church were set about eight feet above the ground, which made them hard to reach without the aid of a stepladder. In the absence of said stepladder, some of the dead had formed a skeleton pyramid, with three corpses providing support for two further corpses, while a final corpse on top was using one of the stone gargoyles, which was complaining loudly, to break the glass. Two of the small panes had already broken, and Reverend Ussher could see a mouth grinning at him through the gap, a mouth with only a couple of broken black teeth still visible, which said a lot about dental care in olden days.

At the same time, more of the dead were thumping at the front door of the church and at the back door that led into the vestry, from which the verger had called the police to inform them of all that was occurring. The verger thought that the policeman who answered the phone had sounded a lot less surprised than he might have done, under the circumstances. In fact, he sounded like the dead rising was the least of his worries.

The vicar and verger had taken the precaution of pushing chairs and pews up against the doors in an effort to hold off the attacking corpses if they did manage to break through. There also continued to be worrying sounds from the vicinity of Bishop Bernard the Bad's tomb, the marker stone of which was piled high with just about every available piece of furniture and statuary stored in the little room. Between the pounding and the laughing they could also hear what sounded like 'Free me!' along with the occasional swear word.

'Bishop Bernard seems most irate,' said Reverend Ussher, as Mr Berkeley returned from checking on the storeroom. 'I do hope you haven't been trying to reason with him again. And he does swear a lot for a bishop.'

'He shouldn't be able to talk at all,' said Mr Berkeley. 'Limestone or no limestone, he's a corpse.'

'Mr Berkeley,' said the vicar patiently, 'in case you haven't noticed, the dead have arisen, there are gargoyles bouncing around on the church lawn, and we have been insulted by a stone monk. Under those circumstances, Bishop Bernard's conversational skills are unremarkable.'

'I suppose you're right,' said the verger. 'We need to do something about those skeletons, though. They'll be on top of us in a minute if we're not careful.'

The vicar grabbed a brass candlestick and moved to the wall of the church. 'Help me up,' he said. The verger leaned down, cupped his hands and with some effort, boosted Reverend Ussher up close to the windowsill, onto which the vicar managed to haul himself with some effort. There were now four broken panes in the window, and the dead had succeeded in breaking the lead that had surrounded them, leaving a considerable gap. As Reverend Ussher steadied himself, a bony hand reached through and grabbed his trouser leg.

'Oh no you don't,' he said as he brought the candlestick down hard upon the skeletal hand. It smashed into pieces, scattering dismembered bones. The rest of the arm was quickly withdrawn.

Through the stained glass, Reverend Ussher could see the pyramid of skeletons tottering He waited for it to draw closer once again, and for the lead skeleton to reach for the glass. When it did so the vicar opened the lower half of the window from inside, whacking the skeleton on the head and over-balancing the pyramid entirely. The three top corpses tumbled hard, and broke various limbs when they hit the ground. Reverend Ussher whooped in triumph, but his delight was short-lived. Dozens of bodies in various stages of decay looked from the vicar to the broken skeletons, then back again. It was hard for skulls without much flesh to look any angrier than they already did, but somehow these managed it.

'Oh dear.'

'Oh dear what?' asked Mr Berkeley from below.

'I think I've annoyed them.'

'And they were a bit miffed to begin with. Well done, Vicar!'

Hurriedly, Reverend Ussher began to close the window, but it now appeared to be stuck. He tugged, but it just wouldn't move.

'Oh dear,' he said again.

'Don't tell me,' said the verger.

'I really think that I should,' said the Vicar.

'Go on, then.'

'The window won't close.'

Below him, the dead began to form not one but two more pyramids. They were about to attack on twin fronts. At the same time, there came a great crashing noise from the storeroom, and a single word was roared from within.

That word was: 'Free!'

'Oh dear,' said the vicar and the verger together.

And then, just as the two pyramids of the dead began to approach the wall, a police car shot round the corner and ran straight at them, turning twelve rather innovative dead people into a pile of rotting limbs and broken bones. The car spun and came to rest facing the skeleton host and Sergeant Rowan's voice resounded across the churchyard.

'Right, you dead lot,' it said. 'This is the police. We're giving you five seconds to get back to wherever you came from, or there's going to be trouble.'

The dead did not move. To be fair, their hearing wasn't great. In addition, none of them had ever seen a police car before, or indeed anything with four wheels that wasn't being pulled by a horse or an ox.

'Your choice,' said Sergeant Rowan. 'Don't say we didn't warn you.'

Constable Peel gunned the accelerator and then released the brake. He'd had enough of demons and Hell. He was tired of the car smelling like poo. This was payback.

The car shot towards the ranks of the dead. Now the dead may not have known a lot about mechanised vehicles, but they'd seen what had happened to the last bunch who'd been hit by the big white cart, and were pretty certain they didn't want the same thing to happen to them. Unfortunately, being dead, they couldn't move very fast. In fact, it had been all that they could manage to move at all. Thus the vicar was treated to the sight of a police car chasing skeletal figures across the churchyard, none of whom was in a position to avoid being run over. The vicar was rather enjoying the show until Mr Berkeley reminded him that some of their troubles were only beginning.

'Er, Vicar,' said Mr Berkeley, just as the door of the store-room was hit with such force that it split in half, the two pieces shooting across the church floor and coming to rest against the far wall. A shadow appeared, then became a shape as Bishop Bernard the Bad made his entrance.

Bishop Bernard had never been a handsome man. He had, to be honest, been uglier than a wart on a toad's bum, and the centuries spent buried beneath the church had done nothing to improve his looks. His skin was dirty brown, like old leather. His nose was gone, leaving only a hole, and his

215

eye sockets were empty, although they now glowed with a cold blue light. He had kept a lot of his teeth, which were long and yellow and, Reverend Ussher thought, a bit sharper than they should have been, as though Bishop Bernard had spent some of his time underground working on them with a file. One leathery hand held a long staff: the bishop's crosier with which he had been buried. He was also wearing the remains of his robes of office. On his head was his bishop's mitre. It was a bit tattered, and the front half lolled forward like a tongue, but it was undeniably there.

As, regrettably, was Bishop Bernard himself, who was now looking at the verger from out of those empty eye sockets, following his progress as Mr Berkeley tried to hide behind the pews.

'He can see!' said the verger. 'How can he see? He's got no eyes. That's not right.'

Above him, Reverend Ussher leaned against the wall, hiding himself from the bishop's view and pressing a finger to his lips.

'Oh wonderful,' said Mr Berkeley to himself. 'Leave me to face him on my own without even a—'

Bishop Bernard raised his hand which like the rest of him looked like old bones wrapped in brown paper, and extended a finger in the verger's direction.

'Thou!' said Bishop Bernard, in a voice like gravel in a liquidiser. 'Thou art the one!'

He began to advance on the verger, who understood immediately that in this case being 'the one' wasn't a good thing. He hadn't won the lottery or, if he had, he wished that he hadn't bought the ticket, because the prize wasn't going to be very pleasant.

'I'm really not,' said the verger.

'Imprisoned in darkness,' continued Bishop Bernard, still advancing. 'My name, a jest. Thou art to blame!'

Mr Berkeley had to admit he had made the odd joke about Bishop Bernard, but it wasn't as if he thought the bishop was listening. After all, he was supposed to be dead. This just didn't seem entirely fair.

'I'm very sorry about that, Your Excellency,' said the verger. 'I thought you were, um, resting. It won't happen again.'

'No, it will not,' said Bishop Bernard, drawing closer and closer. 'Thou wilt be punished. Thou wilt have hot pokers inserted into thy bottom. Thou wilt—'

The vicar landed squarely on top of the bishop, and felt something crack. He rolled across the floor and scrambled to his feet, the candlestick raised to defend himself.

Bishop Bernard the Bad had broken in half at the waist. To his credit, it had barely taken the wind out of him, as the saying goes, not that there was much wind in Bishop Bernard to begin with. He released his grip on his crosier and began to crawl along the floor, his hands clutching at the ends of the pews as he pulled himself along, his attention still fixed upon the verger. Meanwhile, his bottom half climbed to its feet and began bumping into things.

'Vicar!' cried Mr Berkeley. 'He's still coming!'

'Bottoms,' shouted Bishop Bernard. 'Pokers.'

The vicar approached Bishop Bernard from behind.

'I'm very sorry,' said the vicar, 'but this really must stop.'

He brought the candlestick down hard on Bishop Bernard's head. It made a ringing sound, and Bishop Bernard's mitre fell off. The bishop ceased crawling, then twisted his head to look back at the vicar.

'Bottoms,' he said again. 'Thy bottom!'

'Oh, do be quiet,' said the vicar, and hit Bishop Bernard a second time, then a third. He kept hitting him until there wasn't much left of Bishop Bernard and even his severed legs had stopped moving and had just toppled over like two pillars joined at the top.

The vicar wiped sweat from his brow. He put his hands on his knees and tried to catch his breath.

'I don't think,' he said, 'that a vicar is supposed to beat a bishop to death, or even back to death.'

Mr Berkeley looked down upon the remains of Bishop Bernard.

'If anyone asks, we'll say he fell over,' he said. 'Lots of times.'

There was a knocking at the door.

'All safe inside?' said Sergeant Rowan. 'It's the police.'

The vicar and the verger went to open the door. Sergeant Rowan and Constable Peel stood on the step, looking quizzically at them.

'We are most happy to see you, Sergeant,' said the vicar. 'Happy, and relieved.'

'Sergeant—' began the verger, but he was interrupted.

'Let me finish, Mr Berkeley,' said the vicar.

'Spoilsports,' said the voice of the stone monk from above their heads.

'Just ignore him,' said the vicar. 'Now, perhaps—'

'Sergeant,' said the verger again.

'I said, "Let me finish",' the vicar insisted. 'Please! Now, Sergeant Rowan, we've had the most extraordinary experience, one that you might have found hard to believe had you not seen with your own eyes—'

'*Sergeant,*' said Mr Berkeley, with such force that even the vicar was forced to concede the floor to him.

'Well, what is it?' asked the vicar.

'Sergeant,' said Mr Berkeley, 'I think your demon is running away . . .'

Twenty-eight

*In Which Nurd Makes a New Friend, and
Meets Some Old Aquantances*

Nurd had been very much enjoying his trip in the police car,
with its flashing lights and interesting whooping noise.
Furthermore, Constable Peel was a much better driver than
Nurd, although, in his own defence, Nurd had just been
getting the hang of the Porsche when the police stopped him
and confiscated it. Still, he had been learning a lot just from
watching Constable Peel control the machine, and he was
wondering how he might go about making his excuses and
leaving the policemen, in order to apply what he had learned
to his own driving, when they had turned into the churchyard and Nurd had seen the risen dead.

That wasn't helpful. It was all very well for demons to start
pouring into this world from their own – actually, it wasn't
very well at all, come to think of it, but compared to the dead
rising from their graves it was a picnic in the park. It took a
lot of serious demonic energy to raise corpses, and Nurd
could tell that this was a particularly nasty bunch of dead
people. If he'd been wearing a watch, Nurd would have hidden
it in his pocket before passing this lot on the street: thieves
and cut-throats, all of them.

But that wasn't what concerned Nurd. What he was

witnessing was not the result of some accidental breach between this world and Hell itself. No, there was *intent* at work here. Evil corpses just didn't rise up of their own accord; they had to be willed back into existence. And only one being was inclined to go around summoning brigands and murderers from the grave, which suggested to Nurd that a personal appearance by the Great Malevolence was imminent.

It has already been established that Nurd was not in the Great Malevolence's good books. In fact, Nurd wasn't sure that the Great Malevolence had any good books, since he was the font of all evil. It would be a bit like someone who hated flowers secretly filling his house with pansies. Nevertheless he had a list of demons who had disappointed him and he wasn't the forgiving type. He also didn't care much for demonic entities that disobeyed his commands. When you were banished by the Great Malevolence, you stayed banished. If you decided that you'd had enough of banishment, and were tempted to sneak back into Hell's inner circles in the hope of finding a comfortable dark spot in which to mind your own business, the Great Malevolence would inevitably find out, because that was the kind of bloke he was. Demons couldn't die, but they could be made to suffer, and one of the problems with being immortal was that you could suffer for a very, very long time.

Nurd didn't like suffering. He was quite sensitive, for a demon. He realised that the Great Malevolence had obviously been planning this attack on the Earth for quite some time, and Nurd hadn't known about it. After all it wasn't as if he'd received a note saying:

Dear Nurd,

Hi. It's me. The Great Malevolence. I hope you are well. I am well. I am considering launching an attack on the world of men, and avenging myself upon them for all the time I've been forced to spend here in Hell. Love you to be part of it. Call me.

Yours,

TGM (aka The Beast, Satan, etc.)

:-)

No, Nurd had received no such communication, which meant that he was very much *not* part of the Great Malevolence's plans. If he were still here when the big guy arrived Nurd would be given an opportunity to discover just how sensitive he really was, as the Great Malevolence would do his best to inflict as much pain on him as possible for disobeying orders, even if Nurd hadn't done so intentionally.

It was, Nurd had decided, time to go home and pretend that nothing had happened. His plan, if you could call it that, was to find the portal and sneak back through it to Hell, where he would return to his nice Wasteland until everything calmed down a bit. Nurd wasn't quite sure how he was going to sneak back, given that he would be moving in the opposite direction to every other demon and foul creature. Perhaps he could tell them that he'd forgotten his keys, or had neglected to pack clean underwear. Anyway, he'd work it out when he got there.

So, once the policemen had finished mowing down corpses, and had gone to see what was happening inside the church, Nurd had simply slipped out of the car window and, not to put too fine a point on it, done a runner.

Constable Peel briefly gave chase, but seemed to give up

very quickly, Nurd thought. Nurd suspected that Constable Peel was quite happy to see the back of him, especially given how badly he smelled. By now, Nurd was getting tired of smelling himself, so the first thing he did was to take a dip in a local pond to clean himself off, scaring one of the nearby ducks half to death.

He was just finishing washing off his underarms when a large eyeball on the end of an arm popped out of the murk and blinked at him. A second arm quickly followed, this one sporting a mouth.

'I say,' said a cultured voice, 'do you mind? This is my home, not a public washroom.'

'Very sorry,' said Nurd. 'Didn't know this pond was occupied.'

'Suppose I should put up a sign, really. Not to worry, old boy. Just trying to keep a low profile for the moment, don'tcha know. Lot of pillaging and terrifying going on up there. No place for a gentledemon. Still, can't have every Tom, Dick and Harry demon washing his socks in my water, as it were. No offence meant, of course.'

'None taken,' said Nurd. 'I'll be on my way, then.'

'Righty-ho. If anyone asks, you can tell them that this pond has been claimed.'

A third arm appeared, this one holding a homemade flag depicting an eyeball on a red background. It waved the flag in the air.

'Made it m'self,' said the demon proudly. 'All m'own design.'

'Very nice,' said Nurd. 'Very imaginative. Maybe you should put it where people can see it, though.'

'What a jolly good thought,' said the demon. 'You're a clever one, sir, make no mistake.'

A fourth arm grabbed a passing duck and tied the flag to its neck using a piece of pond weed before depositing the startled duck back in the water. The duck made an attempt to fly away, but the demon held it in place until, eventually, the duck gave up and paddled off with the flag hanging limply from its neck.

Nurd stepped onto the bank, smelling faintly of pond, which was better than what he had reeked of before.

'Good luck with everything,' said Nurd.

'Much appreciated,' said the demon. 'You're always welcome to visit.'

The arms plopped back beneath the surface, leaving the pond still and quiet.

'What a nice chap,' said Nurd. 'If only all demons were like him.'

Unfortunately not all demons *were* like the thing in the pond. As Nurd sneaked through the town, trying to make his way to the portal, it became clear that the Great Malevolence's advance guard consisted mainly of some spectacularly vile entities. There was clear evidence of demonic nastiness to be seen: three elderly male members of the Biddlecombe Shooting Club, who had been taking potshots at clay pigeons when the invasion began, had made the mistake of turning their shotguns on a gorgon, its hair a mass of hissing serpents and its eyes so black that they were less organs of sight than dark vacuums, or jellied orbs of nothingness. The shotgun pellets had bounced off the gorgon's body, and the three old gents had immediately been turned to stone when they caught sight of the creature's face, so that they now formed an unusual piece of public statuary outside the post office.

There was rather more blood in the butcher's shop than there should have been, as the smell of raw meat had attracted some very unpleasant carnivores, hunched beings with white flesh that hung from their frames like wax from a melting candle, their heads smooth but eyeless, their nostrils stretched back against their skulls as though unseen fingers had inserted themselves into the holes and pulled hard. The butcher, Mr Morrissey, had only a few seconds to register the awfulness of the creatures that were invading his premises before their mouths opened, and their fine, sharp teeth were revealed, and they descended upon the hanging carcasses and, in their frenzy, upon Mr Morrissey himself. When they were done, only bare bones, animal and human, remained, along with Mr Morrissey's tattered straw hat.

Two members of the Biddlecombe First XV rugby team had been swallowed up during evening training when, somewhat against the laws of nature and, for that matter, rugby, a pair of fins had erupted from the ground and the unfortunate players were dragged beneath it by what very much resembled sharks armed with webbed claws for digging. The rest of the team had promptly harpooned the monsters with the corner flags.

A platoon of imps, two-foot-high red demons armed with small pitchforks, had attacked a florist's shop, only to discover that they were all allergic to pollen. Now they were staggering and wheezing over the street, their eyes streaming and their noses running. This made them easy prey for what was, presumably, the irate owner, a large woman wearing an apron depicting a smiling sunflower, who was beating the imps into submission with a broom.

That was another thing Nurd noticed: the demonic forces

were not having things all their own way. The humans were fighting back. He saw a man on a lawnmower chase a snake demon and turn it into something mushy beneath his blades. A group of schoolchildren dressed as ghouls had encountered half a dozen real ghouls in a park. The ghouls, who were thin and pale and not very interesting-looking, seemed a lot less terrifying than the schoolchildren, who had gone heavy on the artificial blood. This impression was confirmed when they began pelting the real ghouls with stones, forcing them to beat a hasty retreat and barricade themselves in a sweet shop. The members of the Biddlecombe Ladies' Choral Society had trapped a raiding party of demon dwarfs in a car park and reduced them to small piles of pulp with their handbags and hymn books. Nurd saw parties of humans armed with pitchforks, bats and brush handles, determined looks on their faces as they marched out to reclaim their town. He wished them luck, knowing that when the Great Malevolence came it would all be over for them.

Nurd stepped over a wheezing imp that had staggered into his alleyway. The imp sneezed once and then expired, turning to wisps of smoke that drifted away on the night air. Nurd wondered if the Great Malevolence had anticipated what would happen to his forces once they crossed over from their world into this one: they could be killed. Oh, not permanently killed, but temporarily disposed of as it were. Mortal rules applied in this world. There was simply not enough demonic energy here to sustain the entities, so that when they died their essence was dispersed, to be reabsorbed into the larger energy surrounding the Great Malevolence, there to be reconstituted and sent back into battle. The humans couldn't win, not in the end. All they could hope for were small victories over an enemy that in time would simply return.

And even that would change once the Great Malevolence crossed over, for he would bring with him all his evil power and this world would be transformed into a new Hell.

In the distance, behind some houses, Nurd could see a haze of blue lightning, and he knew that there lay the portal, the gateway between worlds. It was his way home. He thought almost fondly of Wormwood. Almost. Then he remembered Samuel, and hoped that the boy was safe. He wondered if he should go and look for him, but what could he, Nurd, do if he *did* find him? Take him back to the Wasteland? No, Samuel would just have to fend for himself, but the thought of the boy in danger, or in pain, made Nurd feel sad and guilty.

Nurd left the alleyway and began moving in the direction of the light. He decided that it would be best to stay off the streets, so he climbed a garden wall and used the hedges and bushes for cover, advancing from garden to garden, sticking to the shadows.

He was in his third garden when his skin began to tingle. There was great power nearby. He could sense it. He peered through a gap in a hedge and spied a pair of creatures, one spiderlike, the other a huge toad, scuttling and hopping down the street. He recognised them both.

Nurd sank to the ground and tried to make himself as small as possible. This was grave news. Those demons were bad enough, but they were merely servants of a greater evil. Where they went something much worse inevitably followed, a being intimately acquainted with Nurd and his wrongdoings. That being was Ba'al. Ba'al, the Great Malevolence's trusted lieutenant, the one who had condemned Nurd to eternal banishment, had already crossed over, and Nurd had a pretty good idea of where the senior demon would be.

Ba'al would be waiting at the portal for its master to arrive.

Twenty-nine

In Which Nurd Proves to Be Rather Decent, Actually

It was Samuel who spotted what now appeared to be a demon hiding behind the hedge in the front garden. Crouching behind a hedge didn't seem like very demonic behaviour to Samuel, whose experiences of demons until now had shown him they were variously frightening, puzzling, or, in the case of the one that had briefly occupied the space beneath his bed, simply not very good at their jobs; but so far he had encountered only one that appeared to be cowardly.

'What do you think of that?' Maria asked him, as they stood in the darkened kitchen, watching the demon.

'Maybe it's planning to jump out at someone,' said Tom.

'It's a him, not an "it",' said Samuel. 'His name is Nurd and he's the one who popped up in my bedroom. He's obviously frightened. You can see that from here.'

'Well, I don't really fancy asking this Nurd about his problems,' said Tom. 'Excuse me, Mr Demon, is 'oo frightened? Is 'oo having a bad day?' I mean, he's a demon. He's supposed to be frightening *us*. It would have to be something pretty terrible to make a demon tremble.'

They were silent as they considered the implications of what Tom had just said. What could be so frightening that even a demon would be terrified? Samuel watched Nurd. He now appeared to be biting his nails. Nurd may have been a demon, but Samuel knew that there was some good in him, even if Nurd had wanted to rule the world. Anyway, what was that old saying, something about an enemy's enemy being your friend . . . ?

He moved to the kitchen door. 'I'm going to talk to him.'

'Are you sure about this, Samuel?' asked Mrs Johnson. Dr Planck tried to protest, but the others shushed him.

'It's worth a try,' said Samuel. 'If he looks like he's about to turn nasty, we can just lock the door again, or Tom can wave his bat at him, but I don't think that's going to happen. To be honest, I rather like him.'

Samuel opened the door and put his head to the crack. 'Psssst!'

Nurd, already somewhat tense, almost wet himself at the sound. He looked round to see the head of a small boy wearing glasses poking through a gap in a doorway.

'What are you doing in my garden?' said Samuel.

'What does it look like?' replied Nurd. 'I'm hiding. Go away, Samuel, it's dangerous.'

'Why are you hiding? Aren't they your friends out there?'

'That lot?' said Nurd, gesturing with a big thumb. 'They're no friends of mine. In fact, if some of them found out I was here, I'd be in terrible trouble.'

'Which brings us back to the whole hiding thing,' said Samuel.

'Exactly,' said Nurd.

'Look,' said Samuel, 'if we let you hide in here, will you help us stop all this?'

Nurd risked another glance through the hedge. He clearly didn't like what he saw, because he nodded briskly.

'I'll do my best,' he said. 'I really would just like to go home.'

'Well, come on then,' said Samuel. He opened the door wider and stepped aside as Nurd shuffled across the lawn and shot through the gap. Once the door had closed behind him, Nurd took a relieved breath and looked around. He saw Samuel, looking thoughtful; Tom, holding a bat as though he were aching for an excuse to use it; Maria, sucking on a pencil and wrinkling her nose at the faint smell of pond coming off Nurd, and, um, was that poo?; and Mrs Johnson, who was clutching a frying pan determinedly. In one corner of the kitchen a man with a beard was trying to hide under a blanket. Nurd knew exactly how he felt.

'Hello,' said Nurd. 'I'm Nurd. Nurd, the Scourge of Five Deities. Actually, just plain old Nurd will be fine. I don't think I want to be the scourge of deities any more. If I never see a demonic deity again, it will be too soon. Mind if I get up from the floor?'

Most of the people in the kitchen looked dubious.

'Honestly,' said Samuel, 'we can trust him.' Eventually Tom said, 'OK, but do it slowly.'

Nurd did do it slowly, mainly because he had hurt his knee while diving into the kitchen. He took a seat at the table and rested his chin in his hands. He seemed very miserable and entirely unthreatening. A single big tear trickled down one of his cheeks.

'I'm really sorry,' said Nurd, wiping it away in embarrassment. 'It's been a funny old evening.'

Everyone looked sympathetic, even if he was a demon. Mrs Johnson put down her frying pan and pointed to a kettle that was currently simmering on a camping gas stove.

'Perhaps you'd like a cup of tea?' she said. 'Everything feels better after a cup of tea.'

Nurd didn't know what tea was, but it couldn't taste any worse than the stuff in the sewer.

'That would be very nice,' he said. 'Thank you.'

Mrs Johnson poured him a cup of strong tea, and added a digestive biscuit to the saucer. Nurd sipped carefully, if noisily, and nibbled at the biscuit. He was pleasantly surprised by both.

'It's nicer if you dunk it,' said Samuel, demonstrating with his fingers.

Nurd dipped the biscuit into the tea.

'That is good, actually,' he said. He dunked the biscuit a second time, but on this occasion he left it in for too long, and half of it fell into his cup. He looked like he was about to cry again.

'Just my luck,' he said.

'Never mind,' said Mrs Johnson, rescuing the soggy biscuit with a spoon. 'Plenty more where that came from.'

'So,' said Samuel. 'Perhaps you could tell us what's happening.'

'Well, it's Hell on Earth isn't it?' said Nurd. 'Gates have opened, demons are pouring out. End of the world, and all that.'

'Can we stop it?'

'Dunno. If you're going to do something, you'd best do it quickly because this lot are just the advance guard. As soon as the Great Malevolence himself comes through, it'll be too late. He'll be too strong for anyone to stop.' Nurd chewed glumly on his second biscuit. 'He really isn't very friendly at all.'

'But you came through the gates with the others, didn't you?' said Samuel.

'No, that's just it,' said Nurd. 'I came on my own. Like I told you before, I keep popping from one dimension into the next. One minute I was sitting on my throne in the Wasteland, hitting Wormwood on the head and minding my own business, and the next moment I was here. Now I appear to have ended up here permanently. I tried to make the best of it. In fact –' Nurd coughed ashamedly into his hand – 'I had hoped to rule the world. Oh, I'd have been very decent about it. None of this terrorising and demonic nonsense. All I really wanted was a bit of adoration, and a nice car. Apart from that, I'd hardly have bothered anybody. Unfortunately I think there's going to be some competition for the position, so I've decided to abandon my hopes and go home.'

'So you just sort of teleported[25] here?' asked Tom, who was a big fan of *Star Trek* and fancied the idea of being transferred from one place to another instantly.

Nurd shrugged, then looked at Maria who was still sucking her pencil and regarding him with an intense gaze.

---

[25] Actually, teleportation is not quite as far-fetched as you might think. Scientists at the Joint Quantum Institute in Maryland recently managed to teleport the quantum identity of one atom to another a few feet away. However, teleportation of humans is a long way off, as the experiment only works once in every 100 million attempts. Therefore the chances of you being teleported and arriving as interesting goo at the other end, if you arrive at all, are very high indeed. You don't want to be the subject of the following conversation:
'Is he there yet?'
'Well, bits of him are . . .'

'Why's she looking at me like that?' said Nurd. 'What've I done?'

'Apart from being a demon, and planning to rule the world, you mean?' said Tom.

'Yep, apart from all that,' said Nurd.

'Maria?' asked Samuel. 'What are you thinking?'

'Nurd here said that he flipped back and forth between worlds. I'm just wondering what that might mean for our plan. It may be that we're wrong about the nature of the portal.'

'What plan?' said Nurd.

Nobody spoke.

'Oh, I see,' said Nurd. 'Don't trust the demon.' He sighed. 'Well, can't say I blame you with that lot outside. And for your information, I didn't just flip back and forth, happy as a demon with two tails. The first time I got crushed, and found myself back in the Wasterland, and the second time a big car thing hit me, and the same thing happened. The third time I was with Samuel, and then I wasn't with him. That was the only time something bad didn't happen.'

He gave Samuel an embarrassed smile.

Maria looked pleased. 'Oh, so the rest of the time you died. Sort of. That's all right then.'

'Thanks very much,' said Nurd. 'It wasn't all right for me. You should try dying sometime. I guarantee that you won't care much for it.'

But now Maria was really interested. 'What's it like, travelling through a portal?'

'It hurts,' said Nurd, with feeling. 'It's like being stretched for miles, and then squeezed into a tiny little ball.'

'That's because of this,' said Maria, pointing at a drawing she had made of an hourglass shape, her pencil poised where the hourglass was at its narrowest. 'That's the point of compression. You shouldn't have been able to pass through it at all, because you should have been torn apart, or squashed to almost nothing. It sounds like this portal has some of the qualities of a black hole, and some of a wormhole. Theoretically, again, it shouldn't exist but then demons shouldn't exist either, and yet one is drinking tea with us at this precise moment.'

'Your point being?' asked Tom, impatient because he couldn't follow most of what Maria was saying.

'My point being,' said Maria, 'that Nurd here may be the solution to our problems.'

'Solution?' said Nurd nervously. 'This solution isn't going to hurt, is it?'

'Might do, a bit,' said Maria. 'Scientifically it has lots of holes in it. It may not work at all.'

'Well, it's better than no plan,' said Samuel. 'Assuming Nurd is willing to try.'

'It can't be any worse than what's happened to me already,' said Nurd gloomily. 'Explain away.'

So they did.

'Right,' said Nurd, when they had finished, 'that sounds so foolhardy, dangerous, and completely impossible that it just might work. Now all we need is a car.'

He looked up from the table and his expression changed.

'There is just one more problem,' he said.

'What's that?' asked Samuel.

Nurd pointed a shaking figure at the window, to where a pair of demons, one a toad, the other a spider, stood at the garden gate.

'Them!'

Thirty

In Which Mrs Abernathy Loses the Battle,
but Sets Out to Win the War

The children crowded at the window, staring out at the demons.

'Ugh,' said Maria, wrinkling her nose at the sight of the ten-legged spider and the great toad. 'They're horrid.'

'The Servants of Ba'al,' said Nurd. 'They look awful, and they *are* awful, but Ba'al is like a thousand of them rolled into one, with added nastiness. I'm in trouble now.'

Samuel stared at the two demons; there was something familiar about them. It took him a second to realise that they still wore the remains of black robes.

'They're not after you,' he said to Nurd. 'I'm not even sure they know you're here.'

'Then who are they after?' asked Tom.

'Me, I think,' said Samuel. 'They're two of the people from the Abernathys' basement, or they used to be. Mrs Abernathy must have sent them.'

'Why?' asked Tom. 'You didn't even manage to stop her. The gates are open. She has what she wanted.'

'I got in her way. I don't think she likes people crossing her. I'm not sure if anyone has ever crossed her before, not like that. She wants to punish me, and you lot as well if you're caught with me.'

He turned to Maria and Tom. 'I'm sorry. I should never have got you involved in all this.'

Tom patted him on the back. 'You're right, you shouldn't have.'

'Tom!' said Maria, appalled.

'Only joking,' said Tom. 'I really was,' he added, as Maria continued to glare at him.

'So what do we do now?' asked Maria. 'Run away?'

'Running away sounds good,' said Dr Planck from some-where beneath the blanket.

'No,' said Samuel. 'We have to face them.'

'Look,' said Tom, 'hitting flying skulls was all very well, but I don't think those two are going to let any of us get close enough to knock them on the head with a bat.'

'We go ahead with the plan,' said Samuel. 'We send Nurd through the portal.'

'There is just one thing,' said Nurd. 'I'd rather they didn't know it was me. Could create difficulties at the other end, assuming I don't get spread over half the universe when the portal collapses. Perhaps you have a disguise of some kind that I could use?'

Mrs Johnson whipped the blanket from Dr Planck, made two holes in it with a pair of scissors, and handed it to Nurd.

'But where do we get a car?' asked Tom.

'Mum,' said Samuel. 'Keep an eye on those things. Tom, stay with her. Nurd, Maria: come with me.'

'Where are you going?' asked Tom.

'To steal my dad's car,' said Samuel, and saw his mum smile.

* * *

Samuel, Maria and Nurd stood in the garage at the back of the house, looking at the car that Samuel's father had spent years lovingly restoring.

'"Aston Martin,"' read Nurd. He stroked the car gently. 'It's beautiful. Is it like a Porsche?'

'It's better than a Porsche, because it's British,' said Samuel.

'Right,' said Nurd. He wasn't sure that he agreed. He really had liked the Porsche, but this was still a splendid car.

'Are you sure you can drive one of these?' asked Maria.

'I drove a Porsche,' said Nurd. 'I got the hang of that fairly quickly.'

Samuel was having second thoughts about letting Nurd have the car. Samuel's dad would go crazy when he found out.

'You will look after it?' said Samuel to Nurd. 'It's such a lovely car.'

'Samuel,' said Maria, 'he's going to drive it through an transdimensional portal and, if things go right, end up back in Hell, or, if things go wrong, in tiny little pieces scattered throughout a wormhole, or even compressed to almost nothing. It's not entirely fair to ask him if he's going to look after it.'

Samuel nodded. 'Perhaps it's better not to know.'

Samuel handed Nurd his father's spare car keys. Nurd climbed into the driver's seat and put the key in the ignition as Samuel raised the garage door that opened on to a lane at the rear of the house. Maria stood beside the open passenger-side window, and spoke to Nurd for the last time.

'Do you know where you're going?'

'Towards the big blue light,' said Nurd. 'It won't be hard to find.'

'No, I suppose not. You'll need to build up quite a head of speed if this is to work.'

'I don't think that will be a problem,' he said.

'Right. Good luck, then,' said Maria. 'And Nurd?'

'Yes?'

'Please don't let us down.'

'I won't,' he said.

'Your dad is going to have a meltdown when he finds out, isn't he?' said Maria to Samuel as he returned from opening the garage door.

'If Nurd fails, or if you're wrong, my dad will have better things to worry about,' said Samuel.

'You'd think so,' said Maria, 'but he'll still find time to kill you.'

'I don't care,' said Samuel. He was not frightened, but neither was he quite as angry as before. In a terrible way, he was getting his own back on his dad for running away. If they weren't quite even, they were getting there.

'Give us a few minutes, then get going,' said Samuel to Nurd. 'We'll distract those things at the gates, just in case they *have* come for you.'

Nurd gripped the steering wheel expectantly.

'I'll count to one hundred,' he said.

'Great,' said Samuel. 'Well, like Maria said, don't let us down.' He patted the car once more in farewell.

'Is your dad really going to be annoyed?' asked Nurd.

'He'll get over it. After all, it's for a good cause.'

'I hope he understands,' said Nurd. 'You just seem . . . like the sort of person who should be understood.'

'I wish you could stay around,' said Samuel. 'I'd like to get to know you a little better.'

'You were the first person who was nice to me . . . ever,' said Nurd. 'That counts for something, whatever happens.'

They shook hands, and then Samuel gave Nurd a hug that, after a moment of surprise, the demon returned. For the first time, Nurd began to understand how it was to feel sorrow at parting with a friend, and even as it hurt him he was grateful to Samuel for giving him the chance to experience something of what it was to be human.

'Come on,' said Maria. 'Let's go and help the others. That will keep your mind off things.'

'I expect being eaten by a spider or a toad will do that . . .' said Samuel.

The demons had not moved. They were simply staring at the house, but it was the huge spider that most concerned Samuel, its mouthparts moving, dripping clear venom that turned the leaves black. Samuel's brain was filled with shrieking voices telling him to run. He had always been frightened of spiders, ever since he was a very small child. He couldn't explain why. Now he was being forced to confront a spider so vile that even in his worst nightmares he couldn't have come up with anything like it, even if it did have a pair of human legs sticking somewhat incongruously out of its bottom.

Samuel opened the front door and stepped into the garden. From the back of the house he heard the sound of the Aston Martin starting up.

A flickering figure like a picture on a cinema screen appeared on the path before him, surrounded by blue light. It was Mrs Abernathy, or a projection of herself.

'Hello, Samuel,' she said. 'I'm sorry I can't be there in person to witness your death, but I'm sure my servants will make it as uncomfortable as possible.' Her head turned, as though she were listening to something; then she clicked her fingers and the toad demon, in response to her command, hopped away.

'Was that the sound of your little friends trying to escape?' sneered Mrs Abernathy, and Samuel knew he had been right: Mrs Abernathy had not been aware of Nurd's presence.

Samuel shrugged.

'Well, they won't get very far. Naroth will find them and kill them. It will be a swift death, pleasant compared to what I have planned for you.'

Her ghostly hand touched the remaining spider demon, causing the hairs on its body to stand on end.

'Chelom,' she said. 'Eat him. Slowly.'

Nurd was approaching the end of Poe Street when a large, dark shape appeared on the road before him, its body tensed to jump. Naroth's face was not capable of showing feeling, but if it had been it would have displayed utter astonishment. Instead of the expected children, and the adult woman, there was a single figure behind the wheel, its body draped with a blanket in which two eyeholes had been cut. Naroth's senses detected something familiar about the figure, but it couldn't decide what it was.

Nurd stopped the car and stared at Naroth.

'Horrid thing,' said Nurd.

As though it had heard the words Naroth jumped on to the bonnet, causing Nurd to shriek in fright. Nurd put his foot down on the accelerator and the car jerked forward, but Naroth was holding on tight with its sticky toes. It spat concentrated venom on to the windscreen, which began to smoke and melt.

'Oh no you don't,' said Nurd. 'I'm not having you messing up this nice car.'

He braked hard, and Naroth was thrown off with such force that it left one of its legs caught in the wing mirror. It landed on its back and began to twist in an effort to right itself. It heard the sound of the engine growling, and re-doubled its efforts, finding its feet just as its head was struck by the front of the Aston Martin and its body was dragged beneath its wheels. It had just enough to time to think, 'Ouch, that—' before it stopped thinking altogether and everything went black.

Nurd looked in the rear-view mirror at the mangled remains of Naroth, and the satisfying green smear that the toad demon had left along the lower half of Poe Street.

'Serves you right for messing with my motor,' said Nurd. 'You should have more respect . . .'

Chelom began to climb over the garden wall, the weight of its body causing the hedge to collapse. It landed heavily and lumbered towards Samuel. As it did so an arrow whistled by Samuel's ear and buried itself in the spider demon's body, causing yellow liquid to spurt from the wound. The spider demon reared up, then resumed its progress as a second arrow flew towards it. This time it struck one of the black eyes on the demon's head and the demon arched its body in agony, one leg raised as if in an effort to dislodge the arrow from its flesh.

Maria appeared beside Samuel, Samuel's toy bow raised, and another arrow already nocked, its tip sharpened with a blade.

'Now, Tom!' she shouted.

Tom emerged from the kitchen carrying a container of fluid from which a plastic pipe connected to a nozzle in his hand. He squeezed the nozzle and a jet of fluid landed on the grass at Chelom's feet. The spider demon reacted as though the ground were hot when the sensitive taste buds at the tips of its legs came into contact with the liquid. Tom kept pumping, and more of the fluid squirted onto the demon's body and into its eyes and mouth. It tried to retreat but Tom pursued it relentlessly until at last the demon began to twist and writhe before falling on its back. Its legs curled in upon its body, and it stopped moving.

Samuel wrinkled his nose.

'What is that stuff?'

'Ammonia and water,' said Tom. 'Maria thought of it.'

But Maria was not listening, and neither, suddenly, was Samuel. Their attention was concentrated on the image of Mrs Abernathy, who was gazing upon them in fury.

'Come and get me,' said Samuel. He wanted to distract Mrs Abernathy from the portal. He had to buy Nurd some time.

But Mrs Abernathy simply disappeared.

Thirty-one

In Which Mrs Abernathy Reveals Her True Colours

Mrs Abernathy stood outside what remained of the house. It was almost time. She had wanted to kill Samuel, but that would have to wait. She would find him and when she did he would wish that the spider had consumed him. Again and again he had defied her, and Mrs Abernathy was not one to tolerate defiance.

The portal had grown to such an extent that all that was left of the house were two walls and a chimney breast. The doors and windows were entirely gone, replaced by a huge spinning vortex with a dark hole at its centre. There were no longer creatures coming through it. All such activity had ceased for a time, and those demons and monsters not otherwise occupied in sowing chaos throughout the town were waiting expectantly for the arrival of their master, the Great Malevolence himself. Winged, purple forms dangled upside down from lamp-posts, like great bats, their heads simply elongated beaks filled with jagged teeth. Around them flew insects as big as seagulls, their iridescent green bodies ending in long, barbed stingers. A phalanx of vaguely human figures had assembled by the corner of Derleth Crescent, dressed in ornate gold armour that was itself alive as the dragons and snake heads with which it was decorated slithered and snapped at the night air, the armour both a means of defence and a weapon. The armour had no face guard, and beneath each jewelled helmet there was blackness broken only by the flickering of red, hostile eyes. Above their heads a banner flew: flames in the shape of a flag, burning in honour of he who was to come.

Mrs Abernathy raised her arms in the air, and closed her eyes in ecstasy as a great cheer arose from the demons before her.

Nurd watched all that was happening from a side street nearby, the Aston Martin purring softly beneath him. He shivered as the woman lifted her arms, blue energy crackling around her.

There were ranks of demons in Hell, but the very worst of them had hidden themselves away with the Great Malevolence, and were rarely seen by the rest. They were monstrous beings, their appearance so awful that they shrouded themselves in darkness, unable to tolerate even the reaction of other, lesser demons to their blighted state.

Yet there was one great demon that felt no such shame, that did not seek to hide itself. It had become the Great Malevolence's most trusted lieutenant, the demon that knew his every secret and to whom he revealed all of his thoughts, a demon that had studied the humans with hateful fascination, altering itself as it did so, its mind becoming both male and female, although it always preferred the female side, sensing that the female was smarter and shrewder than the male.

Even dressed in the skin of Mrs Abernathy, Nurd recognised the entity before him. After all, it had been responsible for his banishment.

It was Ba'al.

He sank back against the wall.

'I'll never get past her,' he said bitterly. 'I'm done for. We're all done for.'

Mrs Abernathy began to speak.

'Our time has come,' she said. 'Our long exile in the void is at an end. Tonight we have begun to claim this world as our own, and soon we will reduce it to a charred ruin. See! Our master approaches. Gaze upon his might! Feel his majesty! Behold him, the destroyer of worlds!'

She stepped aside, and the centre of the vortex grew larger, the dark hole at its heart simultaneously expanding and growing lighter. The gates were almost entirely gone, and the melting metal steamed and boiled. Slowly, shapes became visible through the murk. They were blurred at first, and shrouded in mist, but gradually they became clearer.

It was an army, the largest army ever assembled in any world, and in any universe. All the peoples of the Earth were as nothing before it. Its ranks outnumbered every grain of sand on the planet, every leaf on every tree, every molecule of water in every ocean. Demons of every shape and size, things formed and without form, had assembled behind the remains of the gates. Above the great army towered a black mountain so tall its top could never be seen, its base so wide that a man might walk for a lifetime and never circumnavigate it. At the heart of the mountain was a massive cave, unseen fires glowing within.

A dark form appeared at the entrance to the cave; from its head sprouted a crown of bone. It wore black armour carved with the name of every man and woman who had ever been born on Earth, and who ever would be born, in order that it would never forget its hatred for them. In its right hand it held a flaming spear, and on its left arm it bore a shield made from the skulls and bones of the damned, for in every evil man and woman there was something of the Great Malevolence, and when they died he claimed their remains for himself. He towered above his army, so that they were like insects before him. He opened his mouth, and roared, and they shook before him, for his glory was terrible to behold.

Another cheer arose from the assembled masses. Mrs Abernathy basked in the sound. So consumed was she by the imminent success of their invasion, and the impending arrival of her master, that she failed to notice the cheers had started to fade, to be replaced by mutterings of confusion, and a voice that appeared to be saying, very politely, 'Excuse me . . .'

Mrs Abernathy opened her eyes. Standing before her was Samuel Johnson.

'I have a question,' said Samuel.

Mrs Abernathy was so taken aback that she couldn't reply. Her brow furrowed. Her mouth opened and tried to form words, but none would come. The gates of Hell were about to be opened at last, Earth destroyed, all of its inhabitants torn to pieces, and here was a small boy who seemed to have, not to put too fine a point on it, a question.

Eventually, Mrs Abernathy responded in the only way she could.

'Well, what is it?'

'I just don't see the point,' said Samuel.

'The point?'

'Yes, the point,' said Samuel. 'I mean, if you've all been stuck in horrible old Hell for ages, and now you're about to come here instead, why would you reduce it to a ruin and turn it into somewhere that's just as bad as the place you've left? It doesn't seem to make any sense.'

Beside him, a pink demon with four legs scratched itself in puzzlement. Its form had the consistency of marshmallow, so its fingers got rather lost in the process and jabbed themselves into the demon's brain, but at least it was thinking, or giving the impression of doing so.

'And what would you have us do?' asked Mrs Abernathy. 'Leave it as it is?'

'Well, yes,' said Samuel. 'I mean, it's got trees, and birds, and elephants. Everybody likes elephants. You can't not like an elephant. Or a giraffe. And, personally, I'm very fond of penguins.'

The pink demon gave a little shrug of agreement, or as much of a shrug as something without a neck can give, which isn't very much at all.

'If you destroy it,' continued Samuel, 'then you'll just be back where you started, with a big lump of rock that doesn't have a whole lot in it, except demons. It's not exactly going to be beautiful, is it?'

Mrs Abernathy took a step towards him.

'And why do you imagine that we would want beauty?' she said. 'Beauty mocks us, for we have none. Goodness appals us, because we have no goodness. We are all that this world is not, and we are all that you are not.'

She raised a hand to the stars above her.

'And this world is just the first. We have a universe to conquer. We have suns to extinguish, and planets to crush. In time, each of those lights in the sky will fade to nothing. We will extinguish them like candle flames between our fingers, until there is only blackness.'

The little pink demon, still thinking about penguins, gave a disappointed sigh. Mrs Abernathy flicked a finger and he exploded in a puff of pink and red.

'He goes to the back of the line,' said Mrs Abernathy as Samuel wiped a piece of demon from his sleeve. 'And as for you, I am strangely glad to see you. It means I can kill you now, and enjoy our triumph with the knowledge that you are not alive to spoil it.'

Mrs Abernathy grinned. Her body began to bulge. Her skin stretched under the pressure, opening tears in her face and on her arms, but no blood came. Instead, something terrible moved in the spaces revealed.

'Now, Samuel Johnson,' she said, 'look upon me. Look upon Ba'al, and weep.'

Nurd's finger was poised over the ignition key. He saw Mrs Abernathy step away from the portal, but not far enough.

'Come on, Samuel,' he whispered. The little boy was brave, so very brave. Nurd hoped that Samuel wouldn't die, but the odds in his favour weren't good. The odds in Nurd's favour weren't much better, but he was determined to try. He would be brave, if not for his own sake, then for Samuel's. Mrs Abernathy took another step towards the boy; Samuel retreated in turn. Then Mrs Abernathy started to shudder and swell.

'Oh no,' said Nurd. 'Here we go . . .'

Mrs Abernathy's skin fell away in clumps, withering and turning to dry flakes as it hit the ground. A grey-black form was exposed, wrapped up in tentacles that now began to stretch and move as they were freed from the constraints of skin. Only her face and hair remained in place, like a rubber mask, but it was stretched so tightly over what was beneath that it bore no resemblance to the woman who had once worn it. One of the tentacles reached up, separated itself into claws, and wrenched the skin mask away.

And still Ba'al grew: six feet, then eight, then ten, on and on, larger and larger. Two legs appeared, bent backwards at the knees, from which sharp spurs of bone erupted. Four arms emerged from the torso, but only two ended in clawed fingers. The second pair ended in blades of bone, yellowed and scarred. A great mass of tentacles sprouted from the demon's back, all of them twisting and writhing like snakes.

Finally Ba'al reached its full height, towering twenty feet above Samuel. There was a cracking sound, and what had looked like a bump in its chest was revealed as its head, which now untucked itself. It appeared to have no mouth, merely two dark eyes buried deep in its skull, but then the front of the skull split into four parts, like a segmented orange, and Samuel realised that it was *all* mouth, the four parts lined with row upon row of teeth, a gaping red hole at its centre from which a multiplicity of dark tongues emerged.

Samuel was too frightened to move. He wanted to run, but his feet wouldn't respond. In any case, his back was against the garden hedge. He could go right or left, but he couldn't go any farther backwards. He felt something brush his leg, and looked down to see Boswell, who had escaped from the house and followed his master. Even now, the little dog wanted to be near Samuel.

'Run, Boswell,' he whispered. 'There's a good boy. Run home.'

But Boswell didn't run. He was frightened, but he wasn't going to desert his beloved Samuel. He barked at the nasty, unknown thing before him, nipping at its heels. One of its bladed limbs shot out in an effort to impale him, but Boswell skipped out of the way just in time and the long bone buried itself in the pavement, lodging firmly. Ba'al tried to free itself, but the bone was stuck.

Something in its struggles snapped Samuel out of his trance. He looked around for a weapon and saw a half brick that had been dislodged from the house as the portal expanded. He picked it up and hefted it in his hand. It wasn't much, but it was better than nothing.

With a great wrench, Ba'al managed to pull the blade free, even as Boswell continued to bark and snap. A tentacle, larger than the rest, lashed out at him, catching the little dog around the chest and tossing him into the air. The pincers at the tentacle's end shot out to cut him in two, but they missed him by inches and Boswell fell to the ground, stunned. He tried to get up, but one of his legs was broken, and he was unable to raise himself. He yelped in pain, and the sound cut through Samuel, filling him with rage.

'You hurt my dog!' he shouted. By now he didn't know if he was more angry than scared, or more scared than angry. It didn't matter. He hated the thing before him: hated it for hurting Boswell; hated it for what it had done to the Abernathys and their friends; hated it for what it wanted to do to the whole world. Behind it the portal was visible, and Samuel could see the Great Malevolence approaching, his army parting for him so that he could lead the legions of darkness into this new kingdom.

Ba'al bent down before Samuel, surrounding him with tentacles, those four limbs poised to finish him off. Its skull opened up once more, breathing its stink upon him as it hissed, and Samuel saw himself reflected in those dark, pitiless orbs.

He threw the half-brick straight into its mouth.

It was a perfect shot. The lump of stone landed in the demon's throat. It was too far down to be spat out, and too big to be swallowed. Ba'al staggered back, black blood and drool dripping from its jaws as it began to choke. Around it, the assembled creatures watching the unequal battle, waiting for the boy to be destroyed, gave a collective gasp of shock. Ba'al tried to reach into its mouth with its tentacles to free the blockage, but the gap was too narrow for them to gain purchase. It collapsed to its knees as smaller demons ran to its aid, climbing up its body in an effort to reach its mouth. Carefully three of them entered its jaws and began working at the brick, trying to free it. Samuel felt hands grasp his arms. Two of the figures in gold armour were securing him, their red eyes glaring as he was held in place. He struggled against them, but they were too strong.

There was a thud, and something landed before him. It was the half-brick. Samuel looked up to see Ba'al rising from its knees, and in its black eyes he saw his doom.

At that moment a vintage Aston Martin, driven by a moon-headed figure in a blanket, sped behind Ba'al and disappeared into the portal, leaving behind it only exhaust fumes and a fading 'Goodbyyyyyyyye . . .'

For a second, nothing happened. Everyone, and everything, simply stared at the portal, unsure of what they had just seen. Flashes of white light appeared at its edges, and the portal, which had been spinning in a clockwise direction, reversed its flow and began to move anticlockwise. There was a sense of suction, as though a vacuum cleaner had just been switched on, but it seemed to affect only the demons, not Samuel. First the smaller ones, then the larger, were lifted from their feet and pulled inexorably into the portal. Some struggled against its force, holding on to lamp-posts, garden gates, even cars, but the portal began to spin faster and faster, and one by one they found themselves wrenched from one world and back to the next until the portal seemed to be filled with a mass of legs and tentacles and claws and jaws, demons bouncing off one another as they were drawn towards the centre. Two of them, oddly, were desperately trying to hold on to glasses of beer.

At last only one remained. The thing that had once been Mrs Abernathy was heavier and stronger than anything else that had passed into this world, and it did not want to leave. Every limb, and every tentacle, was stretched to its limit, each clinging to something, however insubstantial, in an effort to fight against the force of the portal, which was now spinning so fast that it was nothing more than a blue blur. Finally it proved too much even for the great demon, until at last only one tentacle remained clinging to the bottom of the garden gate, the rest of the demon's body suspended in mid-air, its legs pointing to the void.

Samuel stepped forward. He stared into Ba'al's pitiless eyes, and raised his right foot.

'Go to Hell,' he said, and stamped down hard on the tentacle with his heel.

The demon released its hold on the gate, and was sucked back to the place from which it had come. The portal collapsed to a small pinpoint of blue light, then disappeared entirely.

Samuel knelt by Boswell and cradled the little dog's head in his arms. A police car pulled up, and people began to emerge from their homes, but Samuel cared only for Boswell.

'Brave Boswell,' he whispered, and despite his pain,

Boswell's tail wagged at the sound of Samuel's voice speaking his name. 'Brave boy.'

Then Samuel looked up at the night sky, and he spoke another name, and his voice was filled with regret, and fondness, and hope.

'Brave Nurd.'

Thirty-two

In Which Nearly Everyone Lives Happily Ever After,
Or So It Seems

It took a long time for Biddlecombe to return to normal. People had died or, like the Abernathys and the Renfields, simply vanished. For months afterwards there were scientists, and television crews, and reporters cluttering up the town and asking all sorts of questions that the townsfolk quickly grew tired of answering. Nutcases, and people with nothing better to do, made journeys to the town to see the place in which, for a time, a gateway between worlds had opened. The problem was that, all damage to people and property aside, and the stories told by those who had encountered the demons, no actual evidence survived of what had occurred, apart from the stone statue of three old gents with shotguns. There were no physical remains of monsters, and those who had taken mobile phone pictures of flying creatures, or who had used video cameras to take shots of demonic entities trampling flower beds in the local park, found that there was nothing but static to be seen. Oh, everyone accepted that *something* had happened in Biddlecombe, but, officially, nobody seemed entirely sure of what that something might have been, not even the scientists responsible for the Large Hadron Collider, who, in the wake of what had occurred, decided that in future they needed to keep a very close eye on their experiments. For now, though, the collider would remain powered off, and Ed and Victor were left to play Battleships in peace, while Professor Hilbert dreamed of travelling to other dimensions, but only ones that didn't have demons in them.

The collider did have three very special visitors in the weeks that followed. Samuel, Maria and Tom were treated with a great deal of curiosity and respect as they toured the facility, and they did their best to answer all of the scientists' questions as politely as possible. Samuel and Maria decided that they quite liked the idea of becoming scientists, although they were pretty certain that, after all they'd seen, they'd be more careful about what they got up to than the CERN people had been.

'I still want to be a professional cricketer,' said Tom after their visit. 'At least I can understand cricket. And nobody ever accidentally opened the gates of Hell during a test match . . .'

Eventually Biddlecombe began to fade from the headlines, and that suited everyone in the town just fine. They wanted their dull, pretty old Biddlecombe back, and that was what they got.

More or less.

Over at Miggin's Pond, a boy named Robert Oppenheimer was throwing stones at ducks. It wasn't that he had anything against ducks in particular. Had there been a dog, or a lemur, or a meerkat at which to throw stones instead he would happily have done so, but in the absence of any more exotic creatures, ducks would just have to do.

He had managed to hit a few birds, and was looking for more stones, when he was lifted up into the air by one leg and found himself dangling over the surface of the pond.

An eyeball appeared on the end of a stalk and, well, eyeballed him. Then a very polite voice said:

'I say, old chap, I do wish you wouldn't do that. The ducks don't like it and, frankly, I don't much care for it either. If you persist, I will have no choice but to disassemble you and put you back together the wrong way. As you can imagine, that will hurt a lot. Do I make myself clear?'

Robert nodded, albeit with some difficulty as he was still upside down. 'Yes,' he said. 'Perfectly.'

'Now say sorry to the ducks, there's a good chap.'

'Sorry, ducks,' said Robert.

'Right, then, off you go. Toodle-pip.'

Robert was put back, surprisingly gently, on the bank. He found that all of the ducks were watching him, and quacking. If he hadn't known better, he might have thought that they were laughing.

Over time, other people reported similar odd encounters at Miggin's Pond, but instead of calling in investigators, or selling tickets, the people of Biddlecombe simply kept quiet about it, and gave Miggin's Pond a wide berth whenever they could.

In the staff room at Montague Rhodes James Secondary School, Mr Hume sat staring intently at the head of a pin. During the Halloween disturbances, Mr Hume had been forced to lock himself in a cupboard while a band of six-inch-high demons dressed as elves shouted at him through the keyhole. The whole experience had shaken him a great deal and when he had learned of Samuel Johnson's involvement in the affair he began to consider that the boy might know something about angels and pins that he didn't.

So he stared hard at the pin, and wondered.

And on the head of the pin, two angels who had been performing a very nice waltz, surrounded by lots of other waltzing angels, suddenly stopped what they were doing as one turned to the other and said:

'Don't look now, but that bloke's back . . .'

One night, almost a month after the events of Halloween, when everyone was getting ready for December, and Christmas, Samuel was in the bathroom, brushing his teeth. Boswell watched him from the doorway, one leg still encased in plaster but otherwise his clever, contented self. Samuel had just taken a bath, and the mirror was steamed up. He reached out and wiped some of the steam away. He glimpsed his reflection, and, standing behind him, the reflection of another.

It was Mrs Abernathy.

Samuel looked round in fright. The bathroom was empty yet Mrs Abernathy was still visible in the mirror. Her lips moved, speaking words that Samuel could not hear. As he watched, she moved forward. A finger reached out and began to write from behind the glass in the steam of the mirror. When she was finished there were four words visible. They were:

THIS IS NOT OVER

A blue light flickered in her eyes, and then she was gone.

Thirty-three

In Which We Bid Farewell to Nurd. For Now . . .

In the great Wasteland, Wormwood stared at the Aston Martin that had accompanied Nurd back to his kingdom.

'What is it?' asked Wormwood.

'It's a car,' said Nurd. 'It's called an Aston Martin.'

Nurd was surprised that the car had made it to the Wasteland in one piece, although not as surprised as that he himself had done so with only minor injuries. After all, it wasn't every day that one went the wrong way through an interdimensional portal wearing a blanket and driving a very fast car. He had already decided that if any curious demons asked him how the car had got here, assuming any of them could be bothered to investigate the Wasteland, Hell being a very big place with more interesting areas to explore, he would tell them that it had dropped out of the sky. After all, who would suspect Nurd, that most inept of demons, of being responsible for thwarting the Great Malevolence and his invading army.

'What does it do?' asked Wormwood.

'It moves. It moves very fast.'

'Oh. And we watch it move fast, do we?'

It sounded like fun to Wormwood, although not much fun. Actually he was quite pleased that Nurd was back. It had been a bit quiet without him, and the throne hadn't been very comfortable to sit on. Funny, that. For so long Wormwood had desired that throne and then, when he'd had it, it hadn't been worth desiring after all.

'No, Wormwood,' said Nurd patiently. His trip to the world of men, and his encounter with Samuel, had mellowed him, and he was no longer immediately inclined to hit Wormwood for being a bit dim, although he had a feeling that this wouldn't last. 'We sit in it, and then we go fast too.'

Wormwood looked doubtful, but eventually he was convinced to sit in the passenger seat, his seat belt fastened and a concerned expression on his face. Beside him, Nurd started the engine. It growled pleasantly.

'But where will we go?' asked Wormwood.

'Somewhere else,' said Nurd. 'After all, anywhere is better than here.'

'And how far will we get?'

Nurd pointed at one of the bubbling black pools that broke the monotonous landscape of the Wasteland.

'You see those pools, Wormwood?'

Wormwood nodded. He'd been looking at the pools for so long that they almost qualified as old friends. If he'd known his birthday, he'd have invited the pools to the party.

'Well,' Nurd continued, 'what's in those pools is remarkably similar to what makes this car go. Hell, Wormwood, is our oyster.'

'What's an oyster?'

Nurd, who didn't know either, but had seen the phrase on a poster in the car showroom and rather liked the sound of it, began to reconsider his decision not to hit Wormwood quite so often.

'It doesn't matter,' he said. He took a paper bag from his

pocket. The bag contained the last of the wine gums that Samuel had given to him. Nurd had been saving them, but now he offered one to Wormwood and took the final sweetie for himself.

'To Samuel,' he said, and Wormwood, who had heard so much about the boy from Nurd, echoed his master.

'To Samuel.'

The multiverse was unfathomably huge, thought Nurd, but it was still small enough to allow two strangers like Samuel and himself to find each other and become friends.

Together, Nurd and Wormwood drove off, the car growing smaller and smaller, disappearing into the distance, until all that was left to indicate that anyone had ever been there was a throne, a sceptre, and an old, rusty crown . . .

Acknowledgments

I would like to thank Alistair and Cameron Ridyard, who were the first two readers of this book. Graham Glusman, and Nicholas and Barney Rees, also came forward with kind words and encouragement at a very early stage. I'm grateful to you all.

Dr Colm Stephens, Administrator of the School of Physics at Trinity College, Dublin, very generously agreed to read this manuscript, and offered advice and clarification. In the interests of fiction I was forced to ignore some of it, and for that I apologise deeply. His input, patience, and expertise were greatly appreciated, and any errors are entirely my own. Thanks also to Sally-Anne Fisher, the Communications Officer at TCD, for her assistance.

I seem to have read a great many books and articles during the writing of this novel, but among the most useful were *Black Holes, Wormholes & Time Machines* by Jim Al-Khalili (Taylor & Francis, 1999); *Quantum Theory Cannot Hurt You* by Marcus Chown (Faber and Faber, 2007); and *Parallel Worlds* by Michio Kaku (Penguin, 2005).

Thanks to Sue Fletcher at Hodder & Stoughton, and Emily Bestler at Atria Books, who I am lucky enough to have as editors; to all of those who work with them, particularly their respective assistants, Swati Gamble and Laura Stern; to Darley Anderson and his staff, without whom I would be lost; and to Steve Fisher, for always thinking visually.

Finally, love and thanks to Jennie, as always, for putting up with me.